BLINDSIDED

FAKE BOYFRIEND BOOK 4

EDEN FINLEY

BLINDSIDED

Edited by Deb Nemeth
http://www.deborahnemeth.com/

Copy-edited by Kelly Hartigan @ Xterraweb
http://editing.xterraweb.com/

DEAR READER

This book belongs to the Fake Boyfriend universe but does not contain a Fake Boyfriend trope.

I've spoken publicly about Talon and Miller's origin—in which they weren't supposed to exist. This book isn't supposed to exist. But Talon was one of those characters who wouldn't take no for an answer, and he decided to drag Miller into it too. So here we are.

Instead of forcing a trope on them that I had no plans for, I let these boys lead their story.

Those of you who have read *Trick Play* will know Talon and Miller's backstory. They sleep with women. They share women. No scenes are graphic in this book, but I wanted to stay true to their bisexuality, because these guys really like boobs. As they should. Boobs are great.

Side note: Tom Brady exists in this universe, but Talon has played for New England for the last six years, so I like to think of Tom Brady as retired in this fictional world. (Even as an Aussie, I know who Mr. Bündchen is.)

DISCLAIMERS/TRADEMARKS

CHAPTER ONE

TALON

NINE YEARS AGO

"Drink up, rook." I hold a red Solo cup out to Shane Miller, the brick shithouse who's gonna protect my ass on the field this year.

He stares me down with his big brown eyes before taking the drink. "You're the type of guy my mom warned me to stay away from. Peer pressure's a real thing, you know."

"Momma's boy, huh?"

Miller snorts and chugs the entire beer. "Nope. If Mom knew the truth, she'd be warning me to stay away from myself. That was like my sixth drink tonight."

I laugh and clap him on his shoulder. "You and I are gonna get along just fine." I've had about that, if not more. I lost count after three.

One could argue it's because football players can't even count past that, but it's actually because I don't give a shit how many drinks go down my throat.

I was there when Coach was reviewing tapes of this guy, and it's no wonder he's on the starting offensive line when he's only a freshman. Miller's as wide as he is tall, and he's only eighteen years old.

"What you in the mood for?" I gesture to the sea of people crammed in my house. "Brunette?" I point to a scantily clad junior who walks by giving us both a wide smile. "Redhead?" I nod toward the sardine-canned living room that's the makeshift dance floor.

Six of us from the team are renting this off-campus house for this reason—parties and drinking without anyone from the school breathing down our necks.

"Blonde," Miller says, his eyes lighting up at the girl approaching us.

"Sorry, man, that one's taken tonight."

She's technically my date, but everyone knows that term is used loosely with me. It's not really a date if I didn't go pick her up and we didn't arrive together, seeing as I live here.

Nikki sidles up to me, and I wrap my arm around her shoulder. "Nikki, this is Miller. Miller, Nikki."

I don't miss the way Nikki eyes Miller, her gaze dragging over him from his short dark hair to his large chest and then narrow waist. Most guys would hate that—their date checking out someone else—but me? I find it hot for reasons I can't explain.

I've never found a reason to be jealous. There's no point. I've never been the jealous type, not just with dates but even girlfriends.

Nikki leans in and whispers in my ear. "Ready to go up to your room?"

Impatient much? I turn and kiss her cheek. "Soon. I'm just gonna talk to my boy Miller for a bit longer."

Miller's eyebrows shoot up as if surprised I'm choosing him over a hookup. We're teammates—that bond can't be broken. He'll learn that. I've decided I'm taking Miller under my wing.

"I'm gonna go dance then," Nikki says, and her arched, perfectly shaped eyebrow is as good as a threat. If she gets a better offer out there, she's gonna take it.

"Have fun," I say.

Again, not jealous. If she finds someone she wants to hook up with, then she should. This is fucking college. No time for drama, bullshit, or serious relationships.

When she saunters away, Miller nudges me.

"Dude, when a girl who looks like that asks you upstairs, you go upstairs."

I huff a laugh. "You'll soon learn there are plenty more books in the library."

He narrows his eyes. "Isn't the saying there's plenty more fish in the sea?"

"I don't like that analogy. Like, if you go fishing and you catch a fish, you don't say 'I think this will taste gross' and throw it back. Doesn't that phrase actually mean that you take the fish home, cook it, eat it, think it's gross, and then throw it out? So, really, that's like saying if it doesn't work out with someone you should kill them. Homicide is not sexy. Books, on the other hand ... you borrow from a library until you find the book you love, and then you keep it. The library won't let you borrow more books until you return it, but you never return it because you'll never need any other book."

Miller looks confused. "You're fucked up."

I grin. "Thanks."

"It actually means if a fish gets away there's plenty more to catch."

I love that Miller doesn't take the shit spewing out of my mouth as gospel like other guys do. It's the athlete effect, and sometimes I push boundaries to see just how much I can get away with. "Well, do women really like being compared to fish? I mean … you know …"

Miller doesn't take the bait—pun totally intended. "I'm getting another drink. You want?"

"Thanks."

I watch him as he walks away, and it's not only girls who turn their heads to stare after him but the guys as well. His presence is demanding. Being a six-five giant probably has a lot to do with that.

When he returns with two beers, he smiles as he hands me mine. "So, what's your plan? NFL, I'm guessing."

"Fuck, yeah. Same for you?"

Miller shrugs. "I guess. I dunno if I'm good enough."

"Are you kidding? I've watched some of your high school games. You're a force to be reckoned with. You can totally go all the way."

Surprise and hope shine in his eyes. "You think so?"

Knowing the chances of the NFL for any of us is small, I should tell him to make sure he gets his degree for a backup first, but I dunno what it is about this guy. It's like when I'm on the field; I have this sixth sense about the game. My gut tells me what plays will work and who to throw the ball to. And even though I only met Miller a few days ago, I know he's gonna make it.

I hold up my drink for him to cheers. "Definitely. You and me. Future Super Bowl winners. I can see it now."

Arms wrap around me from behind. Nikki's back.

I cut her off at the pass. "We can go up soon. We need to hook Miller up first, or he'll want to watch."

It's a total joke. At least, I mean it that way until I see interest flare in Miller's eyes. I turn to Nikki, expecting to be slapped or at least scolded. Nope. She's staring at Miller the same way he is at us.

She shrugs. "I'm cool with that."

I think both Miller's and my mouths drop open. Was totally not expecting her to agree.

Nikki takes my hand and then Miller's and leads the charge upstairs. I'm sure people are probably watching us, and perhaps I should care about that, but I really don't. The thought of having sex while someone else is in the room turns my crank like nothing ever has, and it's not until right this second that I'm learning that about myself.

I'm hard before we even reach my room.

Nikki goes in first, already stripping her skintight tank top off and lowering her miniskirt so she's only standing in her heels and underwear.

"Holy shit," Miller mutters behind me and closes the door fast.

"Thanks." She chuckles.

My room is a shoebox, so Miller brushes by me to get to my tiny study desk and chair in the corner. For some reason, that small contact makes every nerve ending along my skin come to life.

I fumble my way through getting undressed. The button

on my jeans doesn't cooperate, and my T-shirt gets stuck when I try to lift it over my head.

If the other two notice, they don't mention it.

I can't help the way my gaze finds Miller's. His pants are unzipped, his hard dick trying to break through the confines of his underwear.

Miller watching Nikki and me and getting himself off at the same time makes me feel like a god.

Who knew voyeurism was so hot?

I've never been so worked up, so hard, or so ready to explode. It's probably the fastest I've ever come inside someone since losing my virginity, and when I do, I come with my eyes locked on Miller's.

He may not know it yet, but what I said earlier was true. We're gonna get along just fine. I can totally see us becoming the best of friends. And with the way he comes all over his hand, I'd say we're on the same page in knowing this is so going to happen again.

CHAPTER TWO

MILLER

NOW

Shit. It happened again.

My mouth is dryer than if I'd swallowed cotton balls covered in sand, and the tiny drummer in my head pounds against my skull as if playing Van Halen's "Hot for Teacher."

I roll over to a sight I've woken up to many times before, but it's been six years since I last fell into bed with Talon and some random girl. Or in this case, *two* random girls.

The room smells like sex and cheap citrusy perfume.

This was a common occurrence back in the day, but I thought we were past it all—the reckless college phase. When I found out at the end of last season that Talon had signed with the Warriors, the last thing on my mind was going back to our old patterns. I was solely focused on football and how great being on a team with him again was going to be.

Maybe that was my survival instincts kicking in.

He was drafted to New England after he graduated USC

the year ahead of me. I got thrown around from practice team to practice team the first two years after being drafted and eventually got picked up by the Warriors three seasons ago. Because we've been in different conferences, I've barely seen Talon since he graduated. Our contact has consisted of trash talking each other on Twitter and a vague friendship on Facebook.

Now he's permanently back in my life, and it's as if he never left.

And that's why I'm one hundred percent fucked.

Because instead of looking at either woman squished against us, my gaze gets stuck on hard muscles, an unshaven square jaw, and blond hair that's short enough to run my hands through but still grip onto if I—

Nope. Don't go there, Miller.

Never. Going. To. Happen.

Talon may be open to sharing chicks, but there has always been the strict rule that it's about them. Me and him, we don't touch. His hands stay firmly on whoever we're with, and I make sure I keep mine as far away from him as possible. Because if he knew the things going on in my head while we were together, there's no way he'd ask me back to his place ever again.

Hell, if he could know what I'm thinking right now, he'd kick me out of his house buck naked.

The petite body of the blonde woman moves against me as my hard-on for my old best friend digs into her back.

"Mmm, someone's ready to go again," she says, and there's a smile in her voice.

Talon's blue eyes lazily open and lock with mine while a hot-as-hell smirk spreads across his face.

There's no way I can go another round without screwing up our entire friendship. Last night was a mistake. Alcohol and college crushes should never mix.

I pull on my earlobe—our universal sign for *party's over*—and Talon gives me the nod.

"Sorry, girls," he says and stretches. The stretch turns into reaching and bringing them both against him, freeing me to get up. "We have an early practice."

That's a lie. The season hasn't started yet, but the girls don't notice. Most jersey chasers don't know the schedule unless they're the full-on stalker type, but neither woman was interested in actual football talk last night.

A half-assed wave goodbye is all I can manage before I trudge into Talon's bathroom and get in the shower. The three of them remain in Talon's super king bed, which is the size of all of Illinois, and I try not to think about the possibility of them fitting in a quickie.

I put my head under the spray to drown out any possible noises. If I hear them going at it, I don't think I'll have the strength to resist.

And I need to resist before I become the mess I was when Talon left me the first time.

Ugh. Talon didn't leave *me*. There was nothing to leave. There still isn't. He's not ... we're not ... *Gah!*

This is why our friendship is confusing, and why I haven't let myself think much about him.

I'm almost finished in the shower when Talon saunters into the bathroom and pisses in front of me. Does this mansion not have another bathroom?

It's easy to see the difference in our pay grades, and that's just by standing in his bathroom. It's all legit marble tile with expensive fixtures and fancy shower settings. It matches everything else in the Lincoln Park address.

"You mind?" I grumble.

"Nothin' you haven't seen before."

Truth. After three years of being on the same team in college and rooming together for two of those years, I've seen way too much to still be into the guy, but apparently, even unattractive bodily functions won't turn me off him.

"Just like old times, right?" Talon grins. "We should've made an effort to keep in touch over the years."

"Mmm." I duck my head under the spray again. I won't get into why I ignored his messages about catching up whenever we happened to be in the same city. He tried, but I always made excuses. In my defense, it wasn't hard to feign being busy, and Talon understood it. It's not that I didn't want to see him. I did. I was ninety percent sure I was over him by the time I was drafted, but I did worry *this* would happen.

With one night, I'm back where I was six years ago—pining for something I can't have.

"They gone?" I ask.

"Yep. And get this"—he finishes his business and turns to face me, and I have to look at the roof so my gaze doesn't fall to his cock—"I asked for their number, and they giggled as if I was joking and left."

I chuckle. "Someone's ego bruised?"

"I don't get it. It was fun, right? Who wouldn't want more of that?"

"You don't marry the girl who bangs your friend in front of you. They know that."

"Is that slut shaming I hear?"

"No, but normal people kinda prefer it if their partners

don't willingly fuck their friends." I don't know how this concept is lost on Talon.

"I don't get it, man. I'd love a wife who'd let me play with others. Or watch as she played with others."

"That's true love." I rinse off and stop the shower. When I step out, Talon holds a towel out for me as if this isn't weird at all.

He's always been carefree and had an I-don't-give-a-shit attitude. He's comfortable in his skin and doesn't care about our current state of undress. Living in a locker room for over ten years will do that to a guy, but this isn't a locker room, and his assured confidence hasn't wavered.

Me, on the other hand, I'm hoping to hell he doesn't look down and see how much I'm enjoying the view.

Guilt gnaws at me. Not over last night but the three years we were pulling this type of shit in college. I fear he'll figure me out—that I like sharing with him way more than I should. Keeping my secret from him is a betrayal of the utmost degree. Yeah, I like women, but Talon helped me discover all those years ago that I like men too. And after he graduated, I spent a year figuring out exactly what that meant. After experimenting with a few other guys, I came to the conclusion I really like one man in particular. The guys in college proved to me I was bi, but I think I'm technically pan. I fell for Talon because of who he is, not because he's a guy.

"I know your momma told you to share as a child, but I think that's taking it a bit too far."

I hate that my voice comes out croaky, but it's taking all my energy to make words work at all.

"It's ... I dunno ... better when there's more than two people." He looks at me for confirmation of that.

I dry off and wrap my towel around me, hoping Talon can't see the tent in it. "One of the girls kept moaning your full name, even when she was with me. She probably only agreed to a four-way so she could say she bagged *Marcus Talon*. Trust when I say my name and … that other girl's will not be in the retelling of her story."

"I guess that's for the best," Talon says. "Maybe we should get them to sign NDAs beforehand."

I snort. "Hey, ladies, you can't see my dick until I see a signature. Classy as fuck."

Talon laughs.

"But that won't matter anyway. It, uh, shouldn't happen again."

Talon slumps. "Not you too."

"You've seen what the media has put Jackson through the last few months. Can you imagine if this got out? People are freaking out because he has a guy in his bed. *One* guy. What will they think when they find out what we're doing? We're not in college anymore, NDAs aren't foolproof, and if the league—"

"It's not like we're … like Jackson."

"Gay, you mean? You think the media will care about technicalities? You and I have shared a bed on more than one occasion. Yes, there are other people involved, and to us, it's not a big deal, but I don't think that makes it any less scandalous. It probably makes it more." I won't mention contemplating taking magician classes to make the girls disappear—that's a whole other issue.

"Okay, I get it, but it still sucks. We should be able to do whatever the hell we want off the field."

I scoff. "How about you whine to Jackson about that. He'll probably punch you out after what he's been through."

Being the first out guy in the league, Jackson hasn't had it easy.

I go to walk out of the bathroom but pause in the doorway. I shouldn't ask, but the question comes out anyway. "Would you really want a relationship with more than one person? Like ... a permanent arrangement?"

My heart stutters, preparing for an answer I'm not sure I want. A yes would give me hope there was some sort of future with him, but it would also mean I'd continue to make the same mistakes again and again, and nothing between us would change. I'd still be with him but not *with* him.

"What, not for you?"

The fact Talon's deflected and hasn't answered my question isn't lost on me.

I shake my head. "Nah, I couldn't do it. Like you said, this is fun and all, but if I was serious about someone, it'd be just them."

"Oh, to have that type of attention span," Talon says with wistfulness in his tone.

I can't help laughing at the big idiot, and now I'm back where I was six years ago—in his bed but not allowed to touch him. And until last night, I was blissfully unaware of how much I've missed him.

Talk about fucking torture.

CHAPTER THREE

TALON

Miller is ignoring me. *Me.* None of my other friends could get away with that, but Miller's not like anyone else in my life. He's ... I don't know what he is. He's like a brother to me, but that label feels wrong—especially after the shit we've done.

I haven't seen him since the night we took those two women home, and it's been weeks. It hasn't been for lack of trying on my part. I haven't doubted myself this much since I was a freshman and actually had to work to get a girl's attention, and I don't know why it's getting to me so much.

I had expectations signing with the Warriors. Miller and me back together again, us against the world, and winning the Super Bowl and living out our almost decade-long fantasy of holding that trophy up together.

It's always been the dream, so I don't know why he's not the same Miller I knew in college.

Granted, we haven't really known each other these past six

years, but we made a pact his freshman year. It was gonna be us.

Now there's a chance for it to happen, and he's blowing me off, and I don't know why.

Today, he can't avoid me because it's the first day of training camp, and if he thinks I won't call him on it, then he doesn't know me at all.

We don't have to be attached at the hip, but if he's pulling away because he regrets what we did, I may have to slap him upside the head.

It was just sex. Really hot, awesome sex. But it didn't mean anything, and it's not like we touched or nothin', so I don't know why he's being weird about it. It's nothing new for us. I know he's worried the press will find out, and that'll bring a shitstorm upon the team—the team who currently pays me waaay too much to throw around a football—and when I think about it like that, it probably was a mistake to risk it all for an orgy. That still doesn't explain why he's avoiding me though. It won't happen again. No big deal.

After enduring the mother of all press conferences kicking off training camp, Jackson and I are sent to the stadium to meet the rest of the team on the field.

Jackson and I are the only dipshits in suits thanks to the press conference, and DeShawn notices immediately.

"Nice tie." He nudges me. It takes me off guard, and I stumble, because I'm too distracted by wondering why Miller isn't even looking at me.

"Hey, careful with the merchandise. Jackson and I are precious," I say. Because, well, I'm me, and I can't help it.

"*Precious* is one word for it," Miller mumbles.

His mocking snaps the tension between us, and I throw my

arm around his giant shoulders and try to get him in a headlock.

"What was that? Didn't hear you," I taunt.

He fights back but not hard, and I begin to think I've read too much into his radio silence the last few weeks, because this is us. It's what we do.

We goof, we joke, and our antics could be mistaken for that of teenage boys.

Coach Caldwell's voice puts an end to it though. "Cut the shit, Talon. Everyone, take a seat."

There's a round of grumbles, and I don't realize what they're for until Coach starts his speech. It doesn't go the way these things normally do. We're sat down like children and told how to play nice with the new gay kid on the team. That's paraphrasing, and it sucks that Jackson has to go through this at all. I want to yell out that this whole damn thing is unnecessary, but if the glares certain teammates are sending Jackson's way are any indication, it seems we're not all up to date with the love is love movement.

It's a sad day when I'm considered more mature than others.

Once we're released, some of the guys hang around on the field, but Miller stalks off like he's on a mission. He's not gonna get away so easy.

I catch up to him and throw my arm around him. "Dude, where's the fire? Was gonna go for a beer."

His shoulders stiffen under my arm, but that doesn't mean anything. The guy's a tank. His shoulders are probably ninety-nine percent muscle and always that hard.

"I've still gotta put in a few more hours in the gym." He

rubs his stomach. "Definitely ate too much crap over break. Training is going to kill me if Coach doesn't first."

"All right. Guess I better put in the hours anyway."

Miller looks down at his feet, and I'm back on the he's-ignoring-me bandwagon. I grab his arm to stop him from walking down the tunnel toward the locker rooms.

"Are we cool?" I ask.

He pulls back, almost taken off guard or confused. "Yeah. Why wouldn't we be?"

"I dunno, man. You're acting weird."

Miller shakes his head. "Just got a lot going on right now. Not all of us were born superstars like you. We have to actually work for it."

"What the fuck?"

He has never said that kind of shit to me before, and he knows how much I hate it. I may play hard, but I work harder. Everyone only ever sees what they want to, though, and that's usually the fun side of me.

"You know what I mean, Talon. You have more natural talent in your arm than any of us do in our entire bodies."

"That's because I'm Talon-ted ... Get it? *Talon*-ted."

Miller huffs, but I can't work out if it's a true laugh or he's pitying me.

"Well, it's not funny if I have to spell it out," I mumble.

He shakes his head. "I can't lose my place on this team. I ... I need to focus."

"Got it." I think Miller's full of it, but he isn't completely wrong. We should be hitting the weights to get back in top physical form for the season to start.

I let him walk away, and for the first time since I moved

here, I realize things between us can't easily go back to the way they were in college.

Apparently being a grown-up means shit changes, and if that's the case, when the fuck did I get old?

I always figured a life-altering moment would begin with a gut warning or spidey senses telling me something's not right. But no. Apparently, whatever controls my life, whether it be fate, the universe, or a god with a sick sense of humor, whatever it is, they're probably laughing their ass off at me right now.

With Miller being weird, I had the plan to drag Jackson out for a few drinks. The coaches have roomed us together because of my status and his ... gayness. They think having me around Jackson will give him some sort of protection. I'm happy to do it, but I wasn't expecting the eyeful I just got.

It's nothing I haven't seen before being on the road with testosterone-filled athletes who need to blow off stress, but this was different.

Jackson and his boyfriend, Noah, were going at it when I walked in, and I couldn't bring myself to walk away.

I stood, mesmerized by their bodies moving against one another. Hard muscle against Noah's toned frame, miles of bare skin, light against dark ... Even though they were rutting against each other like animals in heat, Jackson whispering claiming words of *love* and *forever* while they got totally lost in one another is what I can't get out of my head.

As soon as they realized I was there, I couldn't get out of there fast enough. I have no idea what I said or did, but my feet led me down to the lobby as fast as they could carry me.

Now, sitting at the hotel bar with a glass of scotch in front of me, I can't bring myself to take a drink in fear I won't be able to swallow it without choking.

It's not from disgust or shock or whatever someone might expect a straight guy to feel when seeing two men naked and writhing, moaning manly sounds and grunts, and covering each other in cum. Nope, it's the utter surprise of how much I liked it that's freaking me out.

Not just liked it but got hard over it, and I don't mean a little twitch of interest. My cock was practically sticking straight up as if volunteering to join them.

I've seen porn where it's been two guys on one girl. Hell, I've lived that with Miller, but doing stuff with him or any other guy had never occurred to me. I didn't even know something like that could turn me on. Seeing Miller's muscular arms wrapped around a woman's petite frame drives me wild, but I always thought it was her or both of them together that was the appeal. Now, I can't help thinking otherwise, because what I just saw flipped a switch ... or opened my eyes. Or something.

I internally groan and refrain from banging my head on the bar in front of me.

I don't know what's worse: making a big deal out of nothing and possibly creating a weird relationship with my roommate or that I can't stop picturing Jackson on top of his boyfriend.

They moved in sync, like they knew each other inside and out. It was frantic but also full of tenderness, like the way Jackson cupped his boyfriend's face as he kissed him slowly, and they were so invested in each other they didn't even hear me come in.

Until this moment, I'd only heard of that type of love existing. People claim it. You see tenderness between lovers when they walk down the street. The kiss of a hand. In the gentle way their mouths come together. But that's all in public. It's tame and appropriate. It's not primal or needy.

When Miller said he could only be with one person, I didn't understand it, but there's no doubt in my mind I just witnessed what he meant by it. All of my relationships have been about having fun, and fun to me is as many sweaty bodies as you can fit in a bed.

I wonder if Miller's ever had that—the elusive single soul to connect with. The way he spoke about being with one person, it sounded like he knew from experience. He didn't have anyone serious in college, but that doesn't mean anything. We've fallen out of touch these past six years. He could've had a harem of women, and I wouldn't know.

I wonder if he's ever looked at anyone like Jackson looks at his boyfriend. I wouldn't even know how to see someone in that light. I've never felt it with any woman I've been with, and I'm pretty sure they've never felt it for me.

After twenty minutes of overanalyzing, I realize I've become a walking cliché—having an existential crisis in a bar.

By the time Jackson finds me, I've almost finished my drink but am no closer to figuring out what just happened or why I'm comparing what Jackson and Noah have with my friendship with Miller.

"So ... uh, that happened," Jackson says.

I snort, but one look in his eyes, and I can tell he's freaking out.

Shit, here I am thinking about me, like always, I haven't even wondered what could be going through Jackson's head.

"Whoa, Jackson. It's okay. Wait, do you think I'm pissed you were hooking up in our room? You think I haven't seen that type of shit before on the road?"

"Not with two guys, no."

That's definitely not the issue I'm having. Or is it?

I try to explain what happened, but I totally dig myself a deeper hole I won't be able to get out of if I keep going. "I feel like a creep. For, like, watching and stuff."

Jackson looks even more freaked out now. Great.

"Not for ages or anything. I was taken off guard, and I couldn't move, and then it was all over, and I had to say something, or you would've thought I'd been there the whole time, but I wasn't, and …" Fuck, kill me now.

"Can we totally forget this ever happened?" Jackson asks. "I'll never sneak Noah into a hotel room again, and if you ask for a new roommate, I will totally understand."

"Not going to ask for a new roommate, dickhead."

Jackson smiles, and just like that, we promise to never mention it again.

Now if it was that easy to forget it too.

"Blue eighteen! Blue eighteen! Set. Hut."

On the field, I become a commanding figure. Everyone sees the fun-loving me on the outside, but when that clock is ticking, there's only one thing I want. The touchdown. The points. The glory.

What I don't want is getting sacked because my offense can't keep defense off my ass.

Training is not going well. The team this year is made up

of newbies, rookies, and a couple of veterans, yet we're all playing like we're in the juniors.

I cough, my lungs hurting from being crushed by Henderson—one of our linebackers and team captains.

"Sorry, Talon," he says as we climb to our feet, but it sounds sarcastic. I've been warned he's a bit of an asshole and thinks he's the best on this team. Well, not anymore. When he sees I'm not playing like he is, he tries the blame game. "Miller fuckin' tripped me."

"No sweat." Just blood.

Stop being dramatic.

Miller at least looks ashamed. Henderson may be hazing me for being the new guy, but Miller's supposed to be my protector. He checks my blindside so I don't have to.

"Where were you on that one?" I bark.

"Sorry. Are you okay?"

"Let's run it again."

Miller turns to go back into position, but I stop him.

"You and I are gonna have words. Tonight. Dinner. And you can't say no this time."

His mouth opens to protest, but he thinks better of it. "Got it."

We get through practice without another complete screwup, which puts me in a better mood than this morning. But when we break for the day and hit the showers, Miller's one of the first guys out the door.

Guess he's gonna blow me off again.

I don't know why I'm trying so hard with him when it's obvious he doesn't want to be friends now or whatever.

Teammates. I can handle that even if I'll hate it. I want to clear the air with him so we can go back to working like an actual team. I've never had to doubt him until today.

Out on that field, he broke more than our friendship. He broke trust.

Yeah, it was only one tackle he let through, but it was a tackle I shouldn't have had to worry about. Not with *him*. If he can't even keep a teammate off me during training, how's he supposed to do it during an actual game?

I dress slowly because defeat weighs me down. Miller doesn't want to hear what I have to say, and I don't know why that gets to me so much. Any other guy I'd write off and not care about, but when we were in college, we were so close it felt like all I needed was him. Girls came and went, and my parents and brother were back home in Denver. Miller and I both had a ton of friends, but they didn't know the real us. They knew the football stars. The big jocks on campus.

I always thought Miller understood that, and what we had wasn't your average friendship, but clearly he's outgrown it. Or maybe we weren't as close as I thought we were.

Outside the locker room, I hate the way my face brightens when I see him there waiting for me.

"What took you so long? Did you have to do your hair to make yourself pretty or what?" Miller reaches over and messes up my hair.

"Fuck off." I swat at his hand. "We doing this?"

"Uh, yeah. Is it all right I invited Jackson too? I figure if you're going to ream me for that tackle today, the new kid can see how much of a hard-ass you can be when we fuck up."

I can't talk about everything in front of Jackson, and Miller either knows this or thinks I only want to yell at him for the shitty practice.

Looking Jackson in the eye after the other day is gonna be fun.

It's not strained between us, but it's not exactly comfortable. I get the feeling he thinks it's because he was with a guy, no matter how much I want to tell him it's not. But if I do that, I have to explain I now feel weird around him because he and his boyfriend made something in my brain short-circuit and I haven't been able to think about much else since it happened. Other than football. And Miller. But all of it seems to tie together in my head, and I don't know why.

"We ready?" Jackson asks behind me, and I startle.

"Uh … yeah. Let's go. Wait, where are we going? What's good here?"

"I know somewhere that won't give us food poisoning," Miller says.

"Sold," Jackson says with a laugh.

CHAPTER FOUR

MILLER

"Hooters?" Talon asks. "You brought us to *Hooters*?"

"What's wrong with that?" Truth is, it's the most manly, most *I'm totally into only chicks and not you* place I could think of.

"Jackson's gay, for one," Talon says.

"They have awesome onion rings here. I'm good," Jackson says. "And I'm starving."

I brought Jackson as a buffer, because Talon should only stick to football talk if someone else is here. He wants to talk to me about what happened a few weeks ago and how blocking him at every chance is a dick thing to do, but the way I see it, there's nothing to discuss. It's not going to happen again, and he's straight. Talking about it will only remind me of how much I fucked up by repeating old mistakes.

As we enter the restaurant and are assaulted by the scent of fried food and toxic masculinity, the hostess greets us with terms of endearment like "sweetie" and "cutie" and "hot stuff."

When we're seated at a table and finish ordering drinks

from the waitress, a weird vibe settles between all of us. Talon refuses to look at Jackson, I refuse to look at Talon, and Jackson looks at the menu as if this is normal. Or maybe he can tell something's up and wants to bury his head.

"So, uh, let's hear it," I say. "Rip me a new one for being distracted today."

Talon looks between me and Jackson and then looks at the table as he casually says, "Don't do it again."

That's all I get?

"That's it?" Jackson asks. "I was expecting some drill-sergeant type shit." He shakes his head. "I'm so disappointed in you, Talon."

The waitress appears with our drinks, and as she puts Jackson's down in front of him, she practically pushes her boobs into his face, which makes Talon and I snicker.

"As disappointing as that experience was?" Talon asks when she moves away.

Jackson takes a sip of Coke. "Eh. They're just boobs."

And that's how I know I'm definitely bi and not gay. "*Just* boobs?"

"Do you know how productive I would be if I had that reaction to boobs?" Talon says. I almost laugh until he turns to me. "Is that why you were distracted today on the field?" His eyes narrow. "Like boobs in general or a certain pair? Are you seeing someone and didn't tell me? Because that's not cool after—" He slams his mouth shut and looks at Jackson again whose eyes are ping-ponging between Talon and me.

"Hey, look at that, my phone's vibrating." Jackson grabs out his phone, which is so not ringing, but that doesn't stop him from pretending it is. "It's Noah. I better take this outside." He rushes out faster than a wide receiver on a breakaway.

"I'm not seeing anyone," I say.

"Then what's going on?"

"What do you mean?" I know exactly what he means, but I'm not gonna spell it out for him in the middle of a restaurant. *Hooters*, at that.

"Why are you avoiding me?"

What if you never see me as anything more than a guy you share girls with? Or worse yet, what if you see right through me and want nothing to do with me anymore?

"I'm not."

"Now you're lying to me? Look, man, I get where you're coming from with the media finding out and all that. I can promise it won't happen again, and I won't ask you about it anymore, but you have to stop pretending like you're too busy for me. I don't want a stupid night of drunken fun to come between us."

He doesn't understand that it wasn't just a stupid night to me, and he never will.

"I can do that," I lie.

"Okay. Problem solved. We go back to being you and me and pretend that night never happened."

If only it was that easy.

Talon moves on as if the issue is now done and buried. "Now, how long do you think we should make Jackson suffer with pretending to be on the phone to his boyfriend?"

I manage a strained smile. "Until we finish off his food, at least."

"Good man. There's the Miller I know and love."

I try hard not to show how my body tenses. If only he knew what saying that kind of shit does to me.

I've heard stories about queer guys crushing on their

straight friends and how hard it is. But hearing about it and feeling it are two completely different things. The twist in my gut when he says something like that makes my chest tighter and tighter until soon his words will be like a tourniquet wrapped around my heart.

The best thing about training camp is we barely get time or have the energy to jerk off let alone go out or do anything. It's made things between Talon and me easier because we can't spend awkward dinners together weirding out Jackson too often. It's only happened once since Hooters, but now Jackson is mysteriously "busy" when Talon mentions going for dinner. Says he spends his alone time Skyping his boyfriend who's in the middle of moving from New York to Chicago for him.

We're so exhausted a few weeks in that when Talon and I do go out to dinner, we're generally too tired to do anything but eat, grunt one-word answers at each other, and leave. And while I'm doing my best to make everything appear normal between us, it's not like it used to be. I think he knows it, but he's dropped it since our last conversation.

I want to put us both out of our misery, but that would include coming out to him, and that's something I haven't done with anyone—not even the guys I hooked up with after Talon had left.

When he graduated, I was so lost I had no idea what was going on with me. There was a hole in my chest, and I had to figure out if it was a Talon thing or a guy thing.

Closet doors are heavy, and college campuses are surprisingly filled with lots of guys happy to experiment behind them.

So I tried, but it never felt the same.

When I made the NFL, I worried about one of my hookups coming forward, but they never did. The thought of the possibility scared me out of trying to hook up with another guy again, though.

Even though I enjoyed fooling around with those guys, I walked away each time satisfied physically but feeling hollow inside. Because while I was with them, I was picturing somebody else. When I'm with women, the ghost of Talon doesn't haunt me.

Now that he's moved here, he can haunt me in real life.

And as I walk into the weight room, and he's over on the other side of the gym on the elliptical machine, I sigh because I can't help it when I look at him. It's a sigh of frustration, appreciation, and longing all rolled into one.

It doesn't help I've never been more nervous on final cut day than this year. I'm only twenty-seven, I still have years of my career ahead of me—hopefully—but I've been off this training camp. The shit between me and Talon is affecting my game, and I hate to say it because he's the best guy I know, but I wish he'd never taken the contract with the Warriors. He should've stayed with New England, or hell, there were rumors Denver wanted him too. He could've gone home to his family, and I could've continued to live without the constant reminder of him.

"You look like you're gonna hurl, Miller," Henderson says from spotting Carter on the bench press. "Someone scared of getting cut?"

For a team captain, he's not very captainly.

I ignore him and tune out the world so I can make it through my workout, but when I'm on the leg push finishing my last set, Talon walks across the room, and I falter like I always do when he lights up whatever Goddamn space he takes up.

Something twinges in my leg, and I let out a grunt of pain —okay, might've been a manly screech—and catch everyone's attention.

Talon, of course, makes his way straight over to me. "You okay?"

I wince. "Yeah, yeah. I'm fine. Think I'm done though. My body's protesting."

Talon grins. "You're getting old, man."

"I'm younger than you, asshole." When I stand, my leg protests. "Oh, fuck."

I almost topple to the ground, but Talon's right there to hold me up, and then Jackson appears out of nowhere on my other side.

"Come on, big guy," Jackson says. "You need to go to the trainer. You might've sprained something."

"Just what I need," I mutter. Another pain I can blame Talon for.

They help me hobble into the trainer's room and onto the massage table. The pain gets worse when I put pressure on the leg, but I'm sure I'm fine. I just pulled something.

The coaches and trainer all wear solemn expressions when I can't keep quiet at the poking and prodding the trainer does to me.

"I'm fine," I reassure everyone, but it's as if I'm invisible.

"It's a sprained hamstring," the trainer says.

"Must've pulled it while working out," I say, trying to be

helpful, but all it does is welcome a "No shit, Captain Obvious" from Talon, who hasn't left my side.

"Get him back to the hotel and make sure he ices that thing," Coach Caldwell says and storms out of the room.

"Such a slacker," Talon jokes. "Come on, lean on my shoulder, but don't break me."

"Yeah, yeah, you're precious."

Athletes push through the agony of injuries all the time. Pain is insignificant, and we're reminded constantly that a broken player is an expendable player. But no matter how many times I tell myself that I'm okay—that the trainer is wrong and I only pulled a muscle or landed on it funny and can shake it out—every time I put a little weight behind it, I want to scream.

Talon's arm around me isn't even enough to forget about how painful it is. Not even the scent of his shampoo that smells exactly like college or the scruff on his chin where he hasn't shaved for days. Everything that has distracted me these past few weeks can't distract me from the burning in my leg.

The university hosting training camp is within walking distance of our hotel, but I can barely make it to the campus entry, let alone a few blocks up the street.

"Let's chill here and get a cab," Talon says.

He lets me go, and I lean against the building, trying to catch my breath.

"Are we sure it's a sprain and not a tear?" he asks, assessing how much I'm struggling. "Like, should we maybe go to the hospital?"

"It's just a sprain," I say. "The trainer wouldn't have let me go if it could be anything worse."

Talon taps away on his phone. "All right. Cab should be here in a few minutes."

He slips his phone in his pocket, and then the awkward silence that's been happening since Talon joined the team reappears once again. At least this time, I can blame my leg.

"So … funny story." Talon rocks back on his heels. "I walked in on Jackson and his boyfriend a few weeks back. Totally naked and grinding all up on each other."

I practically choke on my tongue. "You *what?*"

"Yup. Well, they weren't having sex-sex. Like … gay sex … you know …"

I snicker at him fumbling over the word *anal.*

"They were naked and … yeah … grinding."

"Umm … why exactly are you telling me this?"

Talon shrugs. "Distraction? Is it working? Bet you're not concentrating so hard on your leg when you've got the image of two dudes going at it in your head."

God, the last thing I need right now is a hard-on, so I try not to think about what that would've looked like. Jackson's almost as big as me—big muscles, tall frame. Although, he's only six-three, and I'm six-five. His boyfriend is around six-one and lanky with a lithe but toned body …

Stop thinking about how hot they'd be together.

"Wait, is that why you two have been weird around each other lately?" I ask. "I thought it was because …" *Of us.*

I can't say that out loud because I'm supposed to be going back to normal with him.

Talon frowns. "It's not weird between Jackson and me."

"You refuse to look him in the eye even when you're talking to him."

"That's because I … because I thought … and then I'm all … I mean …"

"Aww, did someone forget how to use their words," I say in the same voice I talk to my niece with.

"Shut up." The tips of Talon's ears turn pink, and now I'm pissed at myself for mocking him. Because if the flush creeping across his face and his awkwardness have anything to say, it's that he might not have entirely hated seeing Jackson and his boyfriend together.

Don't be a fucking idiot, Shane.

Right. Straight guys don't get turned on by gay sex. They just don't.

CHAPTER FIVE

TALON

Standing here in the sweltering July heat, waiting for a cab, I come so close to talking to Miller about walking in on Jackson and Noah and asking him if my reaction is normal, but before I can, my brain reminds me that I've been naked with the man and not just in a locker room.

We've shared a bed and countless women over the years, and suddenly, I'm seeing it in a new light.

My mind thinks of Miller's hard muscles and drops of sweat breaking out over his skin, and I'm not talking about when we've been training or on the field. I remember vividly the sound he makes when he comes. Before now, I didn't realize I'd paid so much attention.

He's right that things between me and Jackson aren't great, and that's eating at me too. I don't want to be awkward around him, but to get over it, I need to get those images of Jackson and Noah out of my head.

I need an explanation ... no, that's not the right word. Clarity? Rationalism? Whatever it is, I don't know how to get it without an outside perspective, but laying it out there like that?

Yeah, I don't want to play that game.

I'm the guy who has it all figured out. Or, I appear to be. Ask me about women, ask me about football, hell, ask me about a diet regime to suit your workout needs, I'm your man. Sexuality confusion?

Fuck, is that even what this is?

I look over at Miller leaning against the wall, his head back against the brick of the building and his eyes closed. His chest rises and falls fast, as if he's breathing through the pain, and as my gaze travels over his large chest, powerful arms, and thick and powerful thighs, I can't help thinking how amazing he looks.

So, uh, yeah, I guess I can definitely say this is confusion. But if I think hard about that, then I have to wonder when it started. Because even though walking in on Jackson and Noah is the thing that made me step back and go ... hang on, that's not a normal reaction for a straight guy, I'm now thinking I've done other things I should've realized before.

Shared a bed with Miller being the main one.

My sarcasm senses tingle, and an annoying voice in the back of my head says: *it's not gay if it's in a three-way.*

I snort, and Miller's head lifts.

"What's funny?" he asks.

Lie. Lie your ass off. "I was thinking we've been through some shit together, haven't we?"

He smiles, and dimples appear. It reminds me of the millions of times I've seen that exact expression on him, and warmth fills my chest.

Yep. Definite confusion.

"Yeah, we've been through some crazy shit."

A memory springs to mind. "Hey, remember that time we got blind drunk and decided it was a good idea for the kid in the dorm across from us to drive us from USC to San Francisco because we just had to see the Golden Gate Bridge?"

Miller laughs. "I vaguely remember Coach yelling at us for missing practice to see Alcatraz and we may as well stay there where we belong."

"He had a right to be pissed. We didn't know how we were getting back to L.A."

Miller's face drops. "What happened to the guy? Is it bad we can't remember his name?"

"Probably. But he was driving home for the weekend, remember? When we're drunk, we don't think about the next day."

Something sparks in his eyes, and his lips twitch. "I think that's an understatement when it comes to us."

And now I'm thinking about every hookup and Miller's big hands roaming over skin. Lots and lots of skin of different colors and shapes. We really didn't discriminate.

I thought the San Francisco story was safe, but nope, I'm back on the *what the fuck is happening* train.

Out of everyone I know, Jackson's the one I should be able to talk to about ... whatever it is in my head that keeps thinking of him pressed against another dude. And why I'm suddenly remembering a whole heap of stuff between me and Miller that I shouldn't be.

The main thing that keeps repeating in my head, and I don't know why, is the way Jackson laid his claim with his boyfriend. The whispered words, the gentle touches even though they were really going at it. I've never felt that with anyone. Hell, I need to have more than one person in my bed just so I can feel *something.*

Aww, poor little star quarterback is bored with his sex life.

Damn, I can be an asshole. Even to myself.

My sarcastic conscience is replaced by my rational one. Contrary to the way I act sometimes, I do have some common sense.

Football.

Forget sex, and focus on football.

Only, that's like telling myself *Don't look over there!* Because now sex is all I want to think about.

And when the cab pulls up, and I help Miller get in the back, I'm conscious of every move he makes in his seat, every breath he takes ... Fuck, now I sound like that stalker song Sting sang.

I force myself to not freak out and get Miller back to his hotel room. Like a pro, I get him settled on his bed, ignore the flashback of him going at it with a girl while I watched, and go to the bedside phone to call the front desk and ask for ice packs.

"I'm not an invalid, you know," Miller says. "Go back to training."

Oh, I want to get out of here all right but not to go back to training. My body's alert and edgy, and while a workout would probably help calm me down, so would a good jerk-off session back in my own room.

"Seriously, go. I'll be fine," Miller says.

"All right." I pick up the phone again and ask them to bring a master key to let themselves in.

"I'm fine," Miller complains.

"Mmhmm, sure you are."

The guy on the line says they'll be right up.

I would stay to make sure Miller doesn't get out of bed, but if I stay in here any longer, I may go insane.

Like you're not already halfway there.

I head for the door but turn back at the last second. "Make sure you ice that leg."

"Okay, Mom."

Giving him a smile, I leave the room and can't get back to mine fast enough.

With Jackson still at training, I have the room to myself, and I don't waste time losing my clothes.

There's no time or enough patience for me to grab my phone and look for porn. My cock was full mast by the time I'd reached my door, so there's no need for it.

I lie on my bed and take myself in my hand and give a few strokes before I need to add spit for smoother friction.

The groan that escapes sounds deep and guttural, and I wonder what it'd sound like in another man's voice.

No, don't think about that.

My brain doesn't listen. It flashes back to Jackson grinding on his boyfriend, me standing there hard as a rock, and those three words I've never said or heard directed at me.

My cock pulses under my hand as I stroke faster, and my heart beats in my throat.

Women. Think about women.

The only problem with this is the times I've been with one woman, it hasn't been as explosive as any of the times I've been there with Miller.

So now *he's* in my head too. And he's beautiful.

No, not beautiful. It's just sex. It was always just sex.

Lesbian porn! Think of that.

Oh, who am I kidding. That's never done it for me. Maybe I'm a voyeur, or maybe I have been oblivious to my attraction to guys for a long time, because to me, there's nothing hotter than watching while Miller takes a girl. Or him watching me.

So, go with that.

The minute my conscience allows me to let go, the need to come hits with full force. Only, when I picture Miller, he's not with a girl.

He stands in front of me with his hard abs, olive skin, and that tattoo over his left pec. *Believe. Achieve.* He got that when we were drunk one night and we were talking about our future pro careers. He thought if he tattooed it to his chest it'd come true.

I video called him the day he was drafted—of course, I did—and I'd be lying if I said I wasn't hoping for him to be picked up by New England, but I knew the chances were slim. We had offensive linemen up to our ears. He was in the fourth round, so it wasn't televised; I wanted to see his reaction when he found out what team had chosen him, but it didn't matter, because his smile was still there when he finally answered my call.

Without warning, my orgasm slams into me, and I come all over my stomach and chest. I keep stroking until I have nothing left and my muscles stop convulsing.

Breathing heavy, I'm thrown into the reality that I jerked off to my best friend. Not his body. Not him banging some girl in front of me. But of the day he was drafted. It was all *him.*

Well, that's new ...

My finger hovers over my brother's name on my phone, but I can't bring myself to press *Call.* We've always been super close, but this ... this might be out of the realm of our relationship. He's the only one outside of this whole situation who I'm comfortable talking to, but even then, admitting to another guy you got turned on by other guys and then jerked it to—

Fuck it. Trey isn't the type of guy to freak out over this stuff. I don't think.

Shit, what if he is? I wouldn't think he'd be like that. Mom and Dad might be religious people, but they believe God created everyone the way they are for a reason and that He loves everyone no matter what, and we were raised with those same values. So, I should call my brother.

Maybe.

If I didn't have a practice game this afternoon, I'd be chugging down all the mini bottles of alcohol in the minibar for some courage.

My leg bounces as I force myself to click on his name.

"Yello," he answers like a douche.

"Green," I say dryly.

"What's up, little brother? Shouldn't you be throwing a football and getting paid big stupid money for it?"

"I, uh, have a completely random question for you."

"Yes, you're still a dork even though you're super famous now."

"Shut up. Can we be serious for a minute?"

The line goes silent.

"Is everything okay?" he finally asks.

"It's fine. I'm just ... curious." My eyes widen at the poor choice of words. "I mean wondering. I was thinking ..."

"What is it? You're freaking me out."

"Well ... you know how Jackson plays for Chicago now?"

"The gay guy? What about him? If you're about to say something homophobic, you're not too old to get a kick in the ass."

I chuckle. "No, but that makes this a little easier. I, umm, kinda ... walked in on him and his boyfriend."

Trey makes a kind of choking sound as if he's trying to hold in laughter. "Awkward," he sings.

"Right. Even more awkward by, umm ..."

"By what?"

"I kinda ... well, I ... and then." There I go losing the ability to talk again. "It's not like I had any desire to join them or anything, but I kinda stood there, and then ... and then ..."

"You liked it?" There's no malice, no disgust, just curiosity.

"Yes? No? I don't know. It's not like I ... you know ..."

"No, I don't know. Remember what Mom always said to us as teenagers. If you can't even say sex, penis, or any of the correct technical terms, you're not mature enough to be having sex."

I feel like a kid again asking my older brother for advice on girls. "I, like, got hard. And I can't stop picturing them together. And—"

I'm cut off by the laugh Trey's been holding in, and I want to die. Just kill me now and put me out of my misery.

"So glad you find this funny, bro."

"I'm only laughing because you're freaking out over *nothing.* Do you find your teammate attractive?"

"No," I say easily.

"His boyfriend?"

"No. He's definitely good-looking in the way movie stars are, but no, I don't find him attractive."

"When you watch porn, are you attracted to the guy on the screen?"

"Where are you going with this? It's obviously a no."

"What about the girls? Are you attracted to them?"

I have to think about that. My immediate response is yes, but I can't even picture a single porn star's face or body. It's more the act than the girls. "Umm, I don't think so."

"Exactly. You got turned on by sex. That's all. Didn't matter it was between two guys. It's still sex."

Could it really be that simple?

"Or, you know, homosexuality is contagious, and you've caught it."

"Can I kick *your* ass for saying phobic shit?"

"Nope, because if you can't tell that I was being sarcastic, we have bigger problems than you getting turned on by two dudes fucking each other."

"They weren't actually fuck—you know what, never mind. I gotta go."

"Stop freaking out, Marcus."

"I'm not freaking out." My voice is unnaturally high-pitched. Am I freaking out? I haven't even told him about jerking off to Miller.

"It doesn't mean anything, and you need your head clear for the season."

I really do. "You're right."

"Of course, I am. I've taught you everything you know."

"Sure you did. That's why I make millions and you're stuck at a desk job in Denver."

"There's nothing wrong with Denver, and you'd know that if you'd signed with our team and come home instead of Chicago."

I don't want to admit to him the real reason why I signed with Chicago, because after what I just confessed, I'm scared he'll take back the whole "It doesn't mean anything." And right now, that makes more sense to me than anything going on in my head. Adding Miller into the situation confuses me more, so maybe it's best if I pretend that amazing jerk-off session where I made myself come harder than I ever had before never happened.

"Chicago offered me more money," I lie. Well, it's not a complete lie. They did offer more money, but had Miller not been a Warrior, I never would've signed with them.

"Well, now you're being greedy. You're already the golden child for buying Mom and Dad a house."

"Hey, I asked if you wanted a house, but you chose a ridiculous sports car to overcompensate for your small dick."

Instead of biting back at me, my brother laughs again. Yeah, I'm fucking hilarious. "Love you, brother. I have to get back to work. You know, what us peasants do."

"All right."

"I'll talk to you later?"

"Before you go. Just ... thanks. For not making a big deal out of this."

He doesn't respond for a long time, and when he does, it's totally not what I expect. "For argument's sake, if it wasn't just the sex, and it turns out guys do it for you, it still wouldn't be a big deal to me."

Something in my gut twists, as if it knows that something in his words holds merit or makes a point.

When I end the call, I have the clarity I was after, but part of me still isn't satisfied with the dismissive answer.

CHAPTER SIX

MILLER

Something weird happens after I sprain my hamstring. Talon becomes *professional.* I've set up a Google alert for apocalyptic events, because I can't think of any other explanation for it.

My leg is still giving me issues, but it's nothing I can't handle. I see the trainer, Tina, a few times a week throughout training camp, but she and team management don't seem to be worried and keep reassuring me my position isn't in any danger.

Going into the season, I'm not at the top of my game, but as a whole, the team shows promise.

That is, until our first official game ends with us scraping by with a win. It's ugly, but we do it. Barely. It's not a great start, and we all feel the tension on the field.

Tension between Talon and me, between Jackson and Carter and a few others who aren't exactly comfortable with a gay guy on the team, and then the tension of playing with a mixed bag of players. We're a new team who has only had a month to get used to each other.

Maybe this is why Talon's turned into quarterback mode, because he won the Super Bowl two years ago, and signing with a team who hasn't even seen the Bowl for over a decade, he needs to prove to the world he made the right choice.

He signed with us even though he had an offer to re-sign with New England or move to Denver—his hometown. Arguably, two of the best teams in the league.

I couldn't make sense of it when I heard the news, but I've never asked him why. I've been too busy trying to keep my crush in check to focus on it too hard.

And just when I think I have a handle on that shit, the man himself walks into the locker room and beelines it right to me.

"How's the leg?"

"Solid," I say even if I don't believe it completely.

We play on sprains all the time. We tear tendons, we break fingers, and we get used to playing with injuries.

"Are you sure?" Talon asks. "I saw you hobbling to see Tina only two days ago."

"It's not one hundred percent, but it's not bad enough to go on the IR list or anything."

"Resting it for a game or two is better than needing to rehab it."

"Thanks, Mom," I mock.

"Your career, man." He slaps my ass in the way we're allowed to as athletes. Smacking asses while doing something manly—the straight guy's excuse to touch some man buns.

Out on the field, we're still trying to work as a team, and the Vikes are out for heads.

They have the heaviest linebacker in the fucking league,

and it's my job to block him. By halftime, I'm bruised and exhausted but still determined.

That is, until the motherfucker breaks me.

We slam into each other, and something in my leg snaps.

Oh fuck, that's a definite snap.

I go down on the field and brace the top of my hamstring. It no doubt looks like I'm trying to grab my ass, but holy fucking shit on a biscuit.

The pain brings bile to the back of my throat and blurriness to my eyes, but at the last second before I close them, I see Talon get sacked.

I'm sorry I let you down.

I should've seen this coming, but I've had my head up my ass. It's the sterile disinfectant smell, the uncomfortable hospital gown, and the small bed that make reality set in.

Complete hamstring avulsion. Six months recovery. I'm out for the rest of the season that just got started.

I'm not the first athlete to injure themselves after thinking they were invincible, but fuck, why did I think it wouldn't happen to me?

It's all fun and games until someone needs surgery.

The annoying niggly voice in the back of my head tells me it's because trying to behave normally the last month since Talon showed up was too hard.

Football, I know. Feelings and shit? They seem more trouble than they're worth. So, I've been holding onto the one thing that doesn't confuse me or have me twisted in knots—

the one thing that doesn't leave a heavy weight sitting on my chest.

I've been pushing too hard, and my body is finally pushing back.

Talon charges into my room the only way he knows how—with the grace of someone high on PCP. His post-game suit is as disheveled as his golden hair, and he looks frantic.

"What's the deal?" His gaze travels from my face to my leg, which is being iced. "I saw Tina out in the hall, but she's busy talking to the doctors."

"I'm out," I say, my voice gruff.

"Please tell me only a couple of games. Six tops."

I force the words past my lips because I don't want to say them out loud. That'll make them truer somehow. "The entire season."

Talon's expression turns to utter defeat as he runs a hand over his head, messing his hair even more. "Surgery?"

"As soon as possible."

"Next season?" His voice cracks.

"They can't say for sure, but the doc said there's no reason to think I won't make a full recovery."

Talon grabs his chest in relief. "Thank fuck."

I'm grateful he knows this isn't a time for *I told you so.* He asked me before we went out on the field, and I basically bit his head off. "I'm sorry for being an asshole earlier."

"When earlier? You're an asshole all the time, so I need specifics."

"When I said I was fine. Should've listened." It's not hard to see why people think athletes are meatheads, because we don't use our fucking heads. What's the point of pushing ourselves past our limits just for the chance to hold a trophy at the end and slip a gaudy ring on our finger?

"Like any of us would've listened if we were in your shoes. We're all pigheaded and stubborn," Talon says.

"Truth. Please tell me you at least won?"

"Of course, we did. I did this whole huddle thing where I talked you up, being all 'We have to win this for Miller!' to get everyone psyched up. Totally worked."

I narrow my eyes. "Why don't I believe you?"

"Okay, fine. Jackson said I was being cheesy and cliché, but we won, so it was totally my motivational speech."

I grin. "What was in your motivational speech?"

"The president's speech in *Independence Day*."

"You didn't."

"Oh, I did. Then Jenkins told me to shut up."

"I think your authority is compromised now."

"We won, didn't we? It's like a loophole. I get to act like a jackass so long as I'm pulling off the wins."

"Ooh, so that explains your behavior for the last ..." I squint as I pretend to count. "Oh, your entire life."

"Ooh, I almost forgot. I brought you something." Talon reaches into his pocket and pulls out his middle finger.

I cough in between muffling the word "Mature."

"Never, under any circumstances, have I ever been accused of being mature."

The conversation is how any conversation between me and Talon would've gone back in the day, and I fucking miss him so much. Having him close has messed with my head like no other person ever has.

"So, umm, yeah, Tina's getting team management approval for me to go home and have the surgery in New York," I say.

"What? Why?"

I think it's panic clouding his eyes.

"I'm gonna be on crutches and need help getting around."

Talon shrugs. "Come stay with me."

My brain cannot emphasize how much of a stupid idea that would be. Like beyond stupid. "Mom's already called me blabbering on about how she's retired now and bored and needs to fuss. She said it's her job to look after me."

Talon used to give me shit in college about being a momma's boy, but I'm not too proud to admit I owe everything to that woman. She worked two jobs to put my sister and me through college. I had a full ride, but she wanted Vanessa to go to the same school as me so I could look out for her. Mom did everything for me and my sister, and she's the reason I'm in the NFL today, so generally whatever she demands, she gets.

"Besides, you'll hardly be there and won't be much help."

Not to mention I need a break from being around Talon. Everything comes back to him and me and everything I'll never have.

Talon pulls up the visitor's chair next to my bed and slumps into it. "I hear that. My mom's still mad I didn't accept the offer from Denver."

That had confused me as well.

"Why *didn't* you go to Denver? Your entire family is there, and you complained about being so far away from them constantly when we were in college. You grew up there—"

"Money. The Warriors offered more."

"Not buying it. Denver would've offered you close to what Chicago did."

"Not trying to sell it." Leaning forward, Talon rests his elbows on the side of my bed and clasps his hands together.

This bed is tiny for a normal-sized human, so he's dangerously close to my thigh, and even though it'd be painful as hell for him to graze his hands over it, I want him to do it.

"This isn't going to make any sense to you, but the only way I can explain it is my gut sent me to Chicago."

"Your gut … because Chicago has such great pizza?"

"I knew you wouldn't understand." Talon, for once, is not in the joking mood, and that's even more confusing than anything else that's happened this last month.

"No, I think I understand," I say. "It's like on the field. You've got a sixth sense out there. It's impressive … and annoying as hell."

He backhands my arm.

"Hey, asshole, I'm injured here," I complain.

"Didn't realize your hamstring's in your biceps. Guess I should've paid more attention in anatomy in school."

"Oh, I'm sure you paid attention. Just to the wrong anatomy."

He smiles. "You're gonna be fine. Next season, we'll kick ass together."

It's the first time since he's been back in my life that it feels like it used to between us, but then he squeezes my good leg, and the nostalgic feeling of having my best friend by my side is gone, and it's replaced with the need I've always had for him. I try to suppress a shiver.

Even in pain—although a lot less thanks to the painkillers they've pumped into me—I still get turned on at his slightest touch.

I throw my head back on the pillow and close my eyes, willing my stupid dick to calm down.

"Shit, are you okay? You in pain?" Talon gets to his feet and leans over me, and fuck, this makes it worse. His face, so close to mine I can feel his body heat without even touching him. "Want me to get a nurse?"

I shake my head. "I'm all good." Distraction, that's what I need. "I do need to take a piss though." Doing that with this hard-on should be interesting.

"You need a hand?"

"Yeah, thanks." I shuffle to remove the ice packs from my leg as I brace myself to get up and try not to let the blanket fall off me. It's the only thing remotely hiding my cock.

I fail miserably.

"Guess the drugs are kicking in."

I follow his gaze to where my dick is trying to say hello under the thin hospital gown.

Way to go, Shane. You're killing it at embarrassing yourself.

"Right. The drugs are doing it." Even though I'm pretty sure limp dick is a usual side effect, not the other way around.

We stare at each other, and I swear the tips of his ears turn pink. Dunno why he'd be embarrassed when I'm the one who's hard.

"You still need to take a leak?" Talon asks. "I carried your ass across campus the other day. Twenty feet is nothing."

If he's willing to ignore the giant boner in the room, then I am too.

"What's your pain level at?" Talon asks when I struggle to get out of bed.

The smirk on his face lets me know he's messing with me. Any time we've got an injury, our trainers constantly ask what the pain level is, and it's beyond annoying.

"I dunno, but my bullshit level is at a zero, so how about not giving me any."

"Clearly, they haven't given you enough drugs if you're this grumpy. Then again, if they give you more, you'd probably poke me with that monster boner you're rocking."

"You wish." The quip rolls off my tongue like it would if I was smack talking any of the team, but this time, it makes me pause. It's different with *him.*

"Maybe I do."

It's a joke, I know that, but my body doesn't. I nearly stumble and fall on my fucking face.

"Whoa." Talon catches me and wraps his arm around my waist, while I put mine around his shoulders. "One joke about your dick, and you're falling for me, huh?"

When I stare at him as if he's lost his head, he acts as if he never said anything out of the ordinary. Either these drugs are better than I thought or he's flirting with me.

It has to be the drugs. Straight guys don't flirt with other supposed straight friends.

"I'm messing with you, man," he says and squeezes me tighter. "If you can't laugh, you're only gonna cry, and you know I'm allergic to that stuff."

"Tears?"

"It's like my kryptonite. It sucks all my awesomeness from me."

I'd like to suck something from him ... Okay, I don't think I can blame the drugs for that thought, but I'm milking the drugged-up situation as long as I can.

He smells of disgusting locker room soap, yet I can't help breathing him in.

Still as pathetic as you were six years ago.

I'm still thinking of the one thing that will never happen

while openly ignoring that reality by pining for and perving on my old best friend.

At least the walk to the bathroom helps deflate my cock with the pain in my leg coming back full force.

It takes two years to get into the bathroom. "Probably shoulda used the plastic urinal thing by my bed," I grumble.

"Need me to hold your dick?"

Yes, please. "I'm all good."

While I drain the snake, Talon stands close. Like, crossing personal boundaries close.

When I'm empty, I drop my hospital gown to cover my cock again. "You mind?"

"It's nothing I haven't seen before."

I'm reminded of the morning we woke up next to those girls and how Talon was so carefree about free balling it in front of me.

It hurts that I can't return the same level of comfort around him, but when he's near me, my skin tingles and my gut tightens with expectation and want.

My brain imagines his hand trailing down my shoulder, my back, and then down to my hip.

"Mmm, these drugs are good." It literally feels like Talon's touching me.

"You okay?" he murmurs, and his voice is impossibly close.

That's when I know it's not the drugs. I'm not imagining this.

Talon's behind me, his hand on my hip and his warm breath in my ear.

"What are you doing?" I garble. It sounds like I've been chewing on gravel.

"Wanna know something weird?"

Is he gonna say the way his hand still rests on my hip over my less-than-sexy hospital gown is weird? Because I'd agree.

"What's weird?" I ask.

"When you went down on the field tonight, my heart stopped, and I wanted to trade places with you. I wish I could take away your pain, because you're the best guy I know, Shane."

He never calls me Shane. It probably doesn't mean anything, but to me, it means *everything*. It means he doesn't see me as just a teammate. Not that I ever thought he did, but the simple use of my first name makes me even more pathetically stupid over him.

"And I can deny it all I want—tell everyone I signed with the Warriors because it was more money—but watching you tonight and helping you struggle right now, I know that it's a lie. I've been lying to myself for months."

"What lie is that?" My question is so quiet, even I barely hear it, but Talon moves in even closer.

"I moved to Chicago because I missed you. It's simple, really."

CHAPTER SEVEN

TALON

What am I doing, and why the fuck am I touching Miller like this? I went from freaking out about all of this to suddenly checking out Miller every chance I get and then waxing poetic about missing him. Not to mention, feeling him up in the bathroom while he's wearing a hospital gown. Because he's injured. And in pain.

Best friend of the year award, right here.

"Shit, I'm sorry." I step back. "That was weird."

Miller turns slowly toward me, struggling with shifting his weight on his bad leg. He doesn't say anything for a long time, and the more seconds tick by, the more embarrassed I become. When he does finally say something, his voice is cautious. "Uh, yeah, I'd say so."

"Ignore me. My head's been messed up since training camp." I realize how that sounds as soon as the words come out of my mouth. "Not that I didn't mean it. I did. All of it. But it's weird, right? It's weird."

"Little bit." His eyes are wide, and he's even more freaked out.

I put my arm around his waist again. "Let's get you back to bed and pump you full of more drugs so you can forget I said anything."

Miller pulls back. "Talon, what's going on?"

"Nothing. Ignore me. A doctor once told me that being too awesome sometimes overloads my brain, and it melts down. True story." When in doubt, bring out the jokes. It's class clowning 101.

I go to move toward the door, but he holds strong.

"No bullshit time."

"Aww, man, you're bringing in the no bullshit rule?"

Miller and I moved in together my last two years of college. The first few months had been a nightmare trying to navigate our way of living on top of each other. Miller and I are similar in so many ways it was surprising to find out we had completely different living habits.

He was a slob, he thought I was too loud, I was an early riser—still am—and he liked to sleep in. It seemed the only time we weren't arguing those first few months was if a girl was over, because even if we were pissed at each other, we never passed up an opportunity to fall into bed together.

We ended up instating a no bullshit policy where if we had a problem we'd say it out loud and the other couldn't be pissed off about it. It worked, and those two years of living with Miller are my favorite memories of college.

"Why did you move to Chicago for me?" Miller asks, and his Adam's apple works his throat like it's hard to swallow.

I know that feeling. "Could we maybe not have this conversation in a hospital bathroom where all I can smell is disinfectant and all I can think is 'I wonder if someone died in here'?"

"We could, but we won't."

My shoulders fall, and I relent, because as I've recently worked out, Miller is my one weakness—the guy I'd fucking kill for if he asked me to. I go to open my mouth, but he cuts me off.

"I need you to be one hundred percent clear here, because I'm pretty sure my meds are making my brain think things I shouldn't."

Things he shouldn't? What does that even mean?

I take a deep breath. "I moved to Chicago for you because I've never had as much fun as when we were roommates. When I think about the happiest times in my life, it wasn't when I was drafted to the NFL. It wasn't when I won a Super Bowl or when I put that championship ring on for the very first time. It's all those nights a million years ago being your roommate and friend."

Miller refuses to look at me as he says, "Not to mention all the sex, right?"

"I thought that might've had something to do with it, but you know what has killed me since you've been avoiding me? Not that you used the media and our position as a way of putting a stop to repeating old mistakes, but that you ignored me afterward. I won't deny the nights sharing a girl with you has been the best sex I've ever had, and I've missed it because I've never trusted another guy the way I trust you, but I wasn't thinking about that when I accepted the Warriors' offer. It was *you*."

Why am I just working this out tonight? And why, when I keep picturing Jackson and Noah together, do they morph in my memory into Miller and some faceless guy? A faceless guy I wished was me?

"Talon—"

I don't know I'm moving because it's so slow, but then I'm suddenly there, pressed against him and catching his scent of sweat and dirt from the field. He smells of where I belong, because if there's one thing in my life I've always been sure of, it's football.

My mouth skims his rough cheek, searching, wanting. I expect him to pull away, but Miller turns his head slightly, moving closer.

Why does this feel so good? So right?

His much bigger body molds against mine. Warmth envelops me, and a sense of home makes my chest ache.

My suit pants become uncomfortably tight, and unlike Miller, I can't blame drugs. But he's not pushing me away either.

"Shane."

"Mmm" is all I get as an answer.

Miller turns his head, and our lips find each other's. The first touch has a weird sensation running down my spine. It's not electricity but a jolt of something else. Realization, clarity ... an epiphany maybe. Our mouths come together to create something that turns all my confusion from the past few weeks into something beautiful and warm and totally unexpected.

My whole body relaxes under his strong hands. The kiss turns up the heat when he slips his tongue into my mouth accompanied by a groan so forceful I feel it in my toes.

The breath gets knocked from my lungs, and I'm freefalling like the time on spring break back in college when

Miller and I jumped out of a plane and were almost killed by both our mothers and our coach when they found out we'd gone skydiving.

The thrill of kissing my old best friend has the same adrenaline effect as extreme sports, and God knows I'm a competitive athlete who wants to win.

What winning means in this situation, I have no idea, but I'm hoping it involves a lot of coming. My dick likes that idea and digs into Miller's hip.

I'm kissing a guy, and my dick is hard.

A few months ago, I thought I knew everything there was to know about life. Turns out I know jack shit.

I cup the back of Miller's head and angle mine to deepen the kiss—a kiss I never knew would be so hot. So consuming.

Miller moans into my mouth, and I savor the masculine sound.

Kissing a man is an entirely new sensory experience. From the roughness and strength in his hold to the scruff on his face scraping my skin, kissing Miller is like nothing I've ever done before. It's incomparable.

"Guys?" a faint voice says. "Hello?"

I tear my mouth from Miller's and step back. "It's Jackson."

"In here," Miller calls out. "We'll be out in a sec."

Our eyes lock, and I have no idea what he's seeing in mine, but his project nothing but wariness. Which makes sense, because I don't know what the fuck is going on either.

"We should get out there," I rasp, but neither of us moves.

We keep staring at each other, almost daringly. Who's gonna mention the giant elephant in the room? The elephant being my very hard cock.

Did my brain just make a dick size joke instead of freaking out about being caught kissing a guy?

Miller takes a deep breath and looks at the roof. His mouth moves silently as if counting or talking to himself, and it's not until I look down I realize he's even harder than before. I wrote it off earlier because of the drugs, but now?

"You're not having another orgy in there, are you? Because I can come back," Jackson says through the door.

"So glad you're able to make jokes about that now," I yell back.

Jackson was out with us the night we took those girls home, and he warned Miller to be careful so the tabloids didn't find out, but he hasn't mentioned it since. I thought it was going to be one of those things we don't mention—like me walking in on him and his boyfriend.

We fumble our way to the door and tumble out into Miller's room while I try to think of disturbing things to deflate my cock like unicorns and cute cats—those evil bastards.

Jackson's eyebrows shoot up when Miller and I leave the bathroom together. Alone ... well, with each other and no girl sandwiched between us.

"Ah, your timing is off," I say. "If you'd been here five minutes ago, you could've held Miller's dick while he peed, because, you know, you're into that."

Shit. Even I know when I tip the smartass scale too far, and that totally came out homophobic and like I didn't like what just happened. Like I'm pulling scared straight guy shit when I'm not.

Scared, that is.

My level of straightness is still up for debate. After that kiss, I'm leaning toward not straight at all.

"Yeah, shame," Jackson says dryly. "Although something tells me you enjoyed it anyway."

My mouth slams shut, because I don't know if he's finally calling me on it or if he's implying he knows I got hard over the thing me and him agreed to never speak about again.

"No one's holding my dick but me," Miller says, "but I do need help getting back to bed, so can you assholes please lose your egos and help a guy out?"

"Sorry," we both mutter and then help him.

"Tina tells me you need surgery," Jackson says. "That sucks."

"What's even suckier is he's going back to New York for it."

Miller scowls at me. "Way to sell me out."

"Was your plan to leave without anyone knowing?" I ask.

"Well, yeah, was kinda hoping. My family wants me back home, and I'm out for the season anyway."

"When do you need the surgery?" Jackson asks.

"As soon as possible. They're trying to figure out a way to get me there that'll be comfortable. It's not like this is an emergency where they can use a medivac or anything."

Jackson pulls out his phone. "I'm on it."

"On what?" I ask.

"Noah has a private plane on standby."

"No fucking way," I say. "I want a private plane. Imagine all the type of mile high shit you could do."

Jackson grins. "I don't need to imagine."

Miller grimaces. "Okay, I'll book a first-class ticket with someone. That's gotta be better than flying in a sex plane, right?"

"It's like I don't even know you at all," I say. "Talon's words of wisdom: never say no to a sex plane."

"It's not a sex plane." Jackson doesn't look up from his phone as he shoots off a text. "I was joking." He lowers his voice and mumbles, "Mostly."

There's a knock on Miller's door, and a nurse walks in. "Hi, guys, I'm sorry, but it's actually past visiting hours."

Flirt switch: turned on. "Aww, precious, can we maybe get five more minutes with our boy here?"

The young nurse blushes but stands her ground. "Don't bat those pretty quarterback eyes at me, mister. I'll give you thirty seconds."

When she walks out, Jackson laughs. "I like her."

"I'm losing my touch," I say, but when I turn back to them, Miller's scowling at me.

We have thirty seconds to talk about whatever happened in the bathroom with Jackson here to hear it all.

"Twenty-five seconds!" The nurse yells from her station.

"Fuck." I run a hand through my hair.

Jackson's phone chimes. "The jet can come get you tomorrow morning first thing."

Miller nods. "Thanks."

Silence falls, and I have no idea what to say.

"So, this is it?" I ask. "You're done for the season." And leaving me to figure this out on my own. But that goes unsaid.

CHAPTER EIGHT

MILLER

Why did I think coming home would be less stressful than recovering in Chicago? Oh right, because it's away from Talon.

I still don't know what happened in that hospital bathroom. Part of me wonders if the painkillers made me loopy and if it actually happened at all.

Marcus Talon kissing me.

Nope, no way. That's what fantasies and wet dreams are made of.

Right now, I'd take dealing with him and my temporary insanity over this torture any day.

I'm in my childhood bedroom where all my football memorabilia and shit from high school hasn't even been touched since I left home for college. The house is a single-story home on Staten Island, and living here again is surreal.

Nothing's changed, but my whole life is different now, so I feel out of place. Days of high school are long gone, bringing girls home and sneaking them into my room while Mom worked double shifts. Shane Miller, star football player bound for one of the top football schools in the country. Now I'm Shane Miller, NFL player who's yet to make a name for himself, stuck in this tiny-ass room, where I can relive all my glory days from when I thought I was awesome. It wasn't until college I realized that being awesome on a field full of semi-decent players didn't mean shit. Fighting for my spot to stay on the USC team was what made me NFL material.

Now look at me. Injured, on the cusp of being cut, and back living at home.

Mom may not have to work double shifts anymore, but that's probably the only thing that's majorly changed. Well, that, and instead of living with my annoying little sister, I now live with her and my five-year-old niece, who takes after her mom.

She wakes me up every morning by pulling my hair. "Uncle Shane, get up."

"Uncle Shane's broken." I try to roll over to get away from her, but then I remember my stupid leg, which sends pain shooting down to my toes.

The kid doesn't quite understand I'm not the same uncle who can carry her on my shoulders or swing her around right now.

"Where's your momma?" I ask.

"At work." She bounces with so much energy I have to close my eyes so I don't get motion sickness.

"Where's Grandma?"

"Making pancakes!" she yells.

Mom appears in the doorway. "Sorry, honey, I told her to let you sleep. How's the leg?"

"The same as yesterday. And the day before. And the day before that. Sore as fu"—my eyes land on the kidlet—"fudge."

"Fudge is nummy!"

I love my niece. She's adorable. But holy fuck, kids need to come with volume control.

My surgery went well a few days ago, but I've never been the type of guy to sit around and do nothing all day, and I have another four days of only getting up when I need to. Bathroom and kitchen are the only places I'm allowed, but Mom sends me away if I try to make any food for myself. I'm appreciative of her helping me out, but I'm already going stir-crazy.

"Come on, Gabby, let's leave Uncle Shane to rest."

"Well, I'm awake now," I say.

Mom smiles. "I'll bring you some pancakes."

"God, they're gonna have to rehab my stomach more than my leg if I keep eating like this."

I think it's ingrained in moms to stuff their kids full of so much food that they'd be able to survive for weeks on fat stores.

My phone pings on my bedside table, and Gabby reaches for it.

"Can I play a game?"

"No, baby, Uncle Shane needs his phone," I say.

"Game." She crosses her adorable little arms across her chest.

"One game."

"Ooh, she's got you wrapped around her little finger," Mom sings as she heads back to the kitchen.

Yeah, she really does. Even if she's loud as fuck.

"Gabby, I need your help decorating the pancakes!"

The kidlet runs off, leaving my phone on the comforter.

Thanks, Mom.

Kinda wish Gabby had run off with my phone when I see the text:

TALON: *JACKSON SAYS YOUR SURGERY WENT WELL. THANKS FOR LETTING ME KNOW.*

I groan. He's calling me out for avoiding him. I thought it'd be easier to ignore him, being eight hundred miles away, but nope. That was pure stupidity on my part, because if there's one thing I've learned over the past six years, it's that distance doesn't make the memory of Marcus Talon any dimmer.

ME: *SORRY I DIDN'T REPLY TO YOUR TEXT WHILE UNDER ANESTHESIA.*

TALON: *SMARTASS. IT'S BEEN THREE DAYS.*

ME: *JACKSON CALLED ME INSTEAD OF TAPPING AWAY ON A PHONE.*

Fucking hell. His name flashes on my screen with an incoming call, and I should've known he'd do that if I taunted him. Yet, I still did it.

Because he's Talon, and I'm me.

"Hey," I say, my voice groggier than when I woke up.

"You sound like crap."

"Miss you too." I wince. Talking to grown-up Talon always brings out college Miller, and breaking old habits like joking about this kind of stuff is hard.

"How's the leg?"

"Why does everyone ask that?"

"Because you had surgery. Duh. It's like proper etiquette and shit."

Is kissing me in a hospital bathroom proper etiquette? Did that really happen or was I super high?

I wish I was on the good drugs now so I had the courage to ask him these things.

"The leg is fine. Drugs are good."

"Evidently," Talon mumbles.

"What's that supposed to mean?"

The line goes silent, and for a moment, I think it's cut out.

"Tal—"

"Are we going to talk about what happened in the bathroom?"

Oh. *Oh.* My tongue searches for the lie I want to say—my mind is blurry on the details. It's not, though. I remember every single thing about it. I just wasn't one hundred percent sure it actually happened.

"I, uh ..." I have absolutely no idea what to say.

Talon laughs, but it's awkward and sounds forced. "Yeah, that's my thoughts on it too. I, uh, dunno what that was."

"I wasn't entirely sure if it was real or a drug-induced hallucination."

There's a pause, because this conversation is awkward as hell, and clearly, we both think it necessary to add to that awkwardness. If it did happen, why? And how?

"Would it have at least been a nice hallucination?" Talon's voice is small, and this whole time I've been wondering if I imagined it because I've wanted him that close to me for so long.

I haven't even had the chance to wonder how *he* felt about it all. "Have you ever ... uh, you know—"

"Been so blindsided by a kiss that I don't know which way's up anymore? Don't know whether I'm going crazy or getting turned on by two guys going at it is normal? Uh, no. That's all new."

"Wait, you got turned on by who?"

"Jackson and Noah."

I thought I saw something in his eye the day he told me he walked in on them, but I'd dismissed it because I thought there was no way.

"Have you ever ..." Talon asks, "kissed another guy?"

I suck in a sharp breath and wonder if *yes* is the wrong answer here. I have kissed guys. Not many, but a handful or so in the year between Talon leaving USC and me graduating the following year.

"Pancakes!" a little—but fucking loud—voice says in my ear, and I jump. I didn't even hear the squirt come in.

I cover my half-hard cock with my blanket, because I really don't want to have to have any sort of grown-up talk with my niece about that. Nope, nope, nope. Anatomy and sex and all that is totally my sister's problem.

"So, I can't talk about this right now," I say into the phone. "Little ears are listening."

"Who's that?" Gabby yells some more.

Talon's laugh is warm. "She sounds cute."

"That's because you're eight hundred miles from all the noise."

Gabby pops her hip out with the attitude of her mother. "Who. Is. It?"

"It's Marcus Talon," I say, and her entire face lights up as she reaches for my phone. "She wants to say hi," I tell him.

"All right." His tone is more amused than annoyed we've been interrupted.

I hand her the phone, and she presses it to her little ear.

"My mom says you get sacked more than anyone else in the league."

"Gabby!"

"It's true," she says.

Talon's laugh is so loud I can hear it from here.

"She said you hold onto the ball for too long, which is why you get tackled all the time."

I take the phone back off her. "Okay, you've had your fun. Go help Grandma with the rest of the pancakes."

She doesn't move.

Talon's still laughing when I put the phone back to my ear.

"So, yeah, that's about the extent of my next few months. I don't think I'm going to get a minute to myself ever. Feel sorry for me."

"How old is she?" Talon asks.

"Five."

"Hmm ... can five-year-olds read yet?"

"Not big words."

"Cool. What I have to say might be easier over text anyway."

Before I can reply, the call ends, and I find myself in a stare-off with a five-year-old. A minute later, a text comes through, and I'm the one to break my gaze from Gabby first.

"Mommy only lets me have half hour screen time."

"I'm pretty sure Mommy doesn't want you to eat pancakes either." I cock a brow at her, and even at her age, Gabby understands my underlying threat.

Then I realize I'm threatening a child. I don't think I should ever be a parent.

Gabby runs off, and I go back to my phone.

TALON: *So your sister thinks I'm bad at football, huh?*

I snort.

Me: *You remember what Vanessa's like. She went to USC too.*

Talon: *Shit. She's a mom now?*

Me: *Yup.*

Talon: *Is the kidlet mine?*

Me: *You better be fucking joking.*

Talon: *HAHAHA. Of course, you fucker. Sisters are off-limits.*

Me: *Not cool, bro.*

There's a long pause before the next text comes through.

Talon: *Kinda feels like we missed out on a lot of each other's lives.*

Me: *Yeah, well, football and life happened.*

Talon: *I meant what I said in the bathroom. That I've missed you.*

Okay, nope. Texting is not easier. My stomach does a weird flip thing, and as I read over it again, it keeps doing it until I feel physically ill. I keep staring at the words that could either mean everything to me or continue to string me along on Talon's hook.

Talon: *And I really liked kissing you.*

I blink rapidly, making sure I'm reading what I think I am. What am I supposed to say to that? My fingers type out three different responses:

I liked it too.

You should have. I'm awesome at kissing.

Are you drunk?

I end up deleting them all, and he beats me to responding.

Talon: *I don't know what that means.*

Well, that one's easy to reply to.

Me: *Neither do I.*

TALON: *KINDA SURPRISED YOU DIDN'T PUSH ME AWAY. OR PUNCH ME.*

It's everything I've ever wanted.

I was too drugged up.

I was two seconds away from pushing you up against a wall and fucking your mouth with my tongue.

Delete, delete, delete!

ME: *IT'S NOT LIKE I HADN'T THOUGHT ABOUT STUFF LIKE THAT HAPPENING BEFORE ...*

I shouldn't send this one either. It's playing with fire. A little voice in the back of my head that sounds a hell of a lot like the Talon I used to know whispers in my ear. "Here are some matches. Have at it."

I hold my breath as I hit send.

TALON: *REALLY?*

Rationalize, my brain tells me.

ME: *WE'VE SHARED A LOT OF GIRLS. DONE A LOT OF CRAZY AND KINKY SHIT WITH THEM. ARE YOU SAYING YOU'VE NEVER THOUGHT ABOUT IT?*

TALON: *NOT UNTIL RECENTLY, NO.*

I shouldn't be surprised or hurt when I knew that was going to be his answer. Instead, I should be focused on the point that he's thinking about it now. But that's the thing. He's only contemplating it now. Experimenting. Thinking he could like dick after seeing two guys get it on. That has nothing to do with me. I did the exploring thing when I was in college. I've played out the fantasies running through Talon's brain right now, and I came to terms with being on the straighter end of the Kinsey scale but still very much bi. What if he doesn't? He could kiss me again and say "Nope. Definitely straight."

Will I resent him for crushing me? Worst of all, would I be able to recover from that?

Marcus Talon has the power to break me, and he doesn't even know it.

Talon: *Have I freaked you out?*

Guess I'm taking too long to respond.

Me: *Nah. Takes more than curiosity to scare me off.*

Talon: *You know what they say about curiosity and the cat.*

Me: *It killed it?*

Talon: *Nah, it turned him gay.*

I can't help but laugh even though I probably shouldn't.

Me: *That's a horrible joke, even for you.*

Talon: *I'm a little out of my element here.*

Me: *Man, if this message thread didn't have so much private stuff on here, I'd have to screenshot that. Mr. Know-it-all is out of his element? Oh shit, does admitting that mean you're no longer eligible for MVP? Don't you multi-time winners know EVERYTHING?*

Talon: *Are you sure you want to taunt me about this? You know what happens when I'm challenged.*

Me: *Somehow, I don't see you becoming an expert in everything gay just to prove a point.*

Talon: *Oh, it's on. Wrong move, Miller.*

Wrong or idiotic? I haven't completely decided yet.

CHAPTER NINE

TALON

I can do this. It's just porn. Gay porn, but that's still porn. It's sex, and who doesn't like that?

My finger hovers above numerous thumbnails of guys in various positions, but some of the titles scare me off. Like: Brutal Fuck. Fast&Hard. Torn New One. Bottom Passes Out. Monster Cock in Tight Ass.

If I'm clenching at the sight of the titles, I'd hate to see how I'll react to watching the damn clips.

I glance at the hotel door and check how long Jackson's been gone. He's using the hotel gym for a light workout before our game tonight, but he hasn't been gone long, so I should have enough time to explore. I've been putting this off since my last conversation with Miller, but busting a nut is a pregame ritual. It helps me relax and clear my mind and get ready to kick ass on the field.

An innocent-enough-looking clip catches my eye—two guys standing fully clothed in a kitchen. The scene begins with them saying cheesy dialogue like every other porno I've watched.

However, unlike others I've seen, this one skips from fully clothed to fully fledged up-close fucking with dicks and balls flapping in all directions.

Well, that escalated quickly.

I frantically hit the giant X in the corner to get the clip to go away. That's not really what I'm looking for.

Maybe I need to start slow. I look up threesomes with two guys and one girl where there's also man-on-man action, but after watching a couple of them, I come to the conclusion the porn industry has a hole in their market: bi guys who actually want to have sex with men as well as women. The ones where the guys do kiss or give blowjobs, it's awkward and looks like they're not doing it willingly. I've heard of gay for pay but thought it'd be a bit more convincing than that. Reluctance is not sexy.

Maybe I'm on the wrong site for the kind of thing I'm looking for.

I never realized how fussy and complicated my dick could be until I go through countless clips, not getting into any of them. They're hot, and I'm hard, but none are giving me that urgency—the need to get off because I can't take it anymore.

Finally, I settle on a clip where there's a guy fucking a girl doggy style while a guy fucks him. And damn, I wanna be that guy in the middle. I don't care if the face he's pulling is fake, but if it is, at least he's a better actor than the others. He looks so completely blissed out. I'm literally jealous.

My mind goes to all those times I've been with Miller, and I wonder what it'd be like to be with him this way instead of our stupid no touching rule. I don't even remember how that rule came about or if we ever had a conversation about it. I think it was a given. He said the other day he'd thought about touching me, but he never, not once, gave any indication he might be into that.

Then again, was I paying that close attention? It never crossed my mind.

Here I am thinking about Miller again with a hard dick and the desire for him to touch it.

I groan. This season without him here is gonna be the longest of my career. I just got him back, and now he's gone.

A loud moan brings me back to the porn, and the guy in the middle has to stop for a moment, and my breathing mimics his—erratic and shallow.

The guy behind him tenderly runs a hand down his arm and leans in to kiss his neck. He turns his head, so their mouths come together in a kiss that's so hot precum leaks from my cock.

The camera zooms in on their faces as they continue to kiss, soft and slow, and I begin to wonder if they're an actual couple, because it looks real. It's more than sex between them.

Then the girl moans, breaking their connection, and what was hot a couple of minutes ago doesn't do it for me now.

I find the names of the stars tagged in the video, click on one of the guy's profiles, and then stalk them on social media. As I suspected, the guys are married in real life, and it's kinda cool how they can be comfortable with each other enough to do porn with other people but still be in a committed relationship.

Whenever I've thought about doing the serious relationship thing—granted most of those thoughts came to me before I'd made the NFL—I imagined getting bored with only one person in my bed. Maybe these guys have the perfect arrangement.

Not that I want to take up porn any time soon.

I watch a few more clips but solo videos of just them, and it doesn't take long for my cock to beg for some attention.

Like in the three-way video, it's more than just sex between them, and I don't know why that turns my crank, but here I am, about to wrap my fingers around my hard dick and jerk off to two guys fucking.

I shake my head. It's not fucking. It's *love.*

My hand stills on my precum-slicked cock as the moment of clarity I've been searching for hits me with full force.

My brother's wrong. It's not the sex I'm attracted to. It wasn't Jackson and Noah that turned me on. It was what they have.

Have I actually reached a level of maturity ready for an honest-to-God relationship?

Shit, I never thought this day would come. Or that it'd turn me on so much.

I work myself over, my hand stroking my cock until my muscles contract, and I'm two seconds away from blowing my load.

And, of course, that's the moment the lock on the hotel door beeps and clicks open.

I frantically try but struggle to put my dick away. "Shit."

Jackson walks in all sweaty and wearing a towel around his neck. He pauses, eyeing my tablet which has two guys still going at it—loudly—takes in my flushed face, and while his eyebrows shoot up in surprise, all he does is nod, say, "We really need to come up with some sort of system," and then turns on his heel and walks back out again.

I throw myself back on my bed, my balls heavy and wanting release but my cock softening and my head even more confused than it was before.

Part of me wanted to do this to prove to Miller I could, but now that I realize how much I'm into it, I can't make sense of it.

It's like I'm living on the outside of my life, watching as I do things and like things old me wouldn't or wouldn't even contemplate, and not understanding how I got here.

I'm not scared of it, just ... confused.

And I don't know how to handle that.

Jackson doesn't come back to the room until twenty minutes before we have to leave for the game. It's plenty of time to get yet another awkward conversation over between us, but he moves about the room as if I'm invisible, never once making eye contact with me.

I'm not ready to talk about ... this ...

Can you even say the word? Say it with me: bisexuality.

I tell my conscience to fuck off.

Even though I'm not ready, I should. At least to clear the air between Jackson and me.

"So, uh, about before," I start.

He freezes. "We don't have to do this."

"We don't?"

He turns to me. "Like, I don't know what's going on with you. Or with Miller. And that's okay. It's none of my business, so you don't owe me any type of explanation."

Relief is the right reaction, but disappointment sneaks in

too. Maybe Jackson's psychic, or maybe because he knows what I'm going through, he senses this shit.

Queer shit?

How have my friends not punched me out with how annoying my sarcasm is?

"If you *want* to talk about any of it, I'm here for you, but don't feel like you need to clarify anything to me if you're not ready."

That's fair. And really good of him.

"I don't think I'm ready."

"Then say no more." Jackson throws me a reassuring smile, and it relaxes my stiff back and neck.

"Thanks."

"We should get ready for the game. How do you think we'll do tonight? The team is getting stronger."

I'm thankful for the subject change. "I wish I could say we're gonna kick ass out there, but you kinda interrupted my pregame ritual, so we're totally gonna blow it."

Jackson laughs. "So, because you didn't get to blow, we will?"

"Exactly."

And sometimes I hate that I'm always right.

We're taken down 23 – 17.

After our next game—a home game, which we win—I'm too wired and a little drunk to go straight to sleep when I stumble into my large and empty house. It's still early in the season, but the team's gelling well, and we have the talent to go all the way, but it sucks Miller's not here.

I sink onto my bed, not bothering to change out of my suit. Not for the first time, I find myself thinking of the one night Miller stayed here with those women. And definitely not for the first time since I started thinking about it in more detail that my cock gets excited over the memory. Only now, in my head, the girls' faces are blurry, and all I can focus on is Miller's hard body.

Gah, I can't go down this road again. Last time I thought about it this hard was right after the away game last week. I got home and basically jerked off until my dick was chafing and I literally had no cum left.

Maybe I need the real deal. I haven't hooked up with someone since ... shit, since that night. That was *months* ago.

Granted, we've been busy with training camp and the beginning of the season, but it's more astounding I hadn't even realized I haven't had sex in months.

I wonder if Miller has, and then the idea of Miller going out in New York doesn't sit well with me, but I don't think he'd be able to anyway when his leg is fucked. Can't do much with a screwed-up leg. Although, the girl could do all the work.

I scowl at that, and now I want to know. No, I *need* to know. I take out my phone and settle back on my pillow.

Me: *I'm so bored.*

And horny. And curious. And for some reason, possessive. I don't say that though.

Miller: *Bitch, you did not just say that to me.*

I laugh. Didn't think he'd like that.

Me: *On a scale of 1 to 10 how insane are you going?*

Miller: *I'd be carted off to the nuthouse if I didn't already live in one. My family is driving me crazy.*

Me: *You haven't had the chance to go out at all? That sucks.*

For you, I want to add but don't for obvious reasons.

Miller: *Jackson gave me his agent's number. He and his boyfriend live in the city. Was thinking about going out with them once I finally get rid of the crutches and start intense PT.*

Quick, come up with reasons why that would be a bad idea.

Me: *If you're worried about what the media will think of us sharing women, I'd hate to see what they'd say about you being spotted at a gay bar.*

Without being an asshole!

Miller: *I didn't realize it was illegal for gay guys to go elsewhere. Jackson says they hang out at a sports bar.*

Where girls would jump at an NFL player just for walking in.

Nope. Don't like that either.

Can I tell him that, though?

One kiss in a bathroom and an awkward text convo doesn't make Miller mine. Or us together.

Is that even what I want?

I don't know what I want.

Me: *Well, have fun, I guess.*

Miller: *I'll remember to have fun under your orders two weeks from now. Until then, I'm all light exercises, crutches, and trying not to kill my family. Fucking sucks.*

Me: *Guess your porn subscription is getting a workout, huh?*

Smooth, jackass.

Miller doesn't respond, and for some reason, my brain thinks it's a good idea to dig a deeper hole for myself.

ME: *SPEAKING OF WHICH, JACKSON WALKED IN ON ME JERKING OFF TO GAY PORN.*

Fuck! Phones need a recall feature for sent messages. My phone pings, and I don't want to look at it.

MILLER: *WHY DO YOU GET TO HAVE ALL THE FUN? I SHOULD ROOM WITH YOU GUYS ON THE ROAD NEXT SEASON.*

Wait ... is he saying he'd be into walking in on that? Or is he referring to watching Jackson and his boyfriend go at it?

Clarify without me having to ask, you stupid ass.

He doesn't listen to me. Or I'm not telepathic. One or the other.

ME: *TOLD YOU I'D ROCK THE GAY THING.*

I bite my lip, awaiting his response.

MILLER: *BECAUSE WATCHING GAY PORN TOTALLY MAKES YOU GAY. *SARCASM**

He adds the eye-rolling emoji.

ME: *IF YOU WERE HERE, I'D SHOW YOU JUST HOW GAY I CAN BE.*

MILLER: *DON'T HAVE TO BE THERE TO PROVE IT, AND I CALL YOUR BLUFF.*

ME: *HOW AM I SUPPOSED TO PROVE IT WHEN WE'RE NOT IN THE SAME STATE?*

Surely, he doesn't want me to hook up with a guy here ... Oh, God, that is what he wants. He's trying to let me down gently. At least, that's what I think until his next message comes through.

MILLER: *VIDEO CALL ME.*

Oh, fuck.

My finger hovers over the button for a lot longer than it

should. I didn't think he'd call me on it. Although, I should have. It's Miller.

It's Miller, I remind myself and come so close to hitting Call. But at the last second, I can't do it, and I don't even know why.

Maybe I've pushed this too far.

CHAPTER TEN

MILLER

I have no idea what happened. One minute, Talon's talking shit that made me think he could've been serious about this bi-curious thing, and the next minute, he's ghosting me.

Our texting was leading somewhere, and then it just died, and now I have no idea what to say to him or where it was heading.

I contemplate calling him to sort it out, and every night for two weeks, after my little niece goes to bed, I stare at my phone, willing it to ring, because I don't think I have it in me to be the one to make the call.

I think I fucked things up by challenging him. Maybe he's weirded out that I called him on his shit, because from what I can tell, no one else does.

The biggest reason for not calling for answers is something I don't want to admit: fear of rejection is crippling.

I never would've thought Talon would be the type of person to mess with me, so logic tells me there's more to it than a simple he was joking.

Was the gay porn a joke too? Did that actually happen or was he playing it up for the challenge I supposedly set for him?

And this is exactly why entertaining any sort of notion about the two of us together is idiotic. Because I will literally drive myself crazy asking all these questions I don't have any answers to.

The idea of video calling me is too much for him, I guess. Which I should be fine with—I should expect him to freak out. It's better for him to walk away now before I truly get my hopes up.

Now, after weeks of thinking about nothing but PT and Talon, I can hobble around without crutches, and Jackson's boyfriend is home to deal with some charity he runs, so he's taking me to meet his friends in the city.

I find him leaning against his Beemer waiting for me as I limp out my front door. He's long and lean, and not for the first time, I give Jackson props for his taste in men. Noah's hot.

"How's the leg?"

We do the whole man-hug, back-slap thing.

"I'm super drugged up right now, so it feels great."

Noah laughs. "Guess taking you to a bar is a dumb idea then. Can you even drink?"

"I'm just happy to be out of the house. You have no idea how crowded my mom's place is. Between my sister living there since her split from her baby daddy, my niece, and my mom, I'm going crazy. I mean, I love them, but, yeah, crazy."

"Damn."

Noah rounds his car, and it takes me so long to lower myself into the passenger seat that he's already buckled up and has the engine revving by the time I even shut my door.

"Sorry. It's still slow going."

"Are they sure you're gonna be okay for next season? You're moving slower than my grandmother who's in a nursing home."

I laugh. "Right now, I feel like a fucking grandmother. Doctors say I should be fully recovered by the time the season's over, and then I've got the off season to recondition. My entire life revolves around physical therapy and not much else." Except making myself crazy by thinking about Talon incessantly.

"Look at it this way, Matt's and Talon's right now revolve around football."

Noah may be good-looking, and I'm sure he's probably smart, but I don't think he's thought that through. He sucks at trying to make me feel better.

"You don't play any sports, do you?" I ask.

"How'd you know?"

"If you did, you'd know that's an athlete's idea of bliss."

Noah glances at me out the corner of his eye. "Matt sure doesn't seem happy with football right now. I'm glad I was called back to the city for a few days."

I pull back. "Huh? Why?"

"Don't you talk to your teammates?"

"Not really."

"Not even Talon? Aren't you two tight?"

I narrow my eyes. "What did Jackson tell you?"

"You sports people and calling everyone by their last name." Noah shakes his head. "*Jackson* didn't tell me anything about you and Talon, but there's so a story there, and I'm so grilling Matt about that when I get home."

"Don't. It's ... nothing. College shit."

"That's a long time to hold onto issues," Noah says.

I'm not touching that with a ten-foot pole. "Maybe I could do with a drink after all."

Noah grins. "Well, this could be interesting."

By the time we wade through city traffic and find a parking spot relatively close by, I'm ready to stretch the leg, but then two blocks later, I'm out of breath, in pain, and asking Noah to give me a second. I brace myself against the wall of a building. It's only been a few weeks since the surgery, so I probably shouldn't be on the leg so much.

"Sorry, I should've dropped you off," Noah says.

"No, no. I'm being a little bitch. I'll be fine." I go to walk when Noah gently pushes me back against the wall so I'm no longer putting pressure on my leg again.

"You remind me of Damon."

Jackson's agent is an ex-baseball player whose career died when he got injured.

"He was the same as you back in college when he was playing ball. Always pushing, always saying he was fine when he wasn't. Do I need to remind you where his career went?"

I give in and relax against the wall holding me up. "No."

"Good. We're already late to meet them. It won't kill them to wait a little longer."

I nod, and then we proceed to stand in complete silence.

Super fun. Not awkward at all.

"So, why is Jackson hating football?" I ask.

He never ended up telling me back in the car.

"Says Talon's riding everyone hard. Whatever's up his ass, it's affecting the whole team."

That's probably my fault. I could singlehandedly be responsible for the Warriors not making the playoffs.

"I'll talk to him when I get home," I say.

"Because he'll listen to you?"

"Something like that."

"There's so a story there ..."

"No story," I bark, a little too aggressively.

Noah puts his hands up in surrender. "Okay, fine, I'll drop it."

"Thank you."

He rubs his chin. "For now. Maybe you should drink after all. Loose lips can be entertaining."

"You're a bad influence."

"You know, Matt says that all the time. I don't get it."

I laugh. "Okay, I'm good to go now."

But as we continue to walk, I can't help wondering what Talon's doing and why he's been riding the boys hard. I wince at my thoughts, because, of course, I think of Talon and riding guys. Not the team. Just in general.

That's a nice image.

I *need* to talk to him.

When we finally arrive at the bar, we make our way over to a table where Damon King and his boyfriend are sitting, too engrossed in each other to sense us approach.

Damon has his arm casually draped over Maddox's chair and is leaning in to say something in Maddox's ear. Maddox's blond hair shines off the neon lighting, but it's his smile that glows. Both he and Damon are all shiny and happy.

I've never seen a more in love couple. Apart from maybe Noah and Jackson. But Noah and Jackson are more primal. I've seen the way they look at each other from across a room, like they can't get home fast enough to tear each other's clothes off.

What I'm seeing in front of me is something just as powerful—actually enjoying each other's company.

There's really only been one person I've had that with, and suddenly, we're in a weird place we can't climb out of because I'm too chickenshit to confront him.

Doesn't help we're apart. Or that we left on awkward terms.

I've imagined what his touch, his lips, his body pressed against mine would feel like for so long I still can't believe he kissed me.

Gah. I shake my head, trying to clear my thoughts. Maybe coming out with Jackson's friends was a bad idea. It's making my brain even more murky when it comes to Talon, which is why I came to New York in the first place—to get away from those thoughts.

Damon notices us first and pulls away from his boyfriend to stand and shake my hand. "Hey, Shane. Good to see you." I'm about to tell him to call me Miller, when he acknowledges Noah. "Dickwad."

"What have I done now?" Noah asks, sinking into his seat.

"You're an hour late. Were you too busy doing your hair?"

I stare at Noah's bald head.

Noah's unperturbed. "It does take forever to look this good."

"He's covering for me," I admit. "My leg's still messed up, and I've been hobbling everywhere."

"How's the recovery going?" Damon asks.

"Slow. So fucking slow."

"Don't push yourself too hard." As if reliving a memory, Damon's face loses some of that couple glow I just witnessed. That is, until Maddox reaches for his hand and gives him a reassuring smile.

All I've wanted for years—is for Talon to stare at me the way Maddox looks at Damon.

Noah must sense my unease or takes pity on me for still being sweaty and panting from the easy walk, because he stands and offers to get me a drink.

"Beer. Whatever they've got on tap."

"Thought you weren't gonna drink," Noah taunts.

"Yeah, me too."

He doesn't question it and disappears to the bar.

"So," Maddox says, "are you currently happy with your representation?"

Damon covers his boyfriend's mouth with his hand. "Ignore him. I told him not to do that, but he's not a very good listener."

Maddox mumbles something behind Damon's hand that sounds like "I listen. I just ignore you."

I smile. "I'll keep you in mind if I run into any issues."

Maddox pushes Damon's hand away. "See. All you have to do is ask."

"It's unprofessional," Damon says.

Maddox waves him off. "Professional smeshional."

I chuckle. "It's cool. Jackson talks you up all the time too, but Hewitt and Locke have been my guys from the beginning—"

"No need to explain," Damon says. "I understand."

Maddox leans in. "But you should know Damon's gonna be the biggest agent in town soon, so you better get in while he still wants you. Fucked-up leg and all."

I find Maddox hilarious, but Damon rolls his eyes and wraps his arm around Maddox to pull him back to his side.

Noah returns with drinks, and before long, one drink turns

to two, and then three, and then I realize why you shouldn't drink while on heavy pain meds. After three beers, I'm pretty loose.

Noah glances at Damon. "Pool table opened up."

Damon's out of his seat less than a second later. "Oh, it's on."

"They're competitive," Maddox says to me as they disappear toward the back.

"I can see that."

When a couple of women walk by, I don't miss the way Maddox's gaze trails after them. They're in tight dresses that show off more skin than they cover. I contemplate what Maddox checking them out means—if anything—and my confusion must show on my face.

"I'm totally allowed to look. Damon gets to check out guys all the time."

"You do know they weren't guys, right?"

Maddox bursts into laughter. "I'm bi, dude."

My heart beats hard, but I try not to let it show. "Oh."

"Wasn't until I met Damon that I considered myself, uh, less than straight."

"Wait, so only Damon? All the others have been women?" *Rude much, inconsiderate asshole?* "Sorry. That's, like, personal." But it's not like I meet anyone I can relate to—probably because I haven't been open about that side of me.

"That's okay, I'm an open book. I used to fool around with my college roommate who may or may not be a certain teammate of yours, but we don't talk about that in front of Damon and Noah."

"Ah. Got it." I take another sip of my beer, but now Maddox is eyeing me warily. "What?"

"You have questions."

How is my mouth still dry? More beer goes down my throat. "Isn't that … wrong to ask questions about that stuff?"

Maddox scoffs and moves into the seat next to mine. "I'm, like, the hardest person to offend. I'm best friends with Damon's sister, and after hearing the shit that comes out her mouth, nothing coming from you is gonna shock me."

"I'm just wondering if you freaked out about it all. Suddenly liking guys."

"Nope. Not at all."

I'm envious of the way he says that so easily and fast. It's not like I had a hard time realizing for myself, but I've never talked about it with anyone, so I guess in my head I'm still working it out.

"I had trouble labeling it," Maddox continues, "but if anything, Damon was the one freaking out. He didn't want to be an experiment and get his heart broken."

My glance darts over to Damon playing pool. "How'd he get over that?" Because it'd be really handy to know.

Maddox does the wary-eyed thing again. "He fell victim to my charming personality."

With another sip for courage, I turn to him. "My very straight best friend kissed me, but now he's ignoring me."

Maddox's mouth turns into an O. "You know how I said nothing could shock me? I was wrong." He reaches for his own drink. "So, I'm guessing you're thinking of taking a walk on the gay side?"

"I … I've … uh, you know, been there, done that."

"So, you're …"

"Yup. Just like you." I don't miss the way I evade saying the actual words, and I don't think he does either. I've never said them aloud though I know them to be true.

"We should start a bi club!"

"We should do what now?"

"Don't mind me. I say impulsive nonsensical stuff all the time."

I let out a small laugh.

"You'll get used to it. So, this friend ... you don't want him or ..."

God, how do I explain Talon and me? I don't think it's possible. "I'm worried he realized he was wrong and is walking away."

"Oooh, so you're the Damon in this situation."

I rub the back of my neck. "I guess?"

"Well, I can't speak for the other guy, but if Damon had never given me a chance, I'd hate to think what we would've both missed out on." He glances over at his boyfriend with the same look he was giving him when we walked in—the look that tells everyone in this bar who Maddox belongs to.

"Okay, but this guy is now ignoring me. Do I push or leave it and wait for him to come to me?"

Maddox purses his lips. "That's a tough one, because while I had no trouble wanting Damon, it's not something everyone would be okay with. Not many guys wake up one day and go *hmm, maybe I'll try dick today*."

I laugh. "That's how it was for you?"

"Sort of. I was more attracted to Damon as a person rather than to his cock. Although it turns out I'm fond of that too."

I love that Maddox has no filter. "Thanks for making me feel better about this, but it's not exactly helping. I'm the one hopelessly and pathetically into the straight guy who's freaking out that he kissed me."

"We need to ask Damon and Noah. They'd have better advice than me. I'm all about diving in and thinking of consequences later." He goes to wave the other two back over to us, but I grab his hand.

"Can we not ... I mean, no one knows about me. Like no one."

Maddox's eyes widen in shock. "Shit, man. Did we, like, just become besties?"

I cock my brow. "Is that the impulsive thing again?"

Maddox waves me off. "Wait, your friend who almost kissed you doesn't know either?"

My gaze tracks Damon and Noah to make sure they're not coming back over. "He thinks I've always been as straight as him."

"I won't say anything, I promise. I already know what Damon would say anyway. He'd tell you to run away from the straight guy as fast as you can. Even if it did work out with me, he's been burned pretty bad in the past."

"What really made him give you a chance?" I ask.

"What, my stunning personality hasn't won you over yet?"

Okay, it has a little bit.

He relents. "Fine. He thought Matt and I were a thing, got jealous, and then decided I couldn't experiment with anyone else."

Well, when he puts it that way, panic claws at my chest. What if Talon ends up finding some other guy because I'm in New York and avoiding him?

No, wait, the ball was left in his court. I challenged him and he backed down ... which Talon never does.

Fuck, maybe I've messed up worse than I thought.

A loud shout from the other side of the bar erupts as Damon cheers, presumably winning their game. As they pass their sticks over to people waiting for the table, I realize I've known Maddox literally fifteen minutes, yet he knows something about me no one else in this world knows. Whether it's the drinks, his eerie similarities to Talon's personality, or just that I've needed to talk to someone about this for so long, I don't know, but now, it's out there.

The others join us again, and more drinks are handed out, but Maddox's words keep running through my head. I've been scared about a lot of things when it comes to Talon: being heartbroken, pining after him like a lovesick puppy, ruining our barely existent friendship, but I haven't actually thought about what would happen if this was our real shot. What if it were to work out? What if I've fucked this up and he gets to experience it all with someone else first?

I stand suddenly. "I have to go."

The other three were mid-sentence, talking about something I should've been listening to, so my abrupt announcement causes them to pause and look at me like I'm crazy.

In their defense, it could be true.

Noah stands too. "You want to crash at my place, or—"

"Uh, nah, that's okay. You stay and keep drinking. I'll catch a cab to the ferry."

"I'll walk you out," Noah says.

Maddox jumps up. "I've got him."

Damon looks at his boyfriend weird but then shrugs, and when Maddox and I make our way outside, he holds his hand out in front of me.

I go to shake his hand when he laughs.

"Your phone, idiot."

"Oh." I hand it to him.

"If you need advice or anyone to talk to or whatever … maybe a new agent who's experienced with out sports stars." Maddox winks.

"Wow. Am I being played right now?"

Maddox grins. "Seriously though. If I'm the only one you've told, I'm all you've got. When I went through the same thing, Damon introduced me to all his friends, and knowing someone else out there could relate to me without even having to talk about it helped."

"Thanks. Can we, maybe, hang out again while I'm in New York?"

Maddox claps me on my shoulder. "Of course. It'll be good to hang out with someone who I can talk football with. Damon's all baseball, baseball, baseball."

"And you want me to sign with him?" I joke.

"He can care about football if he has to. He has Matt."

With a nod, I get in the back of the cab that pulls up curbside.

The trip home gives me enough time to both sober up and freak out. Logic tells me the difference between now and the hour until I get home won't make a difference. It's not like Talon's on his knees right now about to suck off some random guy, and the only thing stopping him is my phone call, but it's hard telling my irrational side that. Once the image is in my head, there's no getting rid of it.

On the ferry, I send off a text.

Me: *You gonna be around in about forty minutes?*

The lights of the disappearing New York skyline become dimmer, and I take in the saltwater stench that's uniquely New

York Harbor.

I stare at the blank screen on my phone, almost not expecting a response, because it's hard to tell if he's avoiding me or I'm avoiding him, but my message was the last one sent. That means it's his—

My phone dings.

TALON: *YEAH, WHAT'S UP?*

My dick. Yeah, I'm not gonna say that.

ME: *BORED.*

TALON: *AREN'T YOU IN THE CITY?*

ME: *HOW DID YOU KNOW I WENT OUT?*

TALON: *JACKSON.*

Of course. And he knows because of Noah.

ME: *CAN I CALL YOU WHEN I GET HOME?*

He doesn't answer me, and when I finally get home and through the door, I don't expect him to pick up when I call either.

My finger hovers over the icons next to his name and hits FaceTime. If he rejects the call, he rejects it. Not much I can do about that.

Surprising me, his face pops up on the screen as I fall back on my bed. With the grace of the two-fifty pound six-five beast that I am, I drop my phone, and it smacks me right on the corner of my eye.

"Motherfucker," I hiss.

Talon's laugh fills my room, and for a brief second, it feels like he's here with me. I've gone six years without him and then spent six awkward weeks with the guy just to end up right back where I was as a twenty-one-year-old love-struck fool, who was devastated by Talon's absence. The words *I miss you* want to fall out my stupid mouth, but I rein them in.

"You good now?" he asks, his voice smooth and effortless.

I grab my phone and hold it above my head, pointing the camera at me. "Yeah."

Talon's face appears on my screen, all perfect, good ol' American charm oozing from him. "Guess it's lucky it's not your job to catch the ball, huh?"

"Yeah, yeah."

Talon's also in bed, shirtless, and his hair is mussed as if he's been there a while. "So, what's with the late-night call?"

"Late night? It's barely midnight, Grandma."

"*Some* of us aren't on vacation."

"Wanna swap places?" I growl.

Talon's smile slowly falls. "Sorry. How's recovery going?"

"Slow. My leg is useless. I couldn't even walk a few blocks tonight."

He frowns, and I think that's more adorable than his smile. "Is that normal?"

"The physio says I'm on track, but I dunno. I thought I'd be further along by now."

"When can you start reconditioning?"

"Not until the end of the season."

Talon's frown deepens. "Is that gonna be enough time? What's your management plan? Where are you working out?" Quarterback Talon makes his appearance. The one who's all business, and one of the reasons I find him so hot.

"I dunno. I'll probably do it all here in New York."

Talon's lips purse. "Nah, we should go somewhere and do it. Like a training retreat. I'll have to go home at some point and see the fam first, but then we can go to the middle of nowhere so there's nothing to do but eat and train."

"Wait, what?"

His blue eyes pierce mine through the screen. “After the season, I’m gonna ride your ass until you’re back in shape.”

CHAPTER ELEVEN

TALON

The words tumble out of me before I can stop them. Miller's mouth drops open, and I wince and fuse my eyes closed, wishing I could put the words back in my mouth.

"Talon." Miller's voice is strained.

"I didn't mean ..." I refuse to open my eyes. "I mean I want to be there to help get you back in form so we can do what we've talked about since we were teenagers."

"Talon," Miller says again, firmer this time. More in control.

I don't want to open my eyes because I'm scared it's going to be written all over my face. What *it* is, I'm still not sure. It's why I've withdrawn from ... whatever game we were playing.

It's not like me to back away from any challenge, but this one was messing with my head and my game.

The season's been rocky, but we're hanging in there. I've been trying to put Miller and whatever feelings I've been having for him as far away as possible. At least until the team finds their feet.

When I finally build up the nerve to open my eyes, Miller's there, the solid presence I needed and that always grounded me during college. Yeah, we did a lot of shit, but I'd hate to see what I would've been like if I'd done it with anyone but Miller.

"You don't need me to win the Super Bowl," Miller says. "You guys can make it all the way. And I'll still get a ring by default. The two games I played count."

I don't know how Miller always knows what I need. Like right now, I need to talk about football, because if we talk about the big gay elephant ... bi elephant? Pan elephant? Who-the-fuck-knows elephant ... I don't want to screw things up between us.

Like they're not fucked up already?

"Default wasn't part of the plan," I say, distracting myself with more football talk. "It was gonna be you and me. So back-to-back Super Bowl wins are the only way."

Miller laughs, deep and warm. "Cocky son of a bitch."

"*Confident*."

"God, I wish I was there," Miller says.

"Here?" I croak. "Why?"

Scenarios run through my head of what Miller could do if he were here right now, and not one of them is PG-rated.

"Why do you think? I'm going batshit and my leg is messed up. I wanna be back on the field."

Ah, he's still talking about football. Duh.

"I'll get you there," I promise.

"You're really going to spend your off season training me? Shouldn't you be taking a jersey chaser or two to a sex island?"

I perk up. "There are sex islands? Think we could recondition there?"

"On second thought, I don't think you should be let loose

on a sex island. You'd probably forget to do important things like eat and drink water, and then you'd die of dehydration."

"Like those animals who literally fuck themselves to death?"

"What?" I ask.

"There are these rat-looking things from Australia. The males literally stop eating so they can have sex until they die. Something about their need to keep their gene pool going."

"I shouldn't be shocked about your weird knowledge of animal sex, but I am."

"Just trying to find my spirit animal." I sigh. "Although lately, I'm more like a panda. If I go much longer without sex, I'll forget how to do it."

Why my brain thinks that's a good idea to tell Miller, I have no idea. Maybe I'm fishing for him to agree with me, or maybe I want him to know that I'm not fucking around with anyone else. Not that I'm fucking around with him either.

"Aww, how long has it been? A few days? A week?" He smiles, but there's something in it that makes me think he's gritting his teeth while he does.

"Try months. That night … with those two girls. That's the last time I …" I wave my hand in a *you know what I'm trying to say* gesture.

"Holy shit, how are you surviving? And what about your pregame ritual?"

"The new calluses on my hands aren't from throwing footballs."

Miller cracks up laughing, and something inside me breaks. What it is, I don't know, but it's like charging the field at the beginning of a game. It's a touchdown in the last minute.

It's putting that championship ring on for the first time. It's … everything.

"Shane," I say, my voice coarse.

His eyes flick to mine through the small screen, and his laughter dies.

My confession is a whisper. "I chickened out."

Miller's brow furrows. "Chickened out of what?"

"This. FaceTiming you."

Miller looks like he's trying to decide to mock me or let me off the hook. I beat him to talking so he can do neither.

"I've wanted to. You have no idea how much."

His expression softens. "I think I have a fair idea. I wasn't calling you on your bluff or taunting you." He lowers his voice and whispers, "I wanted it. I want this."

Miller's gaze burns so hot I expect my phone to overheat. How I've never seen him this way before now is confusing, but not really when I dissect it.

I uprooted my whole life for him. Moved to Chicago to be near him. All because I missed what I had with him, which, up until recently, I thought was just a solid friendship.

Friends don't give up what I did just so they can see their college buddy again. That's illogical. That doesn't stop me from trying to make sense of it. And to make sense of it, I need to do something I've been putting off.

For fear of rejection, fear of discovering some unknown truth that's always been a part of me, I don't know. But I do know Miller doesn't scare me. Doing this with Miller doesn't scare me.

"Take your shirt off," I rasp.

"Talon—"

"Take. Your. Shirt. Off."

Miller's lips quirk, but he does as I say. His voice is muffled by his shirt going over his head as he says, "You know, using that voice for anything but football may backfire."

"What voice?"

"Marcus Talon, the quarterback. Next season, when you call out plays, I'll be blocking linebackers with a hard-on."

The thought of Miller getting hard because of me makes my own dick perk up. Not that it wasn't half there already.

"I've seen your dick. It's impressive but not *that* impressive." I have to joke because I need a dose of reality, and keeping things light between us is the basis of our friendship.

I'm sure if he tried, his dick could tackle someone. Everything about Miller is big, and one thing I have noticed all the times we've been naked together is that he's definitely in proportion to the rest of his giant body.

I've always admired him and his physique on a professional level, but now I'm mesmerized by his body in a new way. Like how he moves his arm under his head, his biceps bunching. Miller's dark hair, usually short during the season, has started growing out, and the slight curls fall over his forehead and almost into his dark eyes.

Why the fuck am I thinking about his eyes? And his muscles? And—

"What are you thinkin' about?" Miller's voice, deep and rumbly, pulls me out of my confusion. Because it's *Miller.* Things have never been confusing with him before, but ever since moving to Chicago ...

"How many times have we seen each other naked?" I ask.

"Countless," Miller answers easily.

"Then why am I only noticing shit now?"

"Shit? Are you calling my abs shit? Because my abs could crush your abs in a fight."

A laugh escapes. "No. I mean why is this the first time I've taken notice of how sexy muscles can be?"

Miller's eyes become hooded. "I'm trying to decide whether to mouth off and tell you you're slow on the uptake or ask you what you want me to do with said muscles."

I smirk. "I love how you found a way to say both of those things without actually saying either."

"There was also a joke about some of the women we've been with being more muscular than me, but I held that one in."

"Respect."

"So ... you were saying something about my muscles."

A breath gets stuck in my throat. "Yeah. I was." Because, apparently, we're doing this, and, apparently, Miller's completely okay with it.

I swallow hard and the question *How are you so comfortable right now?* can't pass my lips no matter how much I want to ask it.

"If you don't want to do this ..." Miller starts.

"I do," I blurt. "I just ... I don't know how ... what ... I—"

Miller leans back, his long arm holding his phone farther away. I can see all of his torso and an impressive bulge in his jeans. Those muscles I've been admiring are on full display, and I bite my lip to hold in any noise. I'm worried if I do it'll all stop.

I can't help wondering what his skin tastes like. Is it different to a woman's? Manlier? Sweatier?

"Are you okay with watching me?" Miller asks. "You don't have to do anything if you don't want to."

I nod, but it's subtle. "Yes."

I'm thankful he's taking the lead here, because as bossy as I can be on the field and in other areas of my life, this is one thing I'm completely lost on.

Miller's hand starts at his collarbone and slowly moves over his chest and down his pec. It hesitates for a second as his fingers trail over his nipple, as if he's contemplating squeezing it, but he keeps moving on.

"Pinch your nipple," I instruct. "I know you want it."

"Yeah? How do you know?" he asks breathlessly.

"You forget I already know what you like. When someone's sucking on your nipple, you get this feral look in your eye, and you sound tortured like it's too hard to hold back."

A flash of surprise crosses his face, and he's probably as shocked as I am that I'd taken that much notice.

Instead of going for his nipple though, his hand moves to his cock and palms it over the denim. His hips roll and lift off the bed, and he grips his cock through the denim.

"What else do I like?" he asks.

My voice shakes as I say, "You like it when your hair is pulled while you're going down on ... someone." I'm trying to avoid pronouns, because reminding him of women while doing this without one present diminishes what we're doing. I want him to only be thinking of me, just like my focus is on him and everything I already know about getting him off. I want to be the one on his mind as he comes tonight.

Miller groans in appreciation, and his wrist flicks the button on his jeans.

"Take them off." Didn't take much for my bossy side to come out.

"Give me a sec." He puts his phone down so I'm staring at his ceiling.

When he appears on my screen again, a shy smile ghosts his lips. "Is it weird that I'm nervous? I mean ... considering the stuff we've done ..."

"This is different," I whisper. "This is us. Only us."

Miller disappears again, and the view goes wonky. I see an arm and a flash of his tat on his pec, and then the picture steadies. Bare ass fills the screen, and I catch a quick peek of his surgical scar running down the back of his hamstring. I don't have time to ask about it, because Miller climbs back onto his mattress, and I can't help loving the image I'm seeing.

He's placed his phone on his dresser, giving me a view of his entire room.

If asked my favorite body part on someone, a few months ago, my answer never would've been Miller's thick and powerful thighs. But as he lies down and lifts the leg closest to the camera, hiding his monster cock, my mouth dries at the sight.

His eyes meet mine. "What do you want me to do?"

"Get yourself off" falls out of my mouth, and I hope he doesn't call me on my obviousness. I'm not so lucky. Of course not. This is Miller. The only guy in the world to truly call me on my shit.

"Oh. I thought you, like, wanted me to knit you a sweater or something."

I go to snipe back, but all playfulness leaves when he drops that powerful thigh and exposes the biggest cock I've ever seen. And I've lived in locker rooms. I've noticed way too many for a supposed straight guy. "I don't think you'd be able to knit with that."

Miller throws his head back and laughs, but then he stares down at his cock as he reaches for it.

His erection is long and thick and only appears bigger when his beefy hand wraps around the hard shaft. He strokes himself slowly, and I swallow hard.

"Are you hard?" he asks, his voice husky.

Am I hard? I don't think I've been so fucking horny in my life.

I palm my cock through my boxers. "Yeah."

He doesn't turn to look at me. Instead, he closes his eyes, and his lips part.

Licking his hand, he uses his spit as lube and strokes himself faster. This isn't the first time I've seen Miller do this—one of our many favorite things we used to do was have him get himself off while he watched me with someone else—but it's the first time I've actually paid real attention to his hand while he's doing it.

Precum leaks in my boxers, and I pull the waistband down and tuck it under my balls so my cock springs free.

Miller doesn't make a move to watch me. When he does open his eyes, his focus stays on his cock as the muscles in his arm flex.

Someone moans, and I think it's me, but I honestly can't be sure. My attention is only on Miller as he works his hand up and down, slowly increasing pace.

His hips buck off the bed as he fucks his own hand, and that's the image that makes me give in to my own need.

The first touch has my whole body shuddering. I'm not going to last long. The last time jerking off felt this good was during training camp, right after I got Miller to his room. These past few weeks, when I've been exploring many, many clips of gay porn, none of those orgasms compare to the one building inside me.

No more words are spoken, and I don't even know if Miller's aware of what I'm doing. He closes his eyes, and his jaw hardens as if he's gritting his teeth, but it's when he makes the telltale grunt right before he comes that has me spilling into my own hand.

My muscles tense to the point of aching and drag out my orgasm until I'm completely spent.

Five seconds later, white ropes of cum cover Miller's stomach, and he collapses back, sinking into his mattress.

The only sound between us is heavy breathing, and Miller still refuses to look at me, but I can't stop staring at his long body.

Miller's hand absentmindedly runs through the cum on his stomach, and the question in my head appears without much though.

I wonder what he tastes like.

"You okay?" Miller asks, pulling my gaze away.

He's finally looking at me, and I wonder how long he's had his eyes open and if he cares about me staring at him with that much intensity.

My lips quirk, and I pan my phone down to show the mess I've made of myself. "Never better. Shame you missed it."

Miller's still breathing heavy. "I didn't want to make you uncomfortable."

Guilt I can't explain consumes me, and when I force myself to speak, I can't get my words above a whisper. "I may not know what's going on with me, but I can say with complete certainty that you could never make me uncomfortable."

Miller's eyes soften, and he looks relieved.

"And what about you?" I ask. "This seems to be a lot easier for you than your average straight guy."

He hesitates. "I told you I'd thought about you in that way."

That doesn't mean this wouldn't or shouldn't be as weird for him as it is for me.

"Have you thought about other guys that way?" I don't know if I want to know the answer.

Miller breaks eye contact again. "I've been with guys before."

Yup, I didn't want to know that. My chest tightens, and while I can't be sure because it's never happened to me before, I think it's jealousy. Which is ridiculous. I've been in the very same room while Miller's been with women. Why does the gender of his hookups matter?

"When?" I ask.

Miller gets out of bed to take his phone from the dresser. He lies back down, and his face is back to being the only thing to fill my screen.

"Do you really want to know?"

No! "Yes."

"There were a few guys senior year of college."

Senior year. After I left. I must make a face or something, because he keeps talking.

"I needed to know if what I felt for you was for you or for guys in general."

"And the answer?" I don't think I truly want to know this either.

"Guys in general. I'm ... uh ... I'm bi."

More inexplicable disappointment.

It's stupid and selfish of me to think any of this could be about *me*. That what's between us is a one-off somehow. If it was just us, it'd give me reassurance that what I want with Miller is bigger than either of us and something out of our control. The thought of going out there and being with other guys doesn't appeal to me, but maybe if I pushed myself—

"You're thinking pretty hard over there," Miller says.

On the small square on the screen where I can see myself, I notice the large frown lines across my forehead.

"I wasn't expecting that," I admit. "But it makes sense after you told me you'd thought about it—us—before. Although I don't know why you didn't think to come to me about it."

He huffs a humorless laugh. "How do you think twenty-two-year-old Talon would've reacted to that?"

"Whoa, why do you say that like you think I was some kind of close-minded asshole back then?"

Miller runs his hand through his hair. "That's not what I mean."

"Then what do you mean?"

"Are we really doing this now?" Miller's reluctance makes me nervous.

"Yes." My voice comes out growly.

"Until tonight, I've never said the words *I'm bi* out loud. I've known it for a long time, but I've never actually said it. The thought of saying it back then to anyone, let alone the straight guy I measured all my hookups against, made me want to crawl into a hole and never come out. Not to mention it was your first year in the NFL and you moved to the opposite side of the country."

Damn.

Asshole of the year award goes to me.

"Seems like tonight's the night for major revelations," I murmur.

Miller cocks his head. "How so?"

"This whole thing, ever since moving to Chicago ... is it too early to have a midlife crisis? I'm twenty-eight, for fuck's sake."

Miller laughs. "So, you've been wondering if your sudden attraction to men means you're going crazy?"

"Well, not ... *crazy*. I dunno. I moved to Chicago for you, and until I saw Jackson and Noah together, I never questioned my motivation behind it. Now I can't think of anything but that. And I don't know if this is an attraction to men or if it's a ... *you* thing. I don't know what it means, I don't know what we're doing here, and I don't know if ..." I can't say it.

"Don't know what?"

"If after all is said and done, that this won't dissolve and we not only screw up our friendship but also the team."

Miller's lips press together. "It's an impossible situation. It's putting everything on the line even thinking about it."

Even though he's right, and I'm scared shitless of all this being some ... temporary insanity—not that being gay or bi or whatever should be equated to insanity—I'm wondering if I've missed Miller on a completely platonic level and somehow my screwed-up brain thinks this is the only way to hold onto him. Which is ridiculous, because if anything, this is going to push him away.

God, I hate my head right now.

"Shane?" I keep using his first name because I can't help loving the way he looks at me when I do. Like he can't believe I'm either being serious or looking at him differently from the rest of the team, who are all on last-name basis only.

He stares at me expectantly. "Yeah?"

"Why'd you call tonight?"

Miller sighs. "Pure jealousy."

"Huh?"

"I was talking to this guy, Maddox, and he told me the story of how he and his boyfriend got together. It made me realize that if you didn't explore with me, you might go to some other guy, and I can't handle that even more than the thought of fucking everything up."

I don't know what that means for us or if I should be flattered or insulted. "Why?" I manage to get out.

"Because even though this is the worst idea in the history of ideas ... it's always been you. Those hookups in college might've shown me that I'm attracted to guys, but you're the only one I've ever truly wanted."

My eyes widen, and he backtracks.

"That's probably too much pressure to put on you right now, but I don't mean it in any other way than what I've said. I'm not going to push you or ask you to do anything you're not comfortable with, and I have no expectations of a future." He blows out a loud breath. "I wanted you to know you can use me. I'm at your disposal to help figure whatever's going on in that head of yours."

God, I want that. I don't think I've ever wanted anything more, but I'm still wary. "I don't want to hurt you," I say softly.

"You never could."

Even I can hear the doubt in his words, but that doesn't stop me from going for this. Right now is a time to be selfless for once and put everything and everyone else first.

Instead, I find myself whispering, "Can we do this again?"

Miller's smile makes the risk worth it.

CHAPTER TWELVE

MILLER

Talon: *I need to change my pregame ritual.*

Me: *To?*

Talon: *You.*

Me: *I'm your new pregame ritual?*

Talon: *Getting off with you is. Did you SEE that game?*

Me: *Wouldn't have missed it. You guys were on fire, and I hate I'm not there with you.*

Talon: *We're finally clicking. Everything was smooth, and it was one of those games where everything fell into place. Like the football gods were watching over us.*

Me: *And I'm somehow to thank for that? Are you saying I'm a football god, because I'll take it.*

Talon: *Dunno, but we should do it again next game. You know … just in case.*

Me: *Right. Just in case.*

TALON: *5 FOR 5, BABY!*

ME: *MY FOOTBALL GOD POWERS ARE STRONG.*

TALON: *CORRECTION: YOUR POWERS IN GETTING ME OFF ARE STRONG.*

ME: *HOW TALENTED OF ME. ALTHOUGH, CAN I REALLY TAKE CREDIT WHEN I HAVEN'T EVEN TOUCHED YOU?*

TALON: *TRUST ME. IT'S ALL YOU.*

After texting every day and a weekly FaceTime call before game nights, we've created this little bubble where the rest of the world doesn't exist and we don't talk about anything real. It's all football and getting off.

I'm letting this go at Talon's pace and not pushing for things I really want, because even though he hasn't freaked out yet, I don't want to overstep. Which is why I hesitate before hitting the Send button on my next text.

ME: *WHAT'S YOUR STANCE ON CELEBRATORY VIDEO CALLS?*

The call comes in seconds later, and I answer with a grin.

"That was quick."

Talon pans the camera down his body. "I was already appropriately undressed and two seconds away from asking you the same thing."

I swallow a groan. My cock goes from a semi to full mast instantly, and his camera isn't even pointing at the good stuff. His bare chest, chiseled arms, and that gorgeous face fill my phone screen, and Talon's blond hair sticks up at all angles from lying in bed.

It's been weeks of staring at him this way—of being allowed to take advantage of it—but I can't get enough. I want more. If only I had the balls to ask for it.

"Eight hundred miles is too far," I complain.

"Ten weeks."

If I weren't so distracted by Talon's body and raspy tone, I'd already have my hand in my boxers.

Ten weeks is way too long.

"Maybe I could skip PT one day this week and fly out—"

"No. Your leg needs to get better for next season. No skipping sessions."

"But—"

"No," Talon barks.

"There's quarterback Talon again, Mr. Bossy."

"You know it." Talon's eyes meet mine, the blue in them taking on a mischievous glimmer. "But I had something else in mind tonight."

My heart hammers as I tell myself to be cool. "Yeah?" Apparently my voice didn't get the message and comes out all gruff with a high-pitched squeak at the end.

"Yeah." Talon's tone is tentative, and he bites his lip.

"I'm pretty sure I can handle whatever it is."

"I want you to boss me around. Like you do with the girls we've been with."

Okay, I was one hundred percent wrong, because Talon asking me to boss him around in bed? I'm in no way prepared to handle that. This is a prank. I have to be being punked right now, because this doesn't happen in real life.

It's not that I'm bossy in bed. I'm the one asking a girl's limits and asking for boundaries, because ever since the first time Talon and I were together, my life revolved around rules and limitations when it came to him. It's about being wary, not about needing to be the one in control.

Now Talon's asking me throw all my rules out the window.

He takes my hesitance as an opportunity to keep talking.

"Ever since we started … fooling around? Is that what you'd call it?"

I grit my teeth. "Get to the point faster, Talon."

"Right. Umm, well, yeah … all I can think about is you telling me what to do. I want to be the one to get you off."

I understand what he's saying. Mostly, when we've done this, it's always been him watching me. I've been the focus of both of us, because I've been letting him run the show. Flipping the dynamic has me excited but scared I'm gonna push too far or fast.

"Remove the sheet," I order.

Talon does as I say, but I can't see anything because he hasn't propped his phone on his bedside table like usual.

"Still can't see anything," I say.

"Impatient much?"

"Very. Now hurry up and show me what's mine."

"Yours?" Talon asks.

"What will be mine," I growl.

Talon places his phone in a position that gives me a view of all his naked glory.

Before, where I felt deceptive looking at Talon's naked body, now that it's what he wants, there's no tearing my gaze away.

The house could catch fire right now, and I wouldn't notice.

He immediately goes to grip his cock when I stop him.

"Nah-uh. You want me to tell you what to do, you have to wait for an instruction." A huge part of me can't believe that just came out my mouth to Talon, but the other part has wanted this for so long that I can't bring myself to dwell on it. Only savor it.

Talon smiles, and his hand falls to his side.

I swallow hard, my mouth still dry at the sight of him. "You know, you'd totally make a good sub if you were into the BDSM thing."

"Fuck off, I would not. I have an issue with authority."

I can't help laughing. "True. You'd get too many punishments for it to be enjoyable."

Talon's expression falls, and he looks right at the camera. "Are you … into that? You haven't been before. At least, not that I've—"

More laughter flies out of me, because his worried face is too much. "No. Not into that. I like this bossing you around thing though. Can we get back to that, or are we gonna lay all our kinks out for each other to judge?"

"You know all my kinks. You've seen them."

Right. The group thing. He really gets off on that.

I push that depressing thought from my mind—the one that leads to voices telling me I'll never be enough for Talon—and focus on what we have here and now even if it's just messing around on a screen.

"Lift your leg on the far side and slip a pillow under your ass so you're kinda facing me."

Talon moves with no question.

"Skim your chest with one hand and pinch your nipple."

His hand makes its descent but pauses. "I don't really have a nipple fetish like you do."

"It's hardly a fetish. It's not like I want nipple clamps or anything."

"Hmm, you with nipple clamps …"

Okay, we're so not going to think about that. "I thought this was about you. Lick your fingers for me. Get them real wet."

Talon eyes me hesitantly.

"Do you trust me?"

"Of course."

"Then do it. If you don't like what I want you to do, you don't have to keep going."

Talon sucks two fingers into his mouth, and he may not be sure about what he's about to do, but his cock is. It twitches like it's trying to do a sit-up off Talon's abs.

"What do you want me to do with them?"

"Massage your balls with the palm of your hand while you tease your hole with your fingers."

Talon cups his sac and does as I say without any question or hesitation. He's so fucking beautiful like this. His skin is flushed, far redder than I've ever seen it on the field or in bed, and I love it. It's sexy and one of the only times I've felt Talon's insecurity.

"You're doing so good," I encourage, which seems to appease him.

"I want ... I want to ... try."

I'm tempted to mock him about using big-boy words, but I don't want to push this. "Try one finger. Slowly."

Even though I can't see from this angle, I know the moment he penetrates himself, because his eyes squeeze shut, and it looks like he's holding his breath.

"It feels weird at first," I say. "That's normal. You need to relax and push out as your finger goes in deeper."

Talon's eyes fly open and pin me to my spot. "Have you done this before?"

"Only with myself. Just like you're doing right now."

"I want to see that."

"Another time. Push your finger deeper—as far as you can get it."

I wasn't kidding when I said he'd make an awesome submissive if we were into that. Talon seems so in control all the time—even when he's goofing off. I think his outgoing and bright, playful nature is who he is to everyone else, his public persona, but anyone who knows him on a deeper level would realize how he can be particular. Especially on the field. The entire team knows what Talon can be like when we lose a game or mess up a play.

He smiles for the cameras and waves off a loss like the rest of us do in front of the media, and even when he's lecturing the guys on a shitty job done, he still has a light tone about him. But underneath it all, he has a penchant for things to be a certain way—his way.

Talon giving me full control and losing himself, letting me call the shots and him doing it without talking back makes me harder than I've ever been.

"If I was there, it'd be my fingers inside you right now."

Talon moans so loud I have to cover the speaker part of my phone. I turn the volume down so he can make as much noise as he wants, because fuck asking him to keep that amazing sound quiet.

"What else would you do?" Talon croaks.

"I want my mouth wrapped around your cock. Lick your free hand for me."

Talon does it and reaches for his dick.

"Nuh-uh. Not yet."

He slumps. "Fuck you."

"Can't wait for that, but fine, take your cock in your hand, but don't move it yet."

Talon's chest rises and falls in quick breaths as if he's struggling to follow my instructions.

"I want you to stroke yourself in time with fingering your ass, but you need to get to two fingers for me. Think you can do that?"

Talon nods like a good boy and does as I say, but when he catches my eye on the screen and he can see me tugging on my dick like a teenager who knows his parents are gonna be home any second and he needs to come right now, Talon scowls.

"If I have to wait, you have to wait."

Okay, so he's not quite ready to give up all control.

I'm a fair guy, so I stop, but it doesn't last long, because Talon begins to jerk himself, and it's like I can feel everything he's doing to himself.

I watch as his hands move in sync, and I'm mesmerized by him. We've done this five times already, but I still have that feeling like I shouldn't be watching him. Like when we've been together in the past. The faces of the women we've been with are probably blurry because I've always focused on Talon even though I knew I shouldn't be. It made me feel dirty doing it.

Now he's giving me full permission to take advantage, but I have to fight the reflexive urge to look away.

"Are you gonna come for me?" I ask. "I want to see you covered in cum."

"Fuck, why do I like the sound of that so much?"

"If you were here, I'd lick every drop off your skin."

Apparently that's all it takes to send him over the edge, and I continue to watch as he writhes through his orgasm. I'm close behind, and when we're both sticky messes, Talon pierces me with his blue eyes.

"February needs to hurry the fuck up."

Weeks feel like months, and if it weren't for my leg still giving me issues, I'd be on the first plane to Chicago, because this distance thing is killing me.

At least, that's what I tell myself. A huge part of me thinks things are gonna get weird in person. Our video calls and texts are the highlights of my day, and they make me so happy that I stop caring about my leg taking longer to heal than they first thought it would. I don't worry about not getting back in shape, because somehow, Talon wanting me has made me believe anything is possible and I just have to be patient.

My leg will get better.

My PT sent me for more scans and tests with my surgeon to be sure, but I think she did it more to shut me up. For a while there, I was convinced something else was wrong, but now, I have a positivity that everything's going to be okay, and I think that's because of Talon.

I haven't even told Talon about my leg issues although I think he suspects something's up. He knows how to read me like no one else can, so the last few video chats have been a mission to pretend like I'm not at least a tiny bit worried.

But as I arrive for my doctor appointment for the latest MRI results, I have a spring in my limpy step, because I've convinced myself I'm being hard on myself, and that's why I'm not as far along in recovery as I want to be.

All the happiness, the positivity, and all-round great mood I've been in since the whole thing with Talon comes crashing down when I take a seat at Dr. Rogers's desk.

Her eyes are sympathetic, her lips pulled into a tight line as

I take the seat in her consulting office. I can already tell her sunny disposition is missing today.

"What is it?" I ask.

"The new scans suggest sciatic nerve injury. We need to discuss another surgery to fix it."

"More surgery?" I slump back into my seat. "What does this mean in terms of recovery?" I can't take more time. I can't.

"We won't know for sure until we remove the scar tissue that's causing it. It may grow back. There are risks. I'm so sorry."

"My career?" I choke on the lump in my throat.

"I know you want answers and a definitive plan, but for the time being, to stop doing any more damage, we need to take a step back. Two weeks' rest and then light exercises."

"How long will this set me back?" I ask, not really wanting to know the answer.

"It's hard to say. Your leg is weaker now. To make a full recovery, we might be talking months. Maybe a year."

"So, I could be out next season too." My last contracted year for the Warriors.

I went from being stupidly happy this morning to watching my future go down the drain.

It's amazing how a few words can change your entire outlook on life.

I make my way home, catching the ferry during peak hour and watching the bustle of New York life.

This could very well be my future. Regular nine to five job, fighting for a spot on public transportation to get to my box of a tiny office ...

Fuck, that's the most depressing thing about this.

A regular job.

There's a game tomorrow night, which means Talon's going to call any minute for our pregame jerk off, and I can't do it. I can't hide something this big from him.

I contemplate staying out so I have an excuse to miss it, but I can't be bothered to deal with other people. I'm exhausted, my leg is aching, and all I want to do is go home to bed and wallow over the death of my career.

The idea of never hitting that field again has me resenting Talon. Just a little.

It's not his fault I'm broken, and it's not his fault he gets to play while I sit on my ass in my childhood home not even being able to exercise because it could do more damage, but jealousy is an ugly thing.

I need another surgery, a full recovery is now uncertain, and the last thing I want to do is face the man who still thinks we can live out some sort of stupid pact we made as teenagers where we'd both make it to the Super Bowl.

When my phone rings with the FaceTime call, I can't bring myself to answer it even if it's the first round of the playoffs tomorrow and we can't afford to lose. One loss and we're out.

Answer it, my conscience says.

I don't.

My heart is breaking for many different reasons, and the love I have for my sport dims. It's like my internal football light is flickering and could blow out completely any minute.

I tell myself not to think about it, but that only makes me do it more.

And the following night when I watch my team take to the field on TV, I want to yell, and cry, and tell them to fuck off all at the same time. At one point, I wish them to lose the game even if it means I lose my last chance at the ring. I'm in a depressed state of *if I can't have it, they can't have it either*, which makes no sense, but my head's all fucked up.

Every play. Every hit they take. Every pass Talon throws on screen … I hate it all, but even worse than that, I already fucking miss it, and not just the way I've been missing it all season. I miss it like I missed my grandparents right after they passed. I miss it as if the sport has died inside me, and I'm yet to let it go.

I stare at McLaren, the kid who took my place, and hate that he's kicking ass. They don't need me. They don't miss me.

Football might be my life, but football will be quick to forget me.

Being told it might not be in my future fucks with my head and my heart, and all I can think is, if they lose tonight, I'd at least get to see Talon sooner than planned.

When the Warriors win easily, I can't bring myself to get excited. Then guilt gnaws at me, because I should be happy for my teammates, but I can't bring myself to muster up any happy feelings right now.

The sterile operating room is freezing. The blanket shouldn't even be allowed to be called a blanket because it does shit all to warm me.

Dr. Rogers' eyes crinkle around the edges as she smiles under her surgical mask. "We'll be going back in using the same incision site as your last surgery, so it won't cause any more scarring. It's a quick procedure, and your leg should be feeling a lot better in six to eight weeks."

Better. Not recovered.

She goes over step by step of how they're going to scrape off the scar tissue causing me issues, but she's already been over this with me so many times I could probably tell *her* how to do it. I think she's trying to distract me while they're still getting everything prepped, but all it does is remind me that this could be a career-ending surgery.

If it goes wrong or doesn't work, not only can I kiss football goodbye, but I run the risk of the scar tissue growing back even worse than it is now. I need to follow the recovery program to the letter, or my future is fucked.

No pressure or anything.

"I bet you'll wake up to a million notifications from your teammates," Dr. Rogers says.

Nope. Because I didn't tell anyone. I've told my agent, and I assume they've informed who needs to know with the Warriors, but I haven't heard from either of them—my agent or team management.

Deep down, I know that can't be a good thing—the whole no news is good news is bullshit in the sporting world—but my focus right now has to be on getting better.

It's why I've gone back to avoiding Talon. It's not that I don't want to tell him. It's that it makes it all that more real. I try not to laugh at that thought—like lying on an operating table doesn't make it real enough.

But I know how Talon will react. He'll be distracted with me when he should be all about football this close to the end.

He'll be positive and confident in my recovery when I'm holding onto the fraying tether attached to my career.

I can't deal with that right now.

I need to be levelheaded and hold onto hope, but at the

same time, I need to be prepared for the harsh reality that I'm about to become a statistic.

An injured athlete losing their career. It's so common it rarely makes the news. You have to be a big name for people to care about that.

And as the anesthetist gives me the good stuff to put me to sleep, I realize the only other person who'd be disappointed if I never play football again is Talon.

I don't want to let him down.

CHAPTER THIRTEEN

TALON

It's the second week in a row he hasn't answered my FaceTime call. Once is circumstance, but twice? He's ignoring me again, like he did the first week of training camp.

Everything was going according to plan until the Warriors made the playoffs. Every week, Miller and I would FaceTime the night before a game, we'd laugh, we'd get off, and it became routine.

I'm ready for so much more. I never thought I'd say that about sex with another guy, but hey, here I am, wanting everything Miller's willing to give.

Which right now doesn't seem like much.

I don't know why he's avoiding me, only that he is. But not completely, so I'm confused. Last week, he sent me a video of him from the neck down with him jerking off into a New England jersey with my old number on it. It made me laugh and gave me enough material for my pregame ritual. This time though, he's not even responding to my attempts to reach him.

I send off a text for him to call me ASAP.

MILLER: *BUSY WITH FAMILY. TALK AFTER THE GAME TOMORROW NIGHT?*

What am I supposed to do? Say *no, you have to talk to me now*?

He's had worried lines across his forehead when we've FaceTimed recently, and his voice has taken on a certain quality I've never heard from him before. It sounds like someone trying to convince everyone around them that they're fine when they're not.

ME: *UNDERSTANDABLE. JUST ... MISS YOUR FACE.*

I hold my breath as I wait for him to respond. We haven't really done the whole affection thing before ... if telling him I miss his face could be called affection. I don't know. If I thought I was out of my element starting something with a guy, it's nothing compared to me realizing I want more than fooling around on FaceTime.

The distance isn't helping. My nerves multiply every day, and with him pulling away, I don't know why I'm nervous. Is it that this could turn out to be nothing, or is it pure excitement that it could turn into something I never saw coming?

When my phone dings, I hesitate to check, but it doesn't last long. I have no self-control when it comes to Miller.

MILLER: *IT IS A PRETTY FACE.*

Okay, at least he can still joke. That has to mean something. I try not to be a petulant child over him spending time with his family instead of taking half an hour to talk to me, but, well, like he always says, I generally get what I want, so him not calling kinda gets to me. I never thought I'd be one of those "Where do we stand?" people.

MILLER: *MISS YOU TOO. PROMISE TO TALK SOON.*

I wish that filled me with more confidence than it has, and

if it weren't for the damn playoffs, I'd push for an explanation, but I have more important things to focus on. Like winning the Super Bowl.

Yet, when it happens for the third week, I'm grumpy, horny, and want some fucking answers. Three weeks. It's been three weeks since I've seen his face, and yeah, he's still texting, but something's up. I can just tell. Call it intuition or that same gut instinct I have on the field. He's not FaceTiming me for a reason, and if I had to guess, it'd be that he's not telling me something, and the minute I see his face, I'll know.

If we win tonight, we're in the championship, and my pregame ritual is nowhere near as satisfying when Miller's not involved.

I throw my gear bag into my cubby with more force than necessary.

"Whoa, what's wrong with you?" Jackson asks.

"Frustrated," I mumble.

"Yeah, you've been frustrated for weeks. You're like a lost little puppy."

I glare at him, but all I see in his brown eyes is worry, and I don't think it's about the game. It's about me. Because Jackson isn't a dick.

My shoulders fall. "I'm being ghosted. Or about to be ghosted. Or … I dunno. Just a bad feeling."

Jackson claps my back. "If it makes you feel any better, Miller's been ignoring me too." He stalks off, but I call after him.

"How did you know it was Miller?"

"What about Miller?" Henderson asks. "They still talking shit in the tabloids about your *bromance*? Careful, man, people will talk about y'all catching the gay with how much you hang around Jackson."

My blood runs cold. Did he really say that?

I scan the locker room, noticing Jackson's out of hearing range.

When Jackson came out, not everyone was happy. We all know it. But as the season's gone on, the easier it's been, and the tension has been missing. Or, at least, I thought so. Henderson shouldn't still have this attitude, especially considering he's a captain.

He's being smart about it though—not mouthing off in front of anyone, especially Jackson, but this time he's mouthed off to the wrong person. Not just because of what's going on with Miller and me. If he'd said the same thing when I thought I was completely straight, I'd call him on it too, because even though I can act like a fool and be the fun-loving guy everyone sees, I'm not a fucking asshole.

"There are bigger things to worry about than the shit they put in tabloids, Henderson."

Henderson shrugs. "I'm just saying. We don't wanna be known as the fag team."

I grit my teeth. "Let's go out there and win the Super Bowl and no one will care what we are off the field."

Right?

For the first time since Miller and I began fooling around, I'm faced with the real repercussions of our ... whatever we are.

No one's that ignorant anymore to believe being gay is contagious, right?

Oh, who am I kidding? Ignorance is like a weed. It seems to grow fast and from nothing.

Great, another thing to distract me.

I try to push that out of my head and focus on these upcoming games. We're only two games away from the end. Two wins until we come out on top. Hopefully.

Even though Miller's ignoring Jackson as well, I can't help feeling edgy about it. It might not be about me, but there's definitely something wrong, and I realize I'm not going to be able to get my head in the game if I don't talk to him now.

Grabbing my phone, I head out of the locker room and down the chute to the empty stadium. People will start pouring in soon, so I need to make this quick, and seeing as he's not going to answer a FaceTime call, I regular call him.

It rings so many times I lose count, and when I think his voicemail's going to kick in, his voice fills my ear, and I let out a breath of relief. Then I'm yelling at him.

"What the fuck, man?"

"Whoa, what's wrong?" Miller's voice is as calm as ever.

"What's wrong?" I lash out. "You've been avoiding me again, and it's been driving me crazy, and now I can't get my head in the game because I'm too worried about you, you big dumbass."

A long sigh comes through the phone, and when Miller speaks again, it feels like a knife cutting through my chest.

"I have been avoiding you."

"Why? Do you regret what happened? Suddenly change your mind about doing this with me? What? Just tell me why."

Miller groans.

"Shane, tell me what's going on."

"I haven't wanted you to worry because you have bigger things to focus on right now. And I can't face you because as soon as you see me, you'll know. You'll just ... *know*."

"You're freaking me out. Did you sleep with someone else?"

We haven't spoken about exclusivity, and it's not like we're really together, but the thought of him with someone else makes me want to hurl. Or punch something. I've never cared about being exclusive with someone before now. I usually encourage the opposite.

"Did you hear me?" Miller asks.

"What?" No, I'm too busy having a revelation over here.

"I said no. I'm not sleeping with anyone but you."

"Although, if we wanna be technical, we aren't sleeping together either." Not yet, anyway. "Hard to do that with eight hundred miles between us."

Miller goes quiet.

"What's wrong?" I ask again.

"It's ... it's my leg. It's fucked. It's really fucked."

My heart sinks. "But we were gonna—"

"I know, but apparently scar tissue from the first surgery was growing over a nerve. It's rare, but it happens. And of course, it happened to me—like I'm not under enough pressure to get back to where I was. They went back in and removed it, but—"

"You had surgery again and didn't tell me? What the fuck?" I would've gone to him. I would've ... wait, no I couldn't. There's no way I could've gotten time off. Miller knows that.

"I was mad. I've been super fucking mad. At the sport. At you. At myself. I didn't want to bring you down."

"But—"

"Super Bowl, Talon. You don't need to be worried about my shit."

"We'll get a second opinion. You'll recondition and train, and we'll—"

"*Marc.*" Miller says, exasperated, but I get stuck on him calling me Marc. No one calls me that—not even my mother. It's always Marcus, a name I haven't really connected with since before I took up football and became *Talon.*

I like it coming from him. Just like I love it when I call him Shane. There's something that's just so ... *us* about it.

His long sigh comes through the phone. "This is why I didn't tell you. Don't worry about me. Focus on the game."

This can't be the end for him. It can't be.

"Is there any hope?" I ask.

"They told me not to give up yet and see how reconditioning goes, but I need to take it easier. More recovery time, shorter training sessions. I'm basically in limbo. They said it might come good, but it's too early to tell for sure."

"Then I guess there's only one thing left for me to do."

"What's that?" Miller's tone takes on that husky side I've only begun to hear since we started fucking around.

I'm guessing he's expecting me to make a joke or say I'll distract him from football with phone sex, but I'm dead serious when I say, "I'm gonna win you a championship ring."

CHAPTER FOURTEEN

MILLER

I should be excited. This is the definition of lifelong dreams coming true. My team has made it to the Super Bowl. I should be pumped and ready to cheer on my teammates to victory. Instead, I'm dreading having to watch the game from the sidelines.

If they win tonight, I don't see how I'm entitled to that ring. I've played two games all season and have sat and wallowed for the rest of it.

Hesitation creeps in as I throw the last of my clothes into a duffle. If it weren't for the plans I had for Talon after the game, I don't think I'd be going.

I don't want to face it. I'm not ready to be back in that world, and I sure as shit don't feel worthy of it.

This doesn't feel like my moment, and the guys don't need my attitude pulling them down.

But I'm dying to see Talon. *In person.*

He's the only reason I'm forcing myself on that plane.

The images of possibilities flood my head for the entire trip to L.A. where the Super Bowl is being held this year.

It couldn't have been a year with a closer venue like New Jersey, or hell, even Atlanta would be better on my leg than fucking Los Angeles Stadium.

The Talon sex images are great at distracting me on the long trip even if I have to cover up my hard-on the entire way. It pulls me from the melancholy of missing out on playing the most important game of my career.

Excruciating self-pity comes screaming back by hour five on the plane when my ass and toes go numb, and a shooting pain down my leg makes me wince. It's a reminder that my leg is truly messed up, and it's all my fault. I pushed too hard and was too distracted with Talon being back in my life that I didn't see the warning signs. Or I ignored them.

Part of me wonders if my internal pain has anything to do with blaming Talon for my injury. On some level. I've never been able to see past the greatness that is Talon, and I'm scared shitless that it's all going to bubble to the surface when I see him again.

The horny side of me is eager to get to him. The more cautious, levelheaded side is worried all this emo bullshit over my leg will make me fuck up any chance we have.

The GM invited me to the Warriors' corporate box for the game, but the thought of wearing a suit and fielding questions all night about my leg makes my anxiety over tonight skyrocket. I was given the option to be on the sidelines with the rest of the team, but so close to the field would be worse. So instead, I've taken Noah's spare seat in the stands with him.

After stopping by the hotel to check in and drop off my bag, I make my way to the stadium and meet Noah, who bought the tickets to get an escape from the Warriors' box. He says the WAGs have been trying to recruit him since the beginning of the season, and no amount of "I'm not that type of gay" keeps them away.

"Thanks for giving me your spare seat, man." I take my ticket, and we head toward our gate number.

"Thanks for keeping me company. I was, like, two seconds away from saying 'Bitch, I'm a person not a handbag' at the last game. They all wanna be my best friend."

"Aww, and here I was thinking you could be my best friend," I say dryly.

Noah smiles.

We reach the usher, and I make sure to keep my baseball cap down and my head low. I'm in a Warriors jacket, but I blend in with the other supporters wearing team colors. Noah's wearing all black—a cashmere sweater and black pants—which makes me laugh. He certainly isn't like any of the WAGs. They'll all be wearing their man's jerseys.

I sink into my seat and take in the stadium and the people filling the stands. It's been a long time since I experienced a game from this side, and the nostalgic feeling of crowd anticipation eases the heavy cloud of depression hanging over me.

It's completely different being on this end of the game, and while the atmosphere is buzzing, it's nothing compared to being in that locker room and getting amped up for the fight. The two are incomparable.

And just like that, my future seems bleak once again. What if this is the only way I get to experience football for the rest of my life?

Maybe I shouldn't have come. Maybe I should ditch Noah and go back to my hotel. But then I'd have to explain why I'm leaving, and I don't want to admit it aloud to myself yet, let alone anyone else.

The big screens at either end of the stadium start with team introductions. One side of the screen goes through head-shots of the guys, and the second screen shows the team in the chute, waiting to run out onto the field.

Talon's up front, of course, his blinding smile visible even through the facemask on his helmet. Jackson flanks him, looking like a scary motherfucker.

Jackson's come a long way this season, and the determination and confidence is written all over him. I'm both parts envious and proud.

That is until his profile hits the main screen and the announcer introduces him. Some asshole a few rows behind us yells a slur.

Noah tenses beside me, and I itch to turn and embarrass the shit outta the guy, but I'm trying to keep a low profile here.

I wait for Noah to maybe say something, but he doesn't.

"I'm sorry," I mutter out the side of my mouth.

Noah shrugs it off, but he hasn't lost the tension in his shoulders. "Not the first asshole to say something. Won't be the last."

"Did you want me to put him in his place?"

"Don't. Last thing I want to do to Matt tonight is bring this issue up again. He's been doing great with the team, and head-lines that read 'Shane Miller and Noah Huntington III in Brawl Over Homophobic Shithead' isn't on my to-do list."

"Fair enough. But I'd honestly pay to see that headline. Especially the shithead part."

Noah bites his lip, unamused. "And, can you maybe not say

anything to Matt? All the Carter stuff at the beginning of the season kinda got to him more than he let on."

I nod, but my stomach sinks, and not only am I now doubting football but also whatever Talon and I are doing.

If we did get involved for real, this would only be the beginning of what we'd have to endure.

Jackson's been facing it all year, and Noah's still worried about him.

When the team storms the field, my Talon beacon seeks him out immediately, and I thank the lord for one thing: football pants. Damn, his ass looks good.

I tell myself to focus on that and drown out the other bullshit.

Talon appears strong and commanding like he always does on a football field. We win the coin toss, so offense is up. The game starts with a completed pass and a textbook delivery. I guess Talon's out to prove his arm's worth every million they pay him.

My good leg bounces with nerves as the team dominates early. They come out in full force and score a touchdown ten minutes into the game. It only reminds me that I'm replaceable.

When those thoughts get too much, I think about what I'm going to do to Talon later ... if he lets me.

We haven't really spoken about what's going to happen tonight, but I have some sort of plan. If we lose the Bowl, I'm going to drown Talon's sorrows with my dick. If we win, I'm going to celebrate with my dick. Totally romantic and effective.

Noah shows the most interest he has all night when the halftime show kicks in, and part of me wonders how he can sit through these games when he has no interest in football.

When I ask him that, he mumbles "Football pants."

I have to laugh. *Great minds think alike.*

The game becomes a nail-biter in the second half when the Warriors choke. There are fumbles, turnovers, and missed conversions. Denver scores back-to-back touchdowns to take a five-point lead.

Suddenly, my shitty attitude and the crushing disappointment in myself is nothing compared to the fear of my team losing this game.

When the cameras pan over the Warriors' bench, it's as if defeat blankets them and they're on the verge of giving up. They're dirty, sweaty, and look utterly dejected.

Talon's the only one who still appears determined. Frighteningly so. He looks pissed.

I may be in limbo when it comes to football, but the resentment I feared I'd have seeing Talon is absent. I don't resent him, but as I watch them continually fumble their way through their chance at victory, I can't help resenting the game. I should be out there with him, helping him bring in the win.

It's where I belong. It's where *we* belong.

I want to not care about that and try to be positive. And while I'm cheering the guys on, there's a small part of me that's as defeated as they look out there.

What happens when the place you belong no longer exists?

CHAPTER FIFTEEN

TALON

Movies and TV will tell you that pure will is enough to win. Fuck talent—it's determination that gets you across that line. That's so bullshit. I've never had to fight so hard for a win in my life. I've won the Super Bowl before. Twice. Both those times were a breeze compared to the fight we put up this time around, but with a few minutes left on the clock, it's as if the football gods whisper in my ear.

"Pass the ball to Jackson."

When I call out the play change, the coaches yell at me in my earpiece. They can't complain when they signed me for this reason, and I have the reputation of being a bit of a cowboy. I know what I'm doing, and it's not the first time I've called out a different play than the one they want me to use.

But this isn't just a Super Bowl win on the line. It's Miller's whole career.

This has to work.

If it doesn't, I won't care what the coaches do or say to me. I only care that Miller will be disappointed, and I can't let that happen.

So pure will and determination might not be enough to win, but they sure as shit are enough for me to risk this. Because I trust Jackson more than anyone else on this field; he can do it.

And I love it when I'm right.

The pass is beautiful—no, magnificent. What could be my best fucking throw of my career.

Time slows as the ball sails through the air and lands in the awaiting hands of Matt-fucking-Jackson, the first out player to win a Super Bowl as of this moment.

This is a win bigger than the NFL. Bigger than Jackson, Miller, and me.

But my motivation had nothing to do with that. It was purely to give Miller everything he ever wanted, and I'm beginning to learn there's nothing in this world I wouldn't do for him.

Loved ones, family, fans, and the entire Warriors crew swarm the field, and we get swamped with back pats, hugs, and just plain screaming in our faces, but there's one face I don't see among the chaos.

I begin to worry Miller didn't end up coming tonight even though last we spoke he was about to get on the plane. I expected him to come join us on the field for the celebrations, but I don't come across him. Not even when the trophy presentation starts.

I find Noah with Jackson. "You seen Miller?" Last I heard, they were going to take the stadium seats for the game.

"Uh, yeah. He's ... somewhere. He said he'd meet us down here—he's slow on his leg."

There's slow and then there's hesitant.

Noah seems like he's holding something back.

"What?" I ask.

"He, uh ... well, it was weird. When you won, he just sat there. Everyone was screaming and going nuts. He sat there, staring at the field."

Shit.

I glance around, hoping with all hope that he'll appear in front of me with a wide smile.

It doesn't happen, and I can't spot him anywhere.

When I take to the podium to accept MVP, I glance out at the crowd, trying to find him. My speech is short, because I'm too distracted. I don't even know if I make sense.

He never shows.

By the time we hit the locker rooms to shower and change into our suits, I'm convinced something's happened to him. Maybe he couldn't handle it and left.

I wonder if it was too much for him to watch the game when he knows he may not get another chance. Maybe he feels like he doesn't deserve to be on that field while we accept the award, but he's as much part of this team as anyone else. We might've lost those first two games had it not been for him, and then we wouldn't be here at all.

But then I think about what it would be like to be in his shoes, and yeah, I can kinda see his point in not feeling worthy. It's easy to say he should feel a certain way; it's a whole other ball game to make him feel it.

I'm almost dressed when the door to the locker room opens, and Jackson calls out, "Miller!"

I spin, and there he is in all his hot as fuckness, but the

imagery of happiness dies there when I notice how he's still limping.

His eyes watch me and send warmth over my skin. He clears his throat for me to flick my gaze to his face and off his leg.

As soon as our eyes lock, the last few months of only talking via text and FaceTime fills the entire locker room with gut-curling tension.

"You're here." My voice is a mix of a worried croak and relieved breath. I want to ask him where he was, I want to go to him, but I don't do either.

Seeing him in person like this ... the pull I've always had toward him has never been stronger.

"What, you think I was gonna miss this?" His words are cocky, but there's something like doubt beneath it all.

Unable to restrain myself, I step forward and take him into a hug. I know immediately that it's a mistake. My body responds as if we're alone. He smells like Miller—like home—and I want nothing more than to kiss him right here in this locker room. But we haven't even begun to define what we are, and after Henderson's comments a few weeks back, I'm beginning to wonder if it's something that could ever happen. Not just in the locker room but in public at all.

When I pull away from Miller, Jackson's looking at us weird, but he shakes it off.

That's when my eyes catch on something in his hand. "Whoa, is that what I think it is?"

Jackson slips a gold band on his ring finger. "Probably not. It's not an engagement ring."

He tells us to follow him out into the hall, where he informs the media he's fucking married. He and Noah ran off and got married almost three months ago and have kept it quiet.

Miller and I chase after him and his new husband, away from the cameras and reporters.

“Where was our invite, assholes?” I ask.

Jackson at least looks a little sheepish. “We didn’t tell anyone but my brother and our best friends.”

I bounce on the balls of my feet like an excitable child. “Fine, but I guess this can only mean one thing tonight.”

“Uh-oh,” Jackson says.

I elbow Miller. “See, the kid does catch on quick. Double celebrations all ’round.”

CHAPTER SIXTEEN

MILLER

"Take me drunk, I'm home." Talon stumbles into my hotel room as I open the door for him.

"I'd love to take you drunk, but you're not home."

I'm not exactly the most sober either, but Talon's completely wasted. It's oddly cute.

Talon struggles with his suit jacket, and he spins to try to take it off. It doesn't work. It just makes him dizzy. When he steadies himself, he holds out his hand to me.

"Whoa, are you okay?" The seriousness in his tone as he stares me in the eyes makes me burst out laughing.

"Come on. Let's get you to the couch, and I'm going to get you some water and aspirin."

Talon's arms come around my waist, and he buries his head in my neck. "Okay."

I help him over to the plush couch of the penthouse suite. Guess my plans for the night are officially canceled. Now I'll be dealing with drunk Talon, which is super similar to dealing with my five-year-old niece when she's overtired.

When I get back to the living room area, Talon's stretched out along the couch.

He grins up at me. "Hey, Miller, guess what?"

I humor him. "What?"

"We fucking won."

I can't help smiling. "Yeah. You did."

Talon shakes his head. "No. *We* did. I did it for you. And you weren't there, but you were there, and I understand why, and—"

"Talon, you're rambling."

"We need to celebrate."

"Think you already did that, buddy. Here. Drink up." I hand Talon the pills and water.

He pulls himself up into a seated position and doesn't take his eyes off me as he swallows it down. He moves the glass to a small side table beside the couch while his free hand grips my hip, holding me in place.

Talon looks up at me again, and I recognize that glimmer in his eyes. I knew it long before he ever directed it at me.

"You're drunk," I say.

"Celebrate." Talon reaches for the button on my jeans.

My hand covers his. "Not like this."

"You're right. We need a bed."

Smartass. "You're incorrigible."

"You know this already." Talon stands and pulls me against him. His lips ghost my cheek. "I missed you."

I close my eyes and take in his words, because I don't know if I'll ever get used to him saying stuff like that. It doesn't seem real.

He pulls back and his glassy eyes meet mine. "Do you

think it's possible to be in love with someone for years and not know it?"

My breath hitches. "W-what?"

"Yeah, I guess you're right," Talon continues to ramble. "There's no way. I mean ... how could you not know, you know?"

I have no idea what he's saying right now. "Okay, you're drunker than I thought. Let's get you to bed."

He smiles. "That's what I'm talkin' about."

"We're not doing anything tonight."

"Why?" He pouts, and it looks ridiculous.

"Because your first time with a guy isn't going to be a fuzzy memory in the morning."

"Aww, thanks for trying to keep my virtue intact, but I'm not a virgin here."

I scoff. "This has nothing to do with your virtue and everything to do with having a crystal-clear memory of everything I do to you so you come begging for more."

Talon groans, and my cock wants to make that sound come out of him again and again. My head might be on right, but clearly, it's not connected to my dick. Either that or it just doesn't understand this is a no-go.

"Come on. Sleep it off, and I promise if you're not hungover when you wake up, I'll do whatever you want me to."

"I'm sober right now. I can prove it. Ask me something."

Oh, Talon wants to play a game?

"How many presidents have there been?" I try to keep a straight face.

Talon looks pensive as he thinks about it, and it's so adorable. "Dude. You need to ask me something I'd know."

I push him toward the huge double doors leading to the master bedroom. "Get in bed already."

Talon spins toward me and almost falls. "Are you at least going to stay with me?"

"I've slept in a bed with you countless times where I haven't been allowed to touch you. I think I can handle it."

Oh God, there's that look again. The mischievous *I solemnly swear I am up to no good* glimmer in his eye.

"Don't even think about trying something, Marc."

Talon's entire face lights up. "Me? Never." His hand slides down my back and doesn't stop.

"Then why are your hands already on my ass?"

Talon glances around me to see. "Huh. How did that happen?"

"Have no idea," I say dryly.

"Can we make out a little?" Talon slurs.

I laugh. "Sure. You're so drunk you're probably not gonna be able to get it up anyway."

Talon pulls me against him, trying to push his half-hard cock into me. "Not able to get it up, huh?"

"Halfway doesn't count."

Talon grumbles as he makes his way to the bed and falls on his back. He covers his eyes with his arm, while his legs still hang off the end of the bed. "I ruined it."

I frown. "Ruined what?"

"Tonight." Talon reaches for me, and I step between his legs. He tries to get up but fails. "Do you know how long I've been thinking about having you all to myself? In the same room? Then I had to go and get wasted off my face."

"You just won the Super Bowl."

"*We* won the Super Bowl."

"Uh-huh." I still don't see it that way, but I'm not gonna argue that with drunk Talon. "I mean you're allowed to celebrate." Even if my balls are blue and I've waited months—no, *years*—for this to happen. "Come on. Shuffle up the bed and get under the covers."

He wriggles his way up so his head hits the pillow. "Fine. But once I'm recovered, your ass is mine. Or mine is yours. I dunno. We haven't worked that out yet, have we?"

We haven't worked out much of anything, but now's not the time for that discussion. Or any discussion, really.

"Maybe we could leave both our asses out of it to begin with. Start slow."

"Oh my God, it feels like we've been moving slower than a fucking tortoise. I've wanted this for six months, ever since training camp."

"Me too. So one more night won't kill us. And then we can talk about it when we're both sober."

"Drunk talking about it seems funner."

"I bet it does." I strip down and join him in bed, but he's still on top of the comforter, and now I'm under the sheets. "You gonna join me under here, or you gonna sleep on top all night?"

Talon tries to roll over and undress without getting up but somehow gets stuck. On what, I'm not sure. "So. Much. Effort." Finally, he gives up and climbs out of bed. He strips out of the rest of his clothes just like I did, only he doesn't stop at his boxer briefs. They go too, and then he lifts the sheets and half-falls back into bed.

Now, he's cuddled up next to me, and all I can think about are the times I imagined this happening—him pressed against me with nothing between us.

I take a deep breath, because I need it to steady my racing heart.

He inches closer and does that thing girls do where they nudge your shoulder like a cat to get you to open your arms for them.

I lift my arm and wrap it around Talon's muscular body as he snuggles into my chest. "Comfortable?" I ask.

"Actually? This kinda feels weird."

I laugh.

"How do girls sleep like this?" Talon moves his head around, trying to get settled in the nook of my shoulder, which makes me laugh even more.

"Hate to say it, but there are plenty of guys who like it too."

Talon stiffens but covers it up by shifting as if he's still uncomfortable. "Do you like it?"

"Wouldn't know. The guys I've been with haven't exactly seen me as the little spoon."

"That's because you're a giant. Let's switch."

Before I can make a *That sounds promising joke*, we change positions so Talon's on his back, and I'm curled into his side.

Talon's strong arms around me feel better than I expected, and I don't know why I've never been the one to be cuddled before. My guess is my large frame probably looks weird and doesn't fit gender norms. Hey, sometimes big guys need hugs too.

I want to sink into Talon's warmth and burrow under it.

"Can I ask you something?" Talon's small voice doesn't fill me with confidence that I'm going to like his question.

"Okay."

"How many guys was it? In college."

My mouth dries. "Why do you want to know?"

"I understand why you never said anything back then, but I kinda hate that we never got the chance to figure this out together. I'm alone in this, and you're treating me with kid gloves."

I don't know if it's the alcohol talking or if it's lowered Talon's inhibitions and filter.

Oh, who am I kidding, Talon has no filter.

"I don't want to fuck this up," I whisper. My head stays on Talon's chest, because I refuse to lift it and look at him.

"So tell me. About the guys."

I sigh. "There's not much to tell." I don't want to tell him that the first time I'd been with another guy, it had been because I hung outside the LGBTQ student support center until I found a forward femme guy to take home. I knew he'd be discreet, because one of the first things out of his mouth was "I can be discreet." I think he knew what I was waiting for. Hell, I dunno, maybe a lot of bi-curious guys did the same thing and he was used to it. Or maybe I was just obvious.

"Did you ... you know ..."

I snort. "No, I don't know. Did I what? Have a relationship with any of them? No. Hook up with them more than once? Only one guy. I don't know what you're asking, Talon."

"Did you have sex with any of them?"

"Define sex."

"You're impossible."

I know what Talon's asking—society's definition of sex which includes penetration—but I don't want to get into it. I don't see the point of him knowing. But this is *Talon*, and I never seem to be able to deny him anything. "I've never bottomed, but I've topped before."

"Does that mean you're a top?" Talon's voice is getting sleepy now, so I continue to humor him.

"No, it means I didn't trust any of those guys or have the guts to ask for what I wanted. I'd let you top me. Every time I was with another guy, I thought of you."

"Mmm, I thought of you too."

"When you were with guys?" I quip.

"Funny. But no. When I was with girls, I always thought of how much fun it'd be if you were there with us."

"You never had another guy in your bed?" I'm not sure if I want to know the answer.

"Like you, I didn't trust anyone enough. One girlfriend—the one my family refers to as The Model—"

"Moxie Burgen?"

"Ah. Saw that in the news then, huh?"

It's one of the only few times I've heard bashfulness come out of Talon's mouth.

"You were being pegged as the next Tom and Giselle. Automatically hated her."

Talon chuckles.

"So, what's her deal? Your family not like her?"

"What do you think? They teased me mercilessly about her because of the Tom and Giselle power couple thing."

I'm doing a sucky job of hiding my jealousy, but just in case Talon hasn't caught on yet, I keep going. "What kind of name is *Moxie*, anyway?"

"A fake one. Her real name ... are you ready for it? Plain ol' Melanie."

I mock gasp. "Scandalous."

"But yeah, I brought up the subject of threesomes with her once. She thought I was asking for a three-way with another girl. When I said it could be another guy if she wanted, she became confused."

I have to try really hard to keep from laughing. "What, she wasn't smart enough to know what goes where?"

"Not at all. She's actually insanely smart. Very business oriented, almost to the point of boring. She was confused as to why I'd want to jeopardize our careers like that."

"Huh." Score one for the supermodel. "Can't say she didn't have a point."

"I know, I know. Heard it all before. We didn't last long after that. And she's the only person I was close enough with to ask, but come to think of it, I don't even think I liked being with her. Nothing against her—she's a great girl. Just ... not my type, I guess. I was with her because it was the thing to do. Star quarterback with the Victoria's Secret model."

"It's a hard life," I say dryly.

"You know what I mean."

"I do," I say solemnly. "A lot of people do something because they think it's the norm. It's staying true to yourself when you don't meet social expectations that's hard."

"That's deep," Talon says sleepily.

"That's what he said."

Talon laughs, but there's no energy behind it.

"Go to sleep. We'll talk more in the morning." I can't help smiling in the dark as I drift off.

CHAPTER SEVENTEEN

TALON

I can do this. It's just sucking a dick. I've received countless blowjobs before, and no one ever choked to death, so it can't be that hard.

Hmm, maybe I should start small. Like a handjob.

Maybe you should wake him up first before you do anything.

Oh, right. That too.

It's been months of thinking about this, of wishing our FaceTime calls were in person, but now it's here, I'm more nervous than the first time we ever took a girl up to my room.

Even though that was probably the most awkward sexual encounter I'd ever had with Miller, it was the start of something indescribable—a feeling I've been chasing and haven't found since graduating USC.

We were both fumbly that first night, not really knowing what to do. It started as a taunt. Seems to be a theme with Miller and me.

Miller rolls onto his back, and the sheet slips down the body I've always admired from a professional perspective, but

—wait ... do truly straight guys stare at other guys and *appreciate* them? I always thought so, but now, I'm not sure.

"If you're gonna puke, use the bathroom." Miller's eyes are still closed, and his voice is strained from sleep.

"Huh?"

One of his eyes cracks open. "I can sense you hovering, and I don't wanna be covered in vomit."

"I wasn't that drunk."

"Dude, you called Jackson your pet unicorn."

I laugh. "He is my unicorn. Without him, we so would've lost the game last night."

"You threw imaginary glitter at him and yelled 'Be majestic, bitch!'" Miller stretches, his long arms reaching above his head and making every muscle in his torso contract.

I run my hand over his chest, my fingers tracing every hard line. "I don't remember that. But I do remember a certain promise you made to me last night."

Miller's dark eyes fill with heat. "Yeah?"

I take a deep breath as I move on top of him. "I'm one hundred percent sober right now."

Miller lifts his hips and grinds his body against mine. "Uh-huh ..."

"And I want to taste you," I whisper.

Miller locks eyes with me and nods. Leaning in, he lifts his head until our lips are almost touching. "Explore me. Use me. Take whatever you want from me."

For so long I've been thinking about his mouth. His lips. Ever since kissing him in that hospital room, I haven't thought of much else other than getting to the Super Bowl, but even then, my motivations revolved around Miller. The sooner we won, the sooner I could present Miller with his first championship title.

Our mouths come together, and it's everything I remember and more. His tongue is lazy at first, teasing me, testing my limits, but it all changes when I take control and dominate the kiss.

I wonder if this is what it's going to be like with Miller. At least in the beginning. He gives the minimum so I have to work for it. Funny thing is, if a woman were to play those kinds of games with me, I'd get over it superfast. But Miller's doing it for one reason only, and I know that without him having to say anything.

He's taking us slow for me. Because, somehow, he always knows what I need.

Right this second, I need to go at my pace and pull back if it's too much, but it's easy to get lost in him.

Miller's hips buck underneath me, his impressive erection digging into me. His hand weaves into my short hair and grips tight.

It's as if I can feel him channeling all his control into that hand, trying desperately to let me take the lead even though he's dying to do it. I can't wait until we're in a place for me to let him take over, but we both know we're not ready for that.

This time is for me to get used to his hard edges and larger body, explore the new sensations, and find out what Miller likes.

I already have a fair idea from what I've observed over the years, so I go for the easy targets first. Like his nipples.

Sliding my way down his body, I capture one with my teeth, biting down a little harder than I normally would with anyone else.

Miller lets out an encouraging moan, so I pinch the other one while I suck and lick the bite pain away.

It's like I'm a kid in a candy store, and I don't know where to sample next. So many things I'd like to do to Miller but probably won't. Not this time around, anyway.

Unable to stay there and take my time, I shuffle down farther, my mouth moving to his stomach. The muscles contract under my tongue, and his cock twitches against my chest.

The wet patch on his underwear somehow turns me on even more. Probably because it lets me know how much he's enjoying what I'm doing to him. My own cock is in a similar state. Harder than I've ever been before and achingly desperate to be touched.

My mouth pauses a little too long at the waistband of Miller's boxer briefs.

"You don't have to do anything you're not ready for." Miller's hips betray his words as they thrust upward in a silent plea to get my head closer to his dick. I know that's what he's doing because I've perfected that move myself over the years.

So this is what it's like to be on the other side of a needy cock. I would mentally apologize to every woman I've ever done it to if it weren't so fucking sexy.

"I'm ready," I murmur against his stomach. "But I need you to help me." I glance up at him only to find his eyes already locked on mine. "Show me what to do."

"Losing my underwear would be a good start."

I can't help smiling as I rise, resting on my knees. My fingers hook into the sides, but I hesitate again.

"Dunno why you're pausing. You've seen my dick a million times."

"Shit, you're right. I'm just ..."

"Nervous? You have nothing to be nervous about. Trust me, I'll like anything you do to me."

"*Anything*?"

Miller sighs. "God, I just set you a challenge, didn't I?" He knows how I love a good dare.

"Tell me if you don't like something I'm doing, because now I wanna try *everything*."

Miller lifts his hips as I pull his underwear off and throw them somewhere behind me. His cock, long, veiny, and thick, bobs against his stomach.

We both groan as my hand wraps around his hard length. I test out a few strokes, getting used to the difference in his thickness compared to mine.

Miller lets out a shuddery breath. "Grip a bit tighter."

I do as he says.

"So good."

I appreciate the encouragement, which gives me the courage to lean in and take the tip into my mouth.

A salty taste fills my mouth, and while it's not exactly pleasant, it doesn't make me gag. Like, no one's gonna bottle and sell a drink that tastes like cock, but as I glance up at Miller and see his hooded eyes, his tight jaw, and the obvious restraint he's forcing himself to hold onto, I understand how people could love the heady flavor. Because it's the taste of pure lust, and I want more of it.

I close my lips over his cock and work my way down until my mouth is filled.

Shit, Miller's huge.

My fingers wrap around his base as I move my mouth up and down.

Miller's breathing comes in short gasps, and I want to drive him to the point where he can't catch a breath. I want to make him come unglued, go crazy, and let out the primal roar I know he holds in.

There've only been a few times I've heard it—not everyone can make him go off like that—but I want it more than I've ever wanted anything.

I pull off him and lick my way down his length, while I move my hand to the head of his cock and keep stroking him.

My tongue runs down the underside, and even though my ass clenches at the size of this thing, I'm curious about what it would feel like inside me.

Apart from our FaceTime sessions when I've used my fingers to explore, I haven't been game enough for any other ass stuff. I want Miller to be a part of that. I want him to be the one I share my firsts with.

I take one of his balls into my mouth and don't let my gaze leave his face as his eyes fill with lust.

"Faster." He reaches for my hand on his cock and jacks himself with my hand.

My own dick aches, and as I flatten onto my stomach, the small amount of friction between me and the sheets is enough for me to almost lose my head ... and my load.

When Miller's satisfied with how fast my hand is pumping, he removes his hand from mine and fists it in my hair, pulling on it tightly but not enough to cause pain.

"God, you look even better doing that than I ever imagined." He pulls my head back farther until his ball falls from my mouth. "But I want you right here."

His hand guides my head back to his cock, and a thrill rushes through me at his demanding presence. I was worried I wouldn't be ready for this, but that didn't last long. He could tell me to rob a bank right now and I'd do it no questions asked.

This time when my mouth closes over his cock, I add a bit of suction and know I'm doing something right. Miller's hips lift off the bed, causing me to almost choke on his dick, but I grip his hip and pin him as hard as I can to the mattress.

"Fuck, sorry."

I want to tell him it's okay, but I don't want to pull off him. Instead, I glance up at him through watery eyes. *It's okay*, I try to say with my mind.

Miller doesn't seem to get it, or maybe he's worried I'm not liking this, because his hesitance is obvious in the way he relaxes under me.

I don't want that. I want him wound tight and ready to explode. To prove how much I want this, I suck him into my mouth as deep as I can—which admittedly isn't very far. I'll have to work on how to deep throat. Who knew it was an actual talent and not something people can automatically do?

"Talon," Miller says.

Damn it. I pull back. "I want to learn how to take you deep."

"You don't have to."

"I *want* to. I want to make you scream."

Miller's dark eyes flare with heat. "Relax your jaw and breathe through your nose."

I lower my head, but right before I get his cock back in my mouth, he grips my hair tight.

"And careful with the teeth."

With a chuckle, I try again and can take him a tiny bit farther this time.

Miller's breathing picks up, but he lies as still as possible. His thigh muscles contract, and as much as I should be worried about his injury, I assume he'll tell me if his leg hurts too much.

My head bobs and my cheeks hollow on the upstroke as I add suction and then release when I push my head back down again.

Miller's hands fumble for a place to go and tremor slightly.

I keep pushing my limits, because every time I go that tiny bit deeper into my throat, it makes him more frazzled and me even harder.

"Fuck, keep doing that."

Miller's encouragement turns me on more than anything ever has in my entire life, and I need friction on my cock. My hips rock against the bed, my dick dragging back and forth against the sheets.

"Holy shit, you're gonna make me come."

I moan around his cock, which sets mine off, and it's the first time I've ever come without someone touching me. My orgasm rocks my entire body, and I lose rhythm on Miller's cock, but he doesn't seem to notice. He's too busy with his head thrown back and his mouth open in ecstasy.

Like I always do when I defile hotel room sheets, I send up a silent apology to the housekeeping staff and make a mental note to leave a big tip.

"Seriously, Marc, pull away."

I shake my head.

"Fuck ... fuck ... fuck! I can't ..." Miller lets out the guttural roar I wanted and bucks into my mouth. More saltiness coats my taste buds, and I remind myself to breathe through my nose when I swallow.

His cock slips from between my lips, and Miller taps my shoulder to get me to climb up the bed.

I wriggle my way up, and Miller's arms come around me. One of his hands moves between us, moving to my softening cock.

"Want me to—"

"Yeah, bit late for that. Making you come was apparently too much for me to handle."

"In that case, you're welcome to do it any time you want. Like, any time. All the time."

I'm surprised he doesn't call me on being fast on the trigger, but no way am I bringing that to his attention. "Well, we have until July to take advantage. In between training, I'll blow you. Make it like a reward system."

"That might not be the best idea. I'm already terrified of getting a hard-on on the field from just being near you. Every time we complete a pass, I might try to push your head into my crotch."

"That'd be a nice halftime show."

We laugh, but Miller's dies quickly.

"Fuck." Miller's tone is dejected. "I'm still talking as if I'm gonna be on the field next season."

"You will be." I'll make sure of it.

CHAPTER EIGHTEEN

MILLER

The day after the Super Bowl, Talon flies back to Chicago while I go home again. He needs a few days to straighten his shit out and then a few more to visit his family in Colorado, so I'm taken off guard when he turns up on my doorstep a day earlier than planned.

Yet, there he is, in all his Talon glory, still basking in his Super Bowl win which has his killer smile on display. His blond hair is covered by a beanie, and his warm breath comes out in puffs of steam. "New York is colder than Colorado."

"Somehow I doubt that," I say. "What are you—"

"Who's ready for some training?" He pushes his way into the house and is way too excited for this time of morning.

I close the door to stop the cold air from coming in. "I guess the correct answer here is me? You're a day early."

"I knew you had your PT appointment today, and I wanted to come so I can talk strategy with your therapist."

"You weren't kidding when you said you were gonna ride me hard, were you?"

Talon's eyes fill with lust, and I shove him.

"I meant with training, you dick."

He shakes his head as if clearing his thoughts. "Don't say *dick* and *ride* and *hard* in the span of fifteen seconds. It short-circuits my brain, and I need a reboot."

"Ah. So, it all comes out. You're a sex robot sent from the future."

"Here at your service for whenever you want." Talon's eyes drift down my body. I don't think I'll ever get used to him looking at me that way. "Seriously, whenever you want."

A little voice from behind me startles me. "What's a sech robot?"

Oh, fuck.

I turn to my niece with a really big smile. "I'll give you a lollipop to never repeat that again."

"Is it a bad word? Mommy says bad words."

"It is a bad word."

"What's a bad word?" Mom says from the other end of the hallway.

"Nothing." I stand up straight.

"I forget already," Gabby says.

I owe that kid a lollipop.

"Marcus Talon, get your butt in here," Mom says when she spots him.

We move away from the entranceway and Talon approaches my mom.

"Hi, Gloria. It's good to see you again." He kisses her cheek.

They met back when we were in college and Mom flew out to check on Vanessa and me.

Mom pats Talon's cheek. "Last time I saw you, the NFL was just out of reach. It's crazy how far you've come since then.

And to think, I thought all those conversations about *Talon this and Talon that, Talon, Talon, Talon* were over. Then you had to go and sign with Chicago, and now it's all I ever hear again."

I run a hand over the back of my neck. "Thanks for the obligatory embarrassment, Mom, and I'd love to stay for more, but we've gotta go now. PT appointment. What a shame."

Talon laughs and follows me back to the door where I put on my jacket and scarf.

He leans in, the smugness in his eyes more prominent than normal—which is saying something. "Talk about me, huh?"

"Shut up," I grumble.

We make our way out to his rental SUV, and I don't miss the way Talon eyes my ever-present limp as we get into the car. It's getting better, and some days, I don't limp at all, but the sciatic nerve is still healing from the second surgery, so I get shooting pain down my leg every now and then, and it's easier to not put pressure on it.

Before I can tell him to quit looking at me like I'm broken and that I'm fine and the doctor assures me it's normal, he says, "I'm guessing your mom doesn't know?"

"Doesn't know what?"

"About us? And the guys in college?"

"There hasn't been a need to tell her."

I think I see hurt in Talon's eyes, but that can't be right. We haven't even discussed what this is with each other; I'm not gonna come out to my mom and—

"I came out to my brother," Talon says.

"You *what*?"

Of course, Talon is just ... so fucking Talon. It's not like I've struggled with my sexuality over the years internally, but externally, I knew there'd be consequences. It was easy to push down the side of me that likes guys because I could still be with women and not feel like I was pretending. But Talon ... he figures out he's bi and comes out of the closet before he even has a chance to climb into it.

It's admirable, but fuck, if I don't resent him a little for it.

"Okay, so, when I started thinking of you in ... that way, and I'd walked in on Jackson and Noah, I called my brother for advice, and he basically said it was nothing but even if it was something that he wouldn't care. When I got home a few days ago, he handed me a beer and asked if it was nothing. I didn't really see a reason to lie to him."

"How'd he take it?"

"He clinked his beer bottle with mine, clapped my shoulder, and that was that. I didn't tell him about you, though."

"What about your parents?"

Talon shakes his head. "Nah. I know them, and they'll probably pry a little too much or boast a little too loud to people they shouldn't. They told all their friends when I lost my virginity, like it was some milestone to be proud of as parents. Considering we don't even know what ... this is ... there're too many non-answers."

I want to ask what this is, but now's not the time. We have until next season to worry about everything else, and right now, we need to focus on my leg and figuring out how we're going to work on our own before we drag the rest of the world into our lives.

"Okay, you're gonna have to tell me where to go, because I got no idea," Talon says. Perfect timing for an abrupt subject change.

I direct Talon to Manhattan, but as soon as we arrive at my physiotherapist's, I know bringing Talon is a huge mistake.

Amelia's eyes light up as we walk in, and I swear cartoonish love hearts beat out of them.

"You're—"

Talon smiles and points to me. "I'm this one's bailiff. I'm here to make sure he's not slacking off, because I really need him next season."

"You did just fine without him, Mr. Super Bowl Winner," she practically purrs. Ugh.

If Amelia were ever to go missing and they looked at security footage of her business, I guarantee I'd be a prime suspect with the way I glare at her as she flirts with my man.

My man. Yup. Talon's mine even if we haven't defined that yet.

I stalk off in the direction of the physio room where my exercises happen, and they follow me while being all flirty.

"You're such a great friend to be here for Miller," Amelia says.

"I really am."

I roll my eyes so hard I see brain.

"We'll have you on the floor, Miller," Amelia says, and I don't even need to look at Talon to know he's waggling his eyebrows at me.

The whole time Amelia stretches me out on the mats, she barely takes her eyes off Talon, and I get it. Hell, I wanna be looking at him the whole time too. And I should be used to this by now. No matter where we'd go, whether it be in college or even during training camp at the beginning of the season, women flocked to Talon because he's a godlike figure in football, and he's always been naturally charismatic.

If this thing with us does go anywhere, we're gonna have to talk about that, because while I've been fine with sharing him in the past, he was never really mine to share. Everything is different now, and the dynamic is still unknown to me.

Talon says he hasn't hooked up with anyone since we started fooling around, but he also hasn't brought up whether or not he expects us to go back to the way things were between us.

Maybe he wants one of those open relationships where someone's invited into our bedroom whenever he feels like more. Maybe he doesn't want an actual relationship at all.

We need to talk about it and set limits and tell each other what we expect out of this, but how do I bring that up? Especially without sounding like a psycho clinger.

"So, you're helping Miller get back on his feet?" Amelia asks.

"His leg, actually."

Amelia laughs as if Talon's cracked the funniest joke in the world.

"We also need to recondition the rest of him." He glances at me. "Give him a really hard workout to build up the muscles that have deteriorated since he's been on his ass for the last four months."

I narrow my eyes at him. I don't know whether to be pissed at him for judging me or turned on by his implication. Either my brain's in the gutter or Talon's trying to torture me. I'm gonna go with torture, because he's Talon.

"Did you just call me fat?" I quip.

"Hey, if the shirt fits … or doesn't, in this case." He gestures to the muscle tee I normally work out in.

"It's supposed to be this tight," I argue.

"Mmhmm."

Amelia's still laughing like Talon's *so* cute. "Are we ready to add more weights to the leg press today?"

I grunt. "Yeah."

"Wait," Talon says, "he was limping before. Is the leg press a good idea?"

For someone who said he was gonna push me hard, he's certainly singing a different tune suddenly.

"He's still on light weights, but he needs to start working the leg more," Amelia says.

"Could that do more damage? Wouldn't it be better to recondition the rest of his body first and save the leg until last to make sure it's all healed?"

Amelia smiles. "I promise I know what I'm doing. If you wanted to maybe grab coffee sometime, I can explain the treatment plan in more depth with Miller's levels of advancement and where he should be at."

I freeze.

"He has set goals and a timeframe to hit them," she continues. "I'd be happy to go over all of that with you."

I bet she would.

I try not to look at Talon, but I can see out of the corner of my eye that he's trying to gauge a response from me.

"Sounds great, seeing as he hasn't discussed any of this with me."

My heart sinks. Did he just accept a date with this woman?

"I'd love to discuss Miller's program with you." Amelia's voice is all breathy. Apparently, she doesn't give a shit about client confidentiality ... wait, is that even a thing with physiotherapists?

"Why don't you do it right now, seeing as both of you are

talking as if I'm not here anyway." And that comes out super harsh. Great.

"Ignore him," Talon says. "He's cranky because I didn't let him have coffee on the way here."

"Oh, I understand," Amelia says. "I'd be cranky without coffee too."

Yeah. Because coffee is the reason I'm an asshole today. Let's go with that.

"We can all go to lunch one day to discuss it," Talon says. "Miller and I are basically inseparable."

Uh-oh. I know that tone. I know that innuendo.

Does he seriously want to have a threesome with my physiotherapist?

Talon's renting an apartment for the off season not far from my mom's house, and as we walk into the gym in the basement of the building, I tell myself to let the Amelia thing go. My mouth doesn't listen.

"You can't be that naïve," I exclaim.

"She did not ask me on a date."

"She so did," I argue. "You're dating my physiotherapist. And you practically asked her to fuck both of us."

Talon sighs in exasperation. "She was being polite, and no, I didn't."

"She was being *unprofessional*, and yes, you did!"

Talon's lips quirk. "Are you jealous?"

"No," I say too quickly.

"You so are."

"So what if I am? Aren't I allowed to be?" My question may come off as rhetorical, but it's really not.

"No. You're not allowed to be," Talon snaps.

"Why not?"

"Why *not*?" he yells and then glances around the empty gym.

It's a small private gym, only open to the residents of the building, but anyone could walk in at any minute. "Because I thought we'd already discussed this before the Super Bowl. You're not dating anyone else, and neither am I. So, I don't know why you'd assume I'd say yes to a date with you right in front of me."

My mouth slams shut.

Talon's smugness is back. Although I have to wonder if it's just a constant thing bubbling under his skin that he can break out at a moment's notice.

"I didn't realize that was the exclusivity talk," I say quietly.

"Are you dating anyone else?" Talon asks.

"Fuck no. I wouldn't do that."

"Well, it kinda sucks that you think I would."

"It's not ... that. It's just ... I don't know. You're you."

"Wow. I must be an asshole in your eyes."

"I've never known you to do the exclusive thing. Hell, I slept with all of your college girlfriends with you right there."

Talon slumps. "Is this going to be an issue with us while we figure this thing out? Or do you want to get it out of the way right now?"

"Get what out of the way?"

"It may've taken me a while to work it out, but you want to know what all those women had in common?"

"They'd do anything for you because you're Marcus Talon?"

Talon playfully slaps the side of my head. "You, you moron. They were all a means to get to you. I got to have you through them, and it's taken me this long to figure that out. Girls came and went, but you've always been there."

A lump lodges in my throat. "What happens when your attention span runs out?"

"Aww. You think I'm gonna get bored of you?"

I shrug. Isn't that what he said always happens?

"Would a threesome with your PT be hot? Hell yeah, it would be. But you've already said that's a hard line for you, and Shane"—Talon pierces me with his blue eyes—"I don't need anyone else. I used to think I did, but that was only because I'd never been with the right person."

The right person. *I'm* the right person?

"I don't need anyone else either," I whisper.

Talon grins. "Good. Then it's settled."

I nod. "Settled."

"Now, get on the ground and give me a hundred crunches."

"I hate you." Yet I do as he says.

Talon positions himself at my feet and runs his hands up my legs and rests them on my knees as he leans forward. "No, you don't. You want me to be your boyyyfriend. Because you liiike me. You want to—"

The door to the gym opens, and a couple of guys step through.

Talon leans back on his heels and drops his hands from me, and while I know it has to be done for obvious reasons, I still hate it anyway. It's not Talon's fault, but it sucks.

As soon as the guys see us, their faces light up in recognition, but they don't say anything. I do feel their constant staring, though. It feels like we're on display.

Talon and I remain professional after that until I'm exhausted, sweaty, and just want to collapse in a heap on the floor.

"Guess we should call it," Talon says after what feels like hours. I look at the clock on the wall and realize it was only an hour. Fuck, I really am unfit. I blame Mom's cooking. I knew that would be my downfall.

Talon leans in and lowers his voice. "We can go upstairs and finish our workout up there."

"What kind of workout can we do up—"

Talon raises that cocky eyebrow at me.

"Oh."

He stands and helps me off the floor, and we can't make it out of the gym fast enough.

CHAPTER NINETEEN

TALON

When I let Miller into my apartment, he looks around the place in confusion. Granted, it has wide windows with a nice view of New York Harbor, but the place is small and not up to my usual standard of living. The furniture which came with the place is dated, and the tiling is covered in mismatched rugs to take the cold out of the floor.

"When you said you'd come to New York, I figured you meant you'd stay in Manhattan and somewhere fancy. This is …"

"This is fine," I say. "I figured it would be better if we were close by. All we're going to be doing for the next few months is training, so it makes sense that we're not far apart."

"I know we talked about possibly going somewhere to do this, but Mom's gone all momma bear on me since coming home. Plus, with Vanessa going through a messy breakup, Mom asked if I could stay and help with Gabby occasionally."

"I'm perfectly fine with it. As long as you're getting the

treatment you need and you'll be back on that field next season, I'll go wherever you need me to."

Miller's lips turn into a thin line as if he already believes he's a lost cause. He's allowed to be skeptical because his entire career is on the line, but I'm not going to give up until the doctors say otherwise, and if he needs me to be that guy for him, then I will be.

"Want a shower?" I ask.

"Like, together?"

I step closer. "Well, I was gonna say to get out of your sweaty clothes, but together works." The little laugh that escapes me has a nervous quiver to it.

"We don't need to do anything you're not—"

I stop him right there. "I thought we went over this that night in your hotel room. No more kid gloves. I know what I'm doing ... okay, well I don't *know*-know, but I want to learn, and I'm not going to freak out."

"It'd make me feel better if we went slow."

"Slow, slow, as in you don't want to do anything or slow as in ..." Wait, what other kinds of slow are there?

Miller closes the distance between us, pressing against me chest to chest. I don't even care he's sweating all over me.

"As in, we try other things before the heavier stuff."

"Other things?"

Miller takes my hand and leads me into my bathroom. Anticipation builds in my stomach in the form of nervous butterflies. He turns the water on, and then turns to me, lifting the hem of my shirt.

Raising my arms, I let Miller undress me, and then it's his turn.

I like the way Miller stares at me, the way his dark eyes appear almost black when he takes in my already hard cock.

I'm excited for anything he has planned for me although I already know I want him to top me one day. I've been thinking about it ever since our FaceTime call where he instructed me to play with my ass.

At home in Chicago, I ordered a dildo online, but I've been too chicken to use it yet. I don't know why. I think, like anything, I want Miller there with me when I use it.

Miller makes everything better.

Even showers.

He gets under the spray first and rinses the sweat from his hair. While he reaches for the shampoo, I duck under the water.

It's a small shower, so the elbows to the ribcage whenever we move about isn't fun. Miller hands me the shampoo and we both wash ourselves off fast. When we're done, we make no move to get out of the shower.

"You were saying something about *other things* we could do?"

My hand trails down Miller's back and over the swell of his ass.

"Want me to get on my knees for you?" I whisper.

Miller's groan sounds like a yes, but when I go to lower myself, he pulls me back up by my arm.

"I have a better idea for that mouth of yours." He cups my face and brings his lips to mine for a chaste, soft kiss. "I love kissing you."

"Then keep doing it." I pull him closer, our wet bodies sliding and pushing against each other.

His mouth descends on mine again, nibbling, sucking, and teasing my bottom lip.

Our hard cocks seek friction, and I can't get close enough no matter how hard I pull Miller to me.

The way Miller kisses, I understand why he loves my mouth. Kissing him is nothing like the kisses I've shared with others before. I've had passionate kisses, warm kisses, kisses that made me feel all cozy, and others that kinda made me bored. But Miller's mouth? It has the power to make my universe crumble. It makes me weak in the knees, and I don't know whether to relax under the comfort of the familiarity of Miller or pin him against the wall and see how far these sparks can fly.

"Shane," I whine, my body conflicted.

"Mmm, I love it when you beg too." Miller's hand reaches between us, and he angles his left hip bone against me to give just enough of a gap for me to see what he's doing.

Miller grips both our cocks in one hand, and my breath hitches. He starts off slow, jacking us in long slow pulls.

I rest my head on his shoulder and continue to watch his soapy hand run up and down our hard lengths.

"Why does that look so fucking hot?" I whisper.

"Forget how it looks. How does it feel?"

Precum leaks from my slit. "Good, but it's not enough. It's a big, fat, fucking tease."

Miller chuckles, his shoulder jostling under my forehead. "What if I do this?" He grips us tighter and thrusts into his hand, making his cock drag along mine, and his hand creates more friction.

"Shit," I hiss.

"I take that as a good sign."

I nod.

Miller keeps going, trying different speeds and twists of his wrist until I'm a panting mess.

"Let's see what else you like," he whispers.

His other hand snakes between us too and massages my balls. I swear I almost come on the spot. I don't even have the ability to voice my approval.

My hips move too, fucking into Miller's hand.

"Oh God, oh God, oh God," I chant.

"You gonna come for me?" Miller asks.

I nod again. Apparently, Miller makes words not work good.

"Want to come in my mouth?"

Just the thought of Miller with his mouth wrapped around my cock has me going over the edge.

"Shiiit." I convulse as streams of cum land on us.

The warm water washes away the evidence of my orgasm, and I don't lift my head from Miller's shoulder until he's shaking with laughter.

"What?" I grumble.

"Seriously, dude? Couldn't hold out? I was looking forward to that."

"I'm totally throwing you a mental middle finger right now."

"Why only mental?"

"Because you've wrung me out. I can barely stand." But I force myself to pull back. Looking down, I notice Miller's still hard. "Oh. You didn't … want me to …" My mouth waters at the memory of swallowing him down.

"I have a better idea. Let's go to the bedroom."

My eyebrows shoot up. "Yeah? What are we gonna do in there?"

"I was thinking of introducing you to the world of frottage."

"Sounds like a kind of cheese."

Miller laughs. "It's like grinding up on each other."

"So, like, dry humping? Totally haven't come that way since I was fifteen."

"Well, you got turned on by Jackson and Noah doing it, right? Isn't that what you said?"

Flashes of Noah writhing under Jackson's big body has my dick twitching like it wants to go again but is not quite ready to.

"You wanna try it?" Miller asks, taunting me because I'm sure he can sense the flare of heat in my gut.

"Fuck, yes."

Miller is so fucking beautiful when he comes. I've seen it before, I've heard it, but when it's me making him do it? It's the best thing in the entire world.

Waking up next to him is even better.

"Come on, lazy-ass. Time to get up." I swat his ass.

His naked and deliciously round, firm, and surprisingly non-hairy ass.

I figured a guy who's built on pure testosterone like Miller would have hair everywhere, but he's smoother than a woman's legs on a third date.

"Fuck off," he mumbles.

"Hmm, it totally sounded like you just told me to fuck off, but that can't be right. Not after the orgasms last night."

"Exactly," Miller complains. "You kept me up half the night, and now I'm fucking tired."

"A brisk walk will wake you up."

"In the snow? I'll probably slip on black ice and injure my leg again. Or worse, the other one."

"Treadmill. Gym. Your PT said you should be walking every day, just not fast."

Miller's phone beeps on the bedside table, and he reaches for it with that long and muscular arm. Seriously, how had I never noticed how sexy a guy's biceps are?

It's like I've been living my entire adult life with tunnel vision. These thoughts had to be simmering under the surface, right?

Or is it like one of those crazy-ass religious cults where *I've seen the light!* I'll have to go to sermons and raise my hand to the gods of dicks, abs, and biceps.

Boom, there's my cult name.

"Oh no. Looks like we'll have to skip the walk," Miller says. "Mom wants me home for breakfast."

"Show me."

Miller hands me his phone, and there is a text from his mom.

"This says I'm invited, so we'll go have breakfast with your family, and then training. Easy."

"I hate you again," Miller grumbles.

"We established yesterday you far from hate me."

"Yes, but I distrust my taste in men, because clearly, you're evil. Am I at least allowed coffee today?"

"Learn how to drink it black, and you can have as much coffee as you want. Creamer is not conducive to your diet."

"The NFL is so lucky to have you," Miller says, but I don't buy it.

"Why do I feel like there's an insult coming?"

He stretches and slowly gets out of bed. "All I'm saying is, if you weren't with the NFL, you'd probably be some personal trainer who makes all his clients cry."

I light up and beam with pride. "You think so?"

"Dude, that wasn't a compliment."

"I'm taking it as one. Who doesn't like making people cry?"

"Normal people?" Miller shrieks. Then he realizes I'm fucking with him. He hastily dresses himself while grumbling, "Yep. Definitely hate you."

"Again, not what you said last night."

"That's because your dick was distracting me."

"Oh, I've heard of that. ADDD. It's like ADHD but it's attention deficit dick-distraction disorder."

I'm still laughing at my lame-ass joke when Miller says, "I'm thinking about telling my mom."

"About your dick disorder?"

"Okay, we're so not calling it that, and no. I mean ... about us."

I can't stop the smile from taking over my face.

"Would you be okay with that? I know we need to keep it a secret from the press, but I figured ... I can tell her just about me if you don't want anyone to know we're together or whatever."

I want to tell him to shout it to the world, but he's right. We can't tell the press. I want this with Miller, and for the first time in my life, I want something real, but what does a future look like with three out players on the same NFL team? What will Miller and I coming out do to Jackson's career? There're too many variables right now to put that kind of pressure on something so new.

It's not that new, my mind reminds me. We've been fooling around for months—just not in person. And we've been dancing around each other for years, but I just never knew it.

"Or I could not do it at all," Miller says when I realize I haven't responded.

"No, no, you should. I want you to tell your mom. And your sister, if you want. I was thinking that it's a shame we can't tell the press or the team or anyone else."

"You want to do that?" Miller sounds surprised.

I approach him and bring him close to me. "If there wasn't a chance of serious repercussions, I'd so want to do that." Leaning in, I kiss his mouth softly. I never told him about the shit Henderson was saying in the locker room, but now's not the time to delve into it. "Let's not think about that right now. Today should be a happy day."

Miller smiles, but it falls just as fast. "Unless Mom flips."

"Do you think she will?"

"Well, no. I didn't think so, but now that I realize I'm definitely gonna tell her, I'm scared she will."

"That's probably normal, right? Otherwise no one would struggle with coming out."

Miller looks like he's going to vomit ... or maybe faint.

I run my hands up and down his arms. "Whatever the reaction, we'll deal with it together, okay?"

He kisses me this time, and it's not chaste or soft. "Promise?"

"Of course."

CHAPTER TWENTY

MILLER

Talon's right. It's probably normal to sweat this much when you're about to come out to your family. I bet he didn't even flinch coming out to his brother, though.

When we arrive, my sister approaches and greets Talon with a hug. "Good to see you again, Marcus."

"Eww, you real-named me. That's gross."

Vanessa laughs. "Still see you're at about the same level of maturity as you were in college."

"Damn straight. Only, you know, according to your daughter, I'm a ball hog."

"Gotta let go of that ball faster, dude."

Talon looks at me. "Your sister is brutal."

"Always has been. That hasn't changed," I say.

"Uncle Shane!" Gabby comes running out from her room and immediately jumps into my arms. "Where'd you sleep?"

Great. Just great. Way to ease me into this, kid.

I carry her into the dining room and put her down in her seat, hoping that ignoring her question will make her curiosity go away. "Here, eat a bagel." I spread the cream cheese for her and put it on her plate.

"Where did you sleep, big brother?" Vanessa asks, and I glare at her. She stares at me with a smug expression I can only guess came from our sperm donor of a father. Dude only stuck around long enough to get Mom pregnant twice before he took off. My sister and I inherited our olive skin and dark hair and eyes from him, but everything else we get from Mom. Right down to our stubbornness.

As we all take our seats, it occurs to me I don't even know how to bring the whole thing up.

Talon digs in and piles his plate high with bacon, eggs, and all the good stuff, while he eyes me when I go for some bacon.

"The more you eat, the farther you have to walk," he sings.

I slump and put the bacon back.

"Are you being hard on my boy?" Mom asks.

Talon practically chokes.

"He's trying to get me ready for next season," I say. "Although I think the choking serves him right for being such a hard-ass."

Talon turns to my mom. "It's all your fault, you know. If I was being fed like this daily, it'd be hard for me to say no too."

My family keeps up small talk with Talon while I tune them out. There's no real correct way to bring this up, is there? It's one of those things you just have to say.

"I'm bi," I blurt.

Talon coughs again, but I think he's choking on his laughter this time instead of food. "Way to bury the lede, man."

"Yeah, probably should've started with something softer," I say.

Mom and Vanessa stare at me, and Gabby glances around the whole table with a cute little scrunch in her forehead.

"What's a bi?" Gabby asks.

"Umm ..." I look at Vanessa for permission to explain it, but Vanessa does it for me.

"It means Uncle Shane likes both girls and boys."

"I like girls and boys!"

"Good for you. It should all be about equality," Vanessa says. "But, uh, how about you go play in your room while Mommy and Grandma talk to Uncle Shane."

Talon tenses beside me, ready to defend me I guess, because sending Gabby away can't be a good thing.

"Okay." Gabby runs off like an obedient little girl. Of course, the one time I don't want her to listen, she does.

A sheen of sweat breaks out on my forehead. "So, uh, yeah. I'm bi, and Talon and I are ... well, you know ..."

"I knew it!" Vanessa says.

"Uh, say what now?" Talon asks. "Knew what? This is new. Like really new."

"Please, all those rumors in college."

"What rumors?" Mom asks.

"That Shane and Marcus liked to share. Like girlfriends and stuff. I always wondered how it worked and if there was more to it, but I didn't want to think about it too hard because, eww, that's my brother."

"That was different," I say. "That was just—"

Mom puts her hands over her ears and sings, "Lalalalalala. I don't want to know."

She doesn't want to know? She wants to pretend I didn't say anything at all? My heart makes a stuttering thud and then beats faster. I must pull a disappointed face or something, because Mom panics.

"No, I don't mean I don't want to know about you and Talon being together. I just don't need to know, like, the intimate details of what you did in college. Or now. Just ... yeah ... If Talon makes you happy, then I'll love him even more than I already do, but like your sister said, eww on the details. Same would go for if you were serious about a woman."

Relief has my heart calming down a notch. "Really?"

"Of course. Were you really worried?"

"I don't know. I mean ... maybe? I figured it's kind of unexpected."

Mom purses her lips. "It's actually not."

My mouth drops open.

"I mean, I'm not going to pretend I've been waiting for this for years or knew ever since you were a little boy, but there was always something in the way you used to talk about Talon. You were so heartbroken when he graduated and left. But then I met that horrible girlfriend you had when you were first signed to the NFL, and I thought I must've been wrong about the whole Talon thing, because you've never been like that with any other man. I chalked it up to hero worship." Mom shrugs. "I'm glad you two got your act together after all this time."

Talon grins. "Hero worshiping, huh? I can totally see that."

I elbow him. Hard. He lets out an "Oomph."

"Well, I'm happy for you," Vanessa says. "Even if it will lead to interesting discussions with the five-year-old."

"Gabby won't care," I say. "She's not an asshole."

Talon snorts. "Best uncle ever."

"I'll make sure she won't care, but what about what everyone else will say?" Vanessa asks.

"There won't be anyone else," Talon says. "Like, no one can know about this anytime soon."

"Why's that?" Mom asks.

"It'd be a PR mess," I say. "We'd need to talk to our agents and come up with some huge coming-out plan. It'd be doable but an absolute nightmare at this point in our careers."

Talon side-eyes me. "Also ..." He hesitates. "Henderson's been saying shit."

"Yeah, what else is new? I honestly think he's worse than Carter on the homophobe scale but is stealthier about it."

"At least Carter admitted he was wrong, and he and Jackson have a civil approach of staying away from each other," Talon says. "But Henderson was pissed at some stupid article that was written about us and how we went to college together and had a 'bromance.' It was an innocent article, but because we've practically adopted Jackson, he says we'll catch the gay and all this other bullshit. If we come out as a couple, it kinda feels like he was right even though he's not. You know he's not gonna be the only one who'll say stuff like that. And then what will that do to Jackson's career? He's been through enough."

Just when I think I can't fall for Talon more, he comes out with that. He's the best friend any guy could ask for. Even though it's potentially putting his happiness on the line, he's trying to protect Jackson, and while I totally understand it, I can't help being crushed by the weight of what being with Talon means.

I knew it'd be like this, but the Henderson stuff makes the reality hit home.

We'll have to live in the closet. Not for a while, but a long while.

Then I remind myself that I've lived without Talon for six years, and the sting of not being able to touch him in public will still be way better than the gut-wrenching hurt of living without him completely.

"That's bullshit," my sister says.

"What's bullshit?" Gabby asks from the entrance to the hallway, and we all flinch.

"She's a freaking parrot," Vanessa mumbles. "Go back to your room, and I'll be in there in a minute to get you dressed for the day." Vanessa stands and approaches Talon. "Make him happy, Marcus, or I'll kick your quarterback ass." She kisses him on the cheek, and he laughs.

"I have no doubt you'll be able to do it too." His eyes meet mine. "And I promise to make him happy."

As soon as we enter Talon's apartment after getting back from my Mom's, I'm on him like white on rice.

I take him off guard, and he stumbles, but with my arms wrapped around him, I save him from falling.

My mouth assaults his, but it's not like he puts up much of a fight. Our tongues tangle, my cock digs into Talon's hip, and he lets out a loud moan.

"I woulda thought you'd still be exhausted after last night."

"I am. And then you said you wanted to make me happy."

"Ah, and your ADDD kicked in. Got it."

I laugh. "Something like that."

Linking our hands, I lead Talon to his bedroom and push him down on the bed so he's on his back.

"What are we trying this time?" he mocks.

"I was thinking you could fuck me, but if you'd rather play more, I'm okay with that too."

Talon's hand pushes down on his cock which is trying to free itself from his pants. "No more playing."

I lower myself to my knees. My leg protests a little but not enough to stop. I take off Talon's shoes and socks and then run my hands up his legs and over his thighs.

"How do you want to do this?" Talon asks. "I mean so it won't hurt your leg."

"We'll find a way," I murmur. "Maybe I'll brainstorm while sucking you off first."

"Nghhrl."

"Is that English?"

"Yes, it's English for *you're a big fucking tease, and I think you might kill me.*"

"No one's ever died from having an orgasm before. Unless, I dunno, if they're eighty or whatever."

I make quick work of his pants and pull them off along with his boxer briefs.

The cock I have memorized, the gorgeous, cut, long, and thin cock, lies against Talon's stomach. Its angry and swollen head begs for attention, and that's the exact reason I ignore it.

Lifting the hem of his shirt, I lean over him and kiss my way up his torso. Talon throws his head back, and I love the sounds he makes as I take a nipple into my mouth. My hands move down his sides, gripping his hip and trailing over his heated skin with light, feathery touches, but I refuse to touch his cock.

"I know if I complain, you're only going to hold out longer," he says through gritted teeth, "but could we maybe move this along a little faster before I lose my load?"

I chuckle and stand up straight. "Sure thing." I lose my clothes and then go back to what I was doing, this time slowly moving my mouth closer and closer until Talon's cock drags along my rough cheek.

It's been so long since I've done this to someone I'm probably gonna be a little rusty, but I don't care. I've been thinking about doing this for so fucking long.

I start small and lick my way over the tip. "Mmm."

Talon's hips jackknife off the bed, and he gasps before releasing a string of curses that makes me laugh.

"What? You're acting like you've never had a guy's mouth on your dick before."

"Funny, smartass. Less talking. More sucking."

"Now who's the bossy one?" I bury my head between Talon's legs instead of giving him what he wants, and my tongue laps at one of his balls.

"Jesus fucking Christ," Talon whispers.

"Name's Miller, actually. But I can be your god anytime."

Talon snorts. "You're as lame in bed with guys as you are with girls, and I still don't know how that line works, but it does. I will gladly worship you for the rest of my life if you keep doing what you're doing."

When I'm done teasing his sac, I run my tongue up his hard shaft and flatten it against the pulsing vein.

"God, I love the feel of your stubble."

He's gonna love it even more in a second. I engulf his whole cock in my mouth, dusting off the deep-throating skills I learned years ago.

Talon's breathing becomes shallow. "I don't want to think about how you're so good at that."

A pang of regret hits me, because part of me wishes we could've had this back then if I'd only ever gotten the courage to say something. But we were both young, and I can guarantee we wouldn't be here today doing this had I mentioned years ago that I've dreamed of this moment.

They say when fantasies become realities, they're always a letdown, because nothing is ever as good as what your imagination can conjure. But when you want something so desperately, the surreal experience of getting it won't let you be disappointed.

Ever since Talon arrived on my doorstep, I've been riding a wave of *I have to make the most of it* and *holy fuck, this can't be real.*

Talon lifts his hips, almost making me gag, but fuck, if it doesn't feel like the best sex I've ever had, even though he's the one getting to have all the fun right now.

He moves in and out of my mouth, and I tell myself to memorize his velvety tight skin and the sound he makes every time the tip of his cock hits the back of my throat.

"Do you want me to fuck you or come in your mouth?" Talon asks. "Because I'm close."

I'm tempted to let him come—he has the stamina to go again later—but I want this too much, and I want it now.

Reluctantly, I pull off his cock, and Talon's breathing slowly evens out.

I go to the bedside drawer where Talon pulled out the lube we used last night and smile when I find a box of condoms too. "You really did come prepared."

"Are you kidding me? I was prepared the night of the Super Bowl, and then I went and got too drunk."

"Thought I'd let you have a go at my ass that night?" I totally would have, but I'm not gonna say that aloud.

I place the supplies on the bed and then lie down next to him on my side.

Talon pulls me in close and presses his mouth to mine. The air between us goes from playful to serious as he reaches for the lube.

His tongue distracts me while he gets his fingers coated.

"Roll over onto your other side," Talon whispers against my skin.

I do as he says, putting my back to him, and he moves my good leg so it's bent but keeps my stupid leg straight.

A finger runs over my surgical scar. "Does it hurt?"

"Bottoming? I guess we'll find out."

Talon laughs. "Your scar, dumbass."

Oh. Self-consciousness makes me want to cover it up, but I don't know why. I've seen the scar in the mirror, and I know it's ugly, but it's not like I'm looking at it constantly. I forget it's even there.

"It doesn't hurt," I say. "It feels weird when you touch it—almost like I have like a Band-Aid or something covering part of my skin. Doctor said I could lose some sensitivity there."

His warm mouth kisses the middle of my back and then my shoulder blade. "Are you sure you're up for this?"

I nod into the pillow. "Do it."

His fingers slip between my ass cheeks, and even though I know what's about to happen, my body tenses when he plays with my rim.

"Relax. We'll go slow," Talon coaches.

I try not to tense again when his finger works its way inside. I chant in my head, reminding myself that this is Talon. This isn't some random hookup from college. This isn't sex for the sake of sex. This is everything I've ever wanted, and he's all mine.

I loosen up enough for another finger to join his first one, and with the feel of his hard cock resting against one of my ass cheeks, and the way his fingers probe my tight channel, it's an overwhelming experience.

I want to reach back and pull him close, turn my head and kiss him, but I'm scared if I move or make even a single sound, I'll lose the sensation I'm quickly learning to like.

"You're doing so good, baby," Talon whispers, and I shudder. "You let me know when you're ready."

I don't know if I am, so I rock my hips back and forth, taking his fingers deeper. The sting of stretching returns. "Try three," I rasp.

Instead of feeling more burn, his fingers leave me completely. I didn't know how full I was until the loss hits me, and I let out a whimper.

"You still with me?" The snap of the lube bottle opening again fills my ears.

"Uh-huh. Keep going."

"You sure?"

"Hurry the fuck up and finger my ass, Marc. I'm almost ready."

Talon laughs. "Mmm, think you're gonna top from the bottom, hey? I've heard about that."

I lean up on my elbow and turn my head toward him. "Where did you hear about that?"

He sheepishly looks away. "Forums and stuff. I wanted to know as much as I could so I didn't feel like such a noob."

"You're far from a noob. You forget I've been there while you've prepped someone before."

"Not with a guy."

"It's really not that different."

Talon's evil glint appears in his eyes. "That's not what I've read."

This time when his fingers enter me, they're on a mission, and it takes no time at all to find their target.

"Oh, holy fucking cheese on a cracker."

Talon laughs again. "Guess I found your prostate."

"Don't stop finding it."

"Wouldn't dream of it." Talon pegs it again and again until his fingers aren't enough and I crave more.

"Talon," I croak.

"Yeah?"

"I need you inside me."

CHAPTER TWENTY-ONE

TALON

No way in the world am I denying Miller's request.

Miller's a quivering mess as I remove my fingers and suit up.

I grip his hip and roll him over that tiny bit more. He's still on his side, but that tight and round ass is on full display. I can't wait for the day where I can have him on his hands and knees begging for me to take him hard and fast, but we both know that day is a while off.

"I kinda like you like this," I say. My mouth ghosts along his back, the rise and fall of his breathing matching mine.

"Pissed off, impatient, and begging for more? Figures you'd like it."

"Aww, someone's just cranky because he hasn't come yet." Or I'll ride it out a little longer, because he's right. Seeing Miller on the brink of losing control is so fucking hot.

"Someone's cranky because I need it right now."

I roll my hips, and my sheathed cock rubs over his crack, settling in between his ass cheeks, but doesn't go near his hole.

He whines, which makes me even harder, but I should put him out of his misery.

"You sure you're ready?"

"Yes!"

This time when I line up my cock, I tease his hole but don't push inside.

"I'm going to fucking kill you," Miller mutters.

"Ah, what's sex without the threat of violence?" Before he can retort, I inch my way inside ever so slowly.

Miller tenses immediately, so I pause.

"I'm good. I promise. Keep going."

The last thing I want to do is hurt him, so I go even slower.

The only sound to fill the room is our combined breaths—mine even and slow as I try to think of anything but the tight heat surrounding my cock, and his, fast and erratic, no doubt trying to forget about the dick in his ass.

My hand makes soothing circles on his hip and his lower back while my lips caress the back of his sweaty neck. "You're doing so good, baby. So good."

Miller nods, but his large biceps contract as he grips his pillow tight.

"Let me know if it's too much."

His hand reaches back and finds mine. "Never too much with you." It's almost inaudible, but it's there—something I never even knew I needed until it comes out of his mouth.

The feeling of being inside him, of being whole—Talon and Miller—it clicks. It's something I've never been able to define, and until recently, I didn't understand it.

But now I do.

My soul mate happens to be a male, and I'm totally okay with that.

"I'm good to go," Miller whispers.

I move slow so he can adjust, and though it takes a little while for him to loosen up, when he does, it's amazing. Like everything since I started this thing with Miller, it surprises the hell out of me that I went so long without realizing what I had in front of me for years.

Everything is better with him. Not just the sex stuff, but life in general. I could spout shit about colors being brighter and food tasting better, but it's none of that bullshit. It's a sense of belonging, of being complete, and everything being *right*.

"Fuck," I hiss when Miller rolls back a little so he can reach for his cock.

Nothing has ever felt like this.

"I don't think I'm going to last." I can barely talk, let alone fuck. "If I go before you, I promise to blow you until you come down my throat."

"Mhfkjuhsgd."

"I'll take that as a yes." Pulling out to the tip, I slam back in, and Miller lets out a hoarse cry. "Again?" I ask.

He chants "Yes, yes, yes, yes, yes."

Miller's hand works his cock so fast there's no way I'd be able to keep up that tempo, but I try. My hips piston, and I go as hard as I can in this position, which isn't easy. I lean up on one elbow and push harder.

I try to pull my orgasm back but fail miserably as a shuddering release sets off fireworks in my groin.

I come harder than I ever have in my entire life, and it seems to last for minutes. The world fades around me, and I'm in a blur until Miller's telltale roar flies out of him as he comes.

I'm vaguely aware of his hand still jacking him through his orgasm, and I tell myself I should help with that, but I'm dead.

Eventually everything slows and goes quiet, as if the world settles around me into relaxed silence.

"Uh, Talon?"

"Yeah?"

"I kinda need my ass back."

"Right. You probably need that." I slip my softening cock from his body slowly, and Miller winces. "You okay?"

"I will be." He smiles over his shoulder at me.

"Good." I snuggle in behind him and kiss the back of his neck. We need to get up and clean ourselves before heading downstairs for training, but I don't want to move.

Miller's back rises and falls hard with his breaths but as they slow, he becomes fidgety.

I feel like I could go back to sleep again. "Stay still."

He laughs. "Can't. I'm uncomfortable and lying in cum."

With a chuckle, I roll onto my back. "Fine."

Miller wriggles his way to the edge of the bed and heads to my bathroom. I close my eyes to the sound of water running in there and almost drift off when warm hands land on my junk.

I crack one eye open. "Wha?"

A deep laugh and warm brown eyes meet me. "I'll get rid of this for you."

"My dick?"

More laughs. "The condom."

Oh. That.

He ties it off and takes it into the living-slash-kitchen area. A cabinet door opens and then another. Miller rummages around for a while, but when the telltale noise of the refrigerator opening hits my ears, I smile and prepare for the complaining I know I'm about to get.

"Hey, Talon?" Miller asks.

I sigh and climb out of bed, finding some boxer briefs and sweatpants to throw on.

Miller's still scanning the contents of my fridge when I emerge. "Where's all the good food?"

"You're staring at it. I went shopping yesterday."

"*You* went shopping? On Staten Island?"

"Okay, fine. I hired a guy to do it."

"Who?"

I shrug. "There's an app where basically you can get anyone to bring you anything." I approach him and wrap my arm around his bare back. My lips land on his shoulder, and I love the way he melts into my side. "I got egg whites, kale, lots of protein. Superfoods for the win!"

Skeptical eyes meet my innocent ones ... well, relatively innocent. "You're going to kill me, aren't you?"

"Not with my cooking, at least. I'm only letting you rest for half an hour before going to the gym."

Miller groans, and unlike a few minutes ago in bed, it's not a happy groan. It's an *I really don't want to* type of groan.

I saw the way he struggled yesterday during his PT session, but I've never known Miller to hate training. He's one of the hardest workers I know. I'm usually the one pulling him away from a workout or practice to do stupid shit. So, seeing him so against training is disconcerting, but I tell myself it's only because he's had months of slacking off while recovering. I know how hard it is to get back into it after the off season. So much so I try not to let myself relax too hard.

"Your leg's not gonna get better until you get off your ass," I say.

"Well, thanks to you, my ass is currently wrecked. Can barely walk."

"We'll go light today, but we need to do *something*."

"Sex counts as a workout."

This isn't working. "Okay, how about this: you give me two hours in the gym, I'll let you have my ass tonight."

I've never seen Miller move faster. Well, since his injury anyway.

"There. Done," Miller pants. "Sex. Now."

He's on his back on the mats in the gym after a set of hand weights, and he can barely lift his arm to try to swat at my ass.

I laugh. "You sure you could handle it right now? You're moving like a rookie with a hangover."

"Nope. Can't move. You're gonna have to ride me right here."

I think he's joking, but I can't be sure. "In the very public gym? Are you stroking out on me?"

He reaches for me, but I hesitate. I really want to climb on top of him, but even though no one's come through the gym doors since we came down here two hours ago, we can't risk it.

Those guys from the other day recognized us, and if they were to walk in again …

"Help me up, jackass," Miller says.

"Oh. Sorry. I thought …" I shake my head. "Never mind."

Miller raises a brow at me. "I'm not actually that dumb as to want to hook up in public."

"Sorry. I know. I just—"

"You freaked out for a second. It's okay. You have to be careful all the time, no matter what, but I'm not used to it yet, and I didn't think. I was just goofing off."

"It sucks even goofing off has lines drawn now." My immediate thought at Miller's joke was to freak out about being caught. It more than sucks. "You getting up?"

Miller doesn't move. "Can't. I live here now."

I try not to let my concern show. Toward the end of the session, Miller finally perked up and became the annoyingly focused guy I'm used to him being in a weight room. But getting there ... it's like he's not one hundred percent committed. He's lagging and slow, and I understand he's had months off, so his body's weak, but I can't help thinking if his mind is holding him back, not his body.

"We should go do something fun tonight," I say.

Miller finally climbs to his feet. "I thought the plan I had was fun." He winces. "But I'm gonna need the use of my arms for that, and I think they're dead."

"Maybe we could go hang out with Jackson and Noah?"

"I'll message their friend Maddox too. He's cool. He's kinda the one who gave me the courage to FaceTime you that first time."

"Ooh, so he's awesome then? That's risky, putting us both in the one room. The world might implode with that much awesome in the same place."

"Mmhmm." Miller grabs his towel and chugs some water and then heads for the door.

I still love the way he ignores my bullshit.

Going out turns out to be a good idea. Miller's blah mood vanishes as soon as we enter the bar where we're meeting

Jackson and his friends. His mood lifts even further when I put a light beer in front of him.

"Really, bailiff? I get an actual beer?"

"Have at it." I worked out today that I'm going about his training all wrong, so I'm going to try a new tactic. Positive reinforcement.

The tough act would've worked with old Miller, but his injury has shifted something in his head. He needs to get excited and retrain his brain to give him the right mentality toward his reconditioning.

We learn about sports psychology through team trainers and our coaches, and while I think some of it is hokey, like visualizing a win, I totally see the correlation between being in the right mindset and succeeding. I need to get him back on track.

Seeing as I know Jackson and Noah and know of Damon King from articles and his baseball days, when they enter, I can only figure the shorter blond guy is Maddox.

He's good-looking, so that counts for something.

Guess I'm noticing the attractiveness of other guys now. Interesting ...

Maddox makes his way over to me, and I see it in his eyes immediately—it's *the look.* I've been getting it since my college days.

"Football fan?" I ask.

He doesn't reply.

Miller nudges him. "Hey, you didn't get all gushy when you met me."

"You're not Marcus Talon."

"Ouch," Miller says. "You're no longer my favorite friend of Jackson's."

Maddox continues to stare at me, but he still hasn't said hi.

Damon's arm goes around his boyfriend's shoulders. "Ignore this one. He's a weirdo."

Maddox snaps out of whatever fanboy trance he was in and turns to him. "A weirdo you're in love with, so what does that say about you?"

"That I'm not only crazy about you—I'm just plain crazy."

Maddox leans into Damon. "Marcus Talon needs a wingman tonight, so I'm gonna go flirt with some girls."

"Uh, I need what now?" I ask. I have to force myself not to turn my head toward Miller.

They ignore me.

Damon kisses Maddox's cheek. "Flirt with girls all you want, babe. You know they can't give you what I can."

"It's a sacrifice I'm willing to make for Marcus Talon."

"Uh, can you stop saying my full name like that?" I ask. "It's weird. Call me Talon."

Maddox lets out a little "Squee," but I think it's by accident. He whispers something to Damon, and Damon nods.

"Go. Have fun."

Maddox puts his hand on my shoulder and pushes me through the crowd.

"Uh, I wasn't really looking for a hookup," I say.

"Single guys are always looking for a hookup."

Before we disappear, I turn back and give Miller eye contact. He has a reserved smile, and as if we're already having those voodoo-reading-each-other's-mind thing couples have, I know he's telling me it's okay to humor Maddox. Or at least I hope he's saying that.

After the PT conversation Miller and I had, it feels wrong flirting with someone else, because we've set our hard limits.

I've never had that before—where I don't see a point in flirting. Maybe it's because in the past I've always kept my options open. Since Miller's come back into my life, my options are definitely closed to everyone but him.

"Damon doesn't care if you flirt with women?" I ask Maddox.

"Why would he? He knows I'm only ever coming home to him."

Huh. I guess that's what complete trust looks like. "How long you been together?"

"Twelve months? I think. Around there. I dunno, we're not keeping track."

Is that how long I can expect to get to that place with Miller? Then again, I have no clue where we'll be in a year. If we were to get to that point, we wouldn't be able to live together without people getting suspicious. What kind of millionaires have roommates?

"Want to play a game of pool instead?" I point to the pool tables at the back.

Maddox turns and cocks his head. "Sure."

He continues to eye me as we head over and interrupt a game with two other guys. One thing I love about my celebrity status is getting my way when I want it.

It only costs me a selfie to get their table.

Again, I glance back at Miller, and I wonder if he has the telepathic thing too when I send him a "Look, I'm being a good boy" vibe.

When he smiles at me from across the room, I turn away again, only to be met with Maddox's inquisitive stare.

Maddox pulls out a stick from the holder while I rack up the balls. "So, you and Miller are good friends?"

"The best. We went to college together." It's not until the words are out of my mouth that I begin to wonder if I've screwed up somehow, because Maddox's eyes widen before he schools his reaction.

Then he throws me some forced nonchalance while nodding once and saying "Cool."

I can't explain my unease as we play.

Maddox scrutinizes me and not in the "I can't believe I'm here with Marcus Talon" way like he did as soon as he saw me. Then there's the way he looks at me. Like I can hear his thoughts: *I know your secret.*

The paranoia makes my ears burn and my chest tighten.

I don't know how this stranger could possibly know for sure, but it's a feeling I can't shake. So much so Maddox kicks my ass at pool when I'm usually the kicker of asses.

"Another game?" he asks.

I smile, but it's tight. "Actually, I might go grab a drink."

CHAPTER TWENTY-TWO

MILLER

When Talon approaches, his skin pale, I have no idea what the fuck happened. He nods in the direction of the entrance of the bar, and I follow him out.

The cold night air hits us, and I shiver because I didn't pick up my jacket.

I shove my hands in my pockets of my jeans. "What's wrong?"

"Does Maddox … did you tell Maddox? About …" He glances around the street, but no one's paying us attention. We're right near a subway station, so it's busy, but everyone's going about their own business. "Us."

"I told him about me, but I never mentioned you specifically. I said my straight best friend kissed me but didn't give specifics."

"That Maddox guy? Not dumb. He knows."

"Oh." I don't know how I feel about that. "What'd he say?"

"Nothing."

"Then how—"

Talon's face is red, but I don't know if it's because he's angry, embarrassed, or just cold from the frigid air.

"Don't ask me how I know. I just do. It's obvious in the way he stares at me. All smug and knowing and shit."

I try not to smile. "Annoying, isn't it?"

Talon cocks his head at me, and I realize now's not the time to joke.

"And are you freaking out that he knows or that it could get out? I don't know him very well, but I trust him. Jackson trusts him."

Talon still seems unsure, so I take my phone out of my pocket and text Maddox.

He appears moments later with both our jackets.

I can't get mine on fast enough. "Thank fuck. I'm freezing my nuts off."

"What's up?" Maddox asks. "Is this about you two fucking around, because you're not exactly being subtle about it."

Talon's mouth drops open.

"He blurts things," I explain. "It's normal."

"But I was right. He knows." Talon's still uneasy.

"We're not telling anyone," I say to Maddox. "We're, uh, trying to figure this whole thing out."

"Figuring it out is the fun part." Maddox winks.

Talon and I don't respond. If anything, Talon tenses more.

"Too soon?" When we don't reply, Maddox nods. "Too soon. Got it. Uh, I'm gonna go back inside. Just know I haven't said anything to anyone about Miller, not even Damon, so please don't freak out about me knowing too much. You guys are rich and could totally afford a hitman to take me out." His face falls. "Oh, God, I'm giving you ideas."

Talon finally smiles and lets out a little laugh. "I do all my contract killing myself."

I sigh. "Figures you two would get along."

"Anyway," Maddox says. "Offer to talk is there if you guys need it. Otherwise, I'm gonna pretend I know nothing. Knowing nothing is my specialty … wait … did I just call myself dumb?" Before we can answer, he shrugs. "Eh. Oh well. See you guys back in there."

He turns on his heel and heads back into the bar.

Talon sinks against the rough brick of the building.

"I think we can trust him," I say.

He shakes his head. "It's not that. It's …" He sighs. "Is this what it's like? What it's going to always be like?" Talon searches the street again as if paranoid people can hear or that we'll be recognized. The only thing that could hear us is random patches of melting snow.

"What is it always going to be like?" I ask.

"When I realized Maddox knew, it was like the ground could crumble underneath me if I said the wrong thing, and I froze up."

I can see it written all over his face. It's the freak-out I expected him to have months ago when we started Face-Timing each other and then again when we began fooling around in person. Only, he's not so much freaking out about us being together but the rest of the world and how they're going to react if they find out. If it was just us and our families, it wouldn't be a problem, but we're not just anyone. We're both public figures—Talon more so than me—but if either of us was outed, it has an impact. On us, on the league, on the fans, but most importantly, on Jackson.

"My life is splashed all over the tabloids enough as it is,"

Talon says. "What if this all comes out, and then those women we've been with come forward? What if you're thrust into the spotlight, Jackson's shit is dredged up again ... Everything flashed through my mind in a split second."

I take a deep breath, because what I have to say probably isn't what he wants to hear. "During college, every time I hooked up with someone, I was self-conscious about it getting out, about them telling everyone. I was constantly looking over my shoulder, and then when I made the NFL, I was terrified one of my hookups was going to come forward, but they didn't."

"Did the paranoia ever go away?"

"It dimmed, but I'm not gonna lie—I still worry about it from time to time."

Talon looks so brokenhearted and defeated, but I don't know how to fix it.

"It's probably something we need to evaluate," I say. "Because this is what being together is gonna be like. There's no way around that."

"Evaluate?"

"If it's worth it."

"Do you need to evaluate?"

I want to tell him the truth—to yell a big fat no, I don't, because it's always been Talon for me. I'd move heaven and earth to be with him. But his uncertainty is clear as day, and I don't want to influence that.

"Maybe we both need it," I lie.

"Man, this part isn't on the brochure, is it?"

"Brochure?"

"When you hear about people coming out, you always picture awkward teens sitting in front of their parents. They come out, parents react—good or bad—and then it's done. Fuckin' nope. You've got friends, work, random people figuring it out in bars ..." Talon grunts. "Whoever the assholes are who say being queer is a choice clearly don't know shit. No one would choose to feel like this."

My heart stutters, and I know that's not a dig at me or what we have, but I can't help being crushed just a little. "Like what?"

Talon stares down at the ground, and it takes all my strength not to press against him and tell him everything will be okay even though I don't know that for sure. As long as I can restrain myself in public, as hard as it is to do, we won't have a problem.

No touching doesn't take away the risk of people finding out, though. Maddox worked it out after meeting Talon for fifteen minutes.

Talon shoves his hands in his pockets. "I don't want to change this side of me, but I don't know how else to describe this—like my privacy is on the line and there's nothing I can do to stop it from being leaked. It's a control issue."

"That's why I want you to be sure before we ... do anything else."

He doesn't respond immediately, and I guess part of me is hoping he'll say "Of course, you're worth it. Duh." But if he's thinking about it, then that's good too, because if he's not sure, it's better to know now.

"You wanna go home?" I ask.

"We haven't been here long. We should go back in there and chill for a bit."

More disappointment, and as we go back inside, I spend the next few hours trying to gauge what Talon's thinking. He seems like his usual goofball self, but he avoids eye contact with both me and Maddox.

When we leave and go home a few hours later, things are so strained that we don't talk the whole way back to Staten Island.

And instead of inviting me back to his place, he pulls up outside my mom's house. I stare at the house and then at him, awaiting some type of excuse that doesn't come. But as I go to get out of the car, Talon reaches for my thigh and gives it a squeeze.

I should ask what it means, because now, I'm going to spend the rest of the night wondering if it was supposed to be reassuring, casual, or bracing me for the bad news to come.

"I just need some time ..."

I told him to think about it seriously, so I can't blame him for actually doing it, but damn, if it doesn't hurt a little.

The loud banging on the front door is what rouses me from sleep.

I can't catch a fucking break. If it's not the kidlet waking me up, it's someone at the front door at some ungodly hour of the day.

I throw my pillow over my head and wait for Mom or Vanessa to answer the door. Hell, even Gabby could answer it right now for all I care.

Uncle of the year award right here. "Answer the door to strangers, honey, so Uncle Shane can get some rest."

Gah, I should get out of bed to make sure she's not being

kidnapped or being asked to convert to Jehovah's Witness, but I'm broken and can't move.

After barely sleeping at all last night because of my idiotic decision to tell Talon to step back and have a think if I'm worth fighting for or not, I'm not gonna be able to function today when I can't get myself to sit up.

"Geez, I give you two beers, and you think you get to sleep in this morning?" Talon's voice startles me, and that finally gets me moving. I bolt upright.

"I … well … yes?" After last night, I wasn't sure I'd see him today.

Talon crosses his arms. He's in his ridiculously cute beanie and sweats, and his cheeks are flushed. "Come on. We're walking back to the apartment and then training all day."

"And the hard-ass is back. I thought after last night he might've been killed off by the nice Talon." On the inside, I'm thankful the hard-ass turned up. It means there's hope.

Something falters in Talon's smile. "No matter what's going on between you and me, I'm still here for a reason, and that's to whip your ass into shape."

I smirk. "I'm not really into whips. Handcuffs on the other hand …"

Talon's eyes flare with heat, but he tries to hide it. "Up. Now. Your mom is making us something to eat, so you've got five minutes to get up and get dressed or you're going in your pajamas."

"You're assuming I'm wearing pajamas." Probably shouldn't poke him, but I want to show him where I'm still at. I don't want to beg him or tell him he has to choose me, but I want him to know nothing has changed on my end.

Talon looks at the roof, muttering something about God giving him strength to keep his dick in his pants.

I don't know where we stand, but that's no different from last night. We're probably not going to work this out immediately. It's something we have to figure out for ourselves.

"I don't see you moving," Talon says.

"It's too early," I complain, trying to get a reaction out of him. It works.

"Don't make me go over there."

My mouth drops open to dare him to do it, but I think better of it. That might be pushing him too far this morning.

Talon shifts on his feet. "Say it."

"Say what?"

"What you were going to say. Taunt me to come over there." His eyes are soft, just like his voice, and it's like he's begging me to give him permission.

"Come here," I say, my voice gruff.

His steps are tentative, but he does it.

When he reaches the bed, I move swiftly and pull him down on top of me. Our bodies collide, and he laughs, but it's cut off when my mouth doesn't know when to let shit go.

"I didn't think I'd see you today."

With our hips lined up against each other, chest to chest, we share a single breath. Talon stares down at me with his baby blues. "Like I said, nothing's gonna stop me from keeping my promise to get you back in shape."

The words neither of us want to hear go unsaid.

This might be too much.

It might be too hard.

It might not be worth it.

A little voice comes from the doorway. "Whatcha doin?"

Talon rolls off me so fast he almost knees me in the groin. I grunt, and he lands on his ass next to me and smiles innocently at my niece.

"Talon fell," I say. "Silly, clumsy quarterback."

I don't think Gabby believes me.

"Your uncle pushed me," Talon says.

She puts her little hands on her hips, and the scowl she gives kills me. She's so freaking adorable. "Don't be a bully."

I try to keep a straight face. "Sorry. You're right. I shouldn't be a bully."

"Breakfast," Mom calls out.

We eat quickly and head out, and I can feel something brewing in my gut—a sense or need to do well and show Talon I appreciate him coming to get my ass out of bed even though things are weird between us after last night.

He thinks I don't see the way he's been looking at me during our training sessions. He knows my head's not in it, and he's worried. If I'm honest with myself, I'm worried too.

An athlete's motivation always comes from the need to win —the need to fight. When I injured my leg, a little of that died for me. And then with the complication after surgery, it died a little more. I don't know if there's enough left to save my career.

Snow fell a few nights ago, but it's all melted away today. The walk to Talon's apartment building warms me a little but not enough, and it's days like this I miss the sunshine and heat of California. I only lived there for four years, but it's like those years erased my entire childhood love of New York winters.

Talon doesn't talk, which is concerning in itself.

It makes me want to do better and show him I can get back

on my feet, even if I don't one hundred percent believe it myself.

So, I begin to walk faster. My leg's good today, and I haven't had any sciatic pain for over twenty-four hours now. I know not to push past my limits, but fear has been keeping me from pushing anything.

If I don't test my limits, I don't know what they are.

And shit, isn't that an accurate phrase for all corners of my life right now. Instead of telling Talon exactly what I want, I'm still letting him lead this.

He asked me what I needed last night, and I lied to him. I said I needed space to think when all I want is for him to be confident in us. Which is unfair to both of us, because how can he be sure when he doesn't even know if I am?

With that thought, I push to prove myself, and we're jogging by the time we make it to Talon's place.

"How's the leg?" he asks as we enter the lobby.

I shake it out. "Good, I think. I want to go harder today."

Talon relaxes into a triumphant grin.

CHAPTER TWENTY-THREE

TALON

Miller gives me one hundred and ten percent for the first time in the three days I've been here.

I don't know what shifted, but something has lit a fire under his ass, and I'm definitely not complaining.

While things are slightly off between us after last night, I know it's not going to last. At least, I hope it won't. Not after I tell him I don't need to think about what I want, because on some level, I've known for years.

Bottom line: I want him.

It's gonna suck having to hide, and I have no idea how this is gonna work long-term, but whatever needs to happen for us to be together, I'll do it.

I hold out my hand and help Miller off the bench press. "Congratulations, you've earned yourself a blowjob when we go upstairs."

Sweat drips off Miller's brow as he scowls at me. "That's *all*? Yesterday I was promised ass, and that was only for two hours. We've been here all day."

"Hmm, true. I do still owe you for that."

The heat in Miller's eyes suggests we may not make it upstairs before he jumps me, and if it weren't for the unpredictability of people coming and going in this gym, I'd totally take him up on it.

Miller's so eager to get upstairs we even take the stairs instead of the elevator that takes a million years to get up to my apartment. Miller slows when we get to the top, and I assume he's exhausted from the day, but once we reach the landing, he winces and kinda hobbles to the door.

"Pushed your leg too far?"

"Shoulda taken the elevator."

I spin on my heel as I open my apartment door and pull him inside by his shirt. He stumbles a little, and I grimace.

"Okay, change of plans. We'll shower fast, and then we'll go to bed where I'll do all the work. You need to rest your leg."

Miller smirks and leads me into the bathroom.

After a quick shower with lots of grabby hands, I throw Miller a towel. "Dry yourself off and then lie in the middle of the bed."

Miller's eyebrows shoot up in surprise. "Think you're gonna be the bossy one this time around?"

"My ass, my rules."

He looks like he wants to argue, but he keeps his mouth shut and does as I say.

When I finish drying myself, I make my way to the bedside table for supplies and throw them on the bed next to Miller.

I never thought the sight of a man waiting in bed for me could turn my crank the way it does. Miller's hard lines and muscles take up most of the king bed, but my gaze lands on the massive cock pointing straight up toward his stomach.

I can do this. Just like I hadn't sucked a cock up until recently, this is the same deal. No woman ever died from anal. I'll be fine. Although a few did say they felt like they were being ripped apart ...

Then again, I always thought that was to stroke my ego. You know, like how they're all so "Oooh, you're so big." Please ... I've seen a hell of a lot of cocks bigger than mine, and that's just in the locker room.

"You freaking out?" Miller asks.

"Nope." Hey, at least my fake confidence is working.

"You sure?"

Okay, maybe not.

"Because we don't have to do this."

"I *want* to do this, because, you know, it's what you do in a relationship."

Miller leans up on his elbows. "Fun fact. Only around thirty percent of guys in a same-sex relationship have anal sex."

Huh. "Really? That seems like such a low number."

"It's not a big deal if you don't want to. And you know I'd be happy to—"

"I still want to try it. When I was watching all that gay porn—you know, for research purposes—"

Miller snorts. "Of course. Research."

"Right. Well, yeah, there was this couple I loved watching. They're married in real life, and I dunno, they make it seem ... I dunno." My cheeks flush. I never get all weird and shy about sex. Like, ever.

"You know porn is, like, the worst depiction of what sex is really like, right?"

I roll my eyes. "Duh. But these guys ... they're different."

"Show me." Miller beckons me onto the bed with him, but I hesitate.

"You want to watch porn?"

"I want to see what you want."

I find my phone and pull up the app, and it automatically opens to the couple I've basically stalked since seeing that first video months ago.

As I join Miller on the bed, he sits up and pulls me to his side.

"Oh, I've seen these guys, but they had a chick with them."

"That's where I found them." Is it weird I'm excited we have the same taste in porn? It makes sense seeing as we've been sexually compatible since way back in college. I pull up the threesome scene which was my rabbit hole into the world of these guys.

It's a clip that jumps straight to the middle—no foreplay, just fucking—and it takes about thirty seconds of watching before Miller's hands wander. Then his lips. They lay light kisses to my neck as his fingers trail down my side.

I go to put the phone down, but he stops me.

"Keep watching."

His mouth and hands continue to explore my body, while I keep my eyes on the screen.

The moans coming from my phone speaker are broken by one of the guys saying "Take that fat dick," which, of course, makes Miller and I crack up laughing.

"Hey, Talon, you gonna take my fat dick?" He chuckles into my neck.

"I, uh, can mute the sound." I put my phone on silent.

"Get on your hands and knees."

I do as he says and place my phone on the bed facing me.

Miller's ingenious idea to distract me with porn totally works, because while he covers his fingers in lube, I'm too busy getting worked up at the people going at it on screen to be nervous.

He kneels behind me, and when he teases my hole, I imagine what it's going to be like being the guy on screen—with Miller's cock buried so deep in my ass I can't feel anything but him.

The first breach of his fingers gives me the same sense of awkwardness like when I do this to myself, but Miller's gentle and patient, and he works me slowly. So slowly that I'm easily distracted by the video again.

I don't realize he's two fingers deep until he hits that spot inside me that I was never quite able to reach. "Holy son of a fucking god bitch."

Miller chuckles. "God bitch?"

"I'm sure God has bitches and hos around him all the time."

All I get is laughter at my nonsensical rambling. Of course.

Miller continues to fuck me slowly with his fingers until I'm involuntarily rocking back onto his hand.

"Do you think you're ready?"

"I ... I think so." Maybe. Shit, I don't know. Is anyone truly ready to shove something the size of Miller's dick in an out hole?

I'm unsure when Miller suits up, but when he removes his fingers, the feel of latex dragging along my ass crack makes me shiver in anticipation. And maybe nerves. Okay, a lot of it is nerves.

His cock lines up with my hole, and I brace myself for something that doesn't come.

"Change of plans," Miller says. "Move over."

"What? You can't tease me like that. I—"

"You froze up as soon as you knew it was my cock. I want you to ride me so you set the pace. It's way too much pressure for me to handle, and I'm scared of hurting you."

Typical Miller. Always trying to protect me.

"I'm not gonna break."

"I might. My leg won't hold up this way for long anyway."

I'm sure he's stretching the truth for my benefit, but when Miller lowers himself onto his back, I'm quick to crawl on top of him and straddle his waist so he can't get away.

We're doing this.

I reach behind me and grip his cock to keep it still as I sink down on him. He tries to hide the concern on his face, and I try to cover the pain, but it's a struggle. Every fat inch that makes its way inside my body, the more my ass protests.

Miller grips my ass cheeks and holds tight. "Take your time or it'll hurt more."

I still and close my eyes, trying to concentrate on anything else but the ache in my ass.

"Talon, breathe."

Yes. Miller giving orders is what I need right now. Handing him that control relaxes me—settles something inside me somehow.

He massages my lower back and ass while I concentrate on my breathing, and our eyes meet. It's the encouragement I need. Miller is amazingly patient with me like he always is. It's always been our dynamic. I'm the loose cannon he reins in, and I make him loosen up.

Although, right now, he's anything but loose. His body is

wound tight, his jaw set hard, and as I take more of his cock, it becomes apparent he's trying to restrain himself.

I slowly rotate my hips and take him in shallow thrusts until I'm fully seated.

I can't stop looking at Miller's dark eyes, hooded in pleasure. The sting lessens when I know how much he's enjoying this, and then as it fades away, the pain turns into need.

I lean down and kiss Miller's addictive mouth while I take a few more minutes to adjust. With his cock deep inside me, I've never experienced this kind of want before. I want to move, I want to stay still, I want to beg ... Basically, I want everything and nothing, and now I'm not even making sense.

My mouth nips and teases his while I test out small thrusts that have me seeing stars. Miller moans, the sound so raw.

When he thinks I can handle it, his hands grip my hips and give a little push. It takes him deeper than I've tried, and the sting comes back, but I don't care, because his cock pegs my prostate, and I shudder.

"Shane." My voice comes out pleading.

Miller takes that as encouragement and does it again, and then again, until I have the confidence to do it.

Sitting up straight, I place my hands on his chest for leverage and begin to fuck myself on his cock. Over and over, I want to feel that push of pleasure, that burst of need.

"Lean back," Miller orders. "Put your hands on the mattress beside my legs."

As I do that, Miller grips my thighs and thrusts upward.

Unintelligible things fall from my mouth, because I didn't know this could get any better. Miller's trying to kill me, I'm sure of it.

"Do it again," I say.

Miller breaks out into a cocky smile and begins a slow pace but quickly picks up speed.

All I can do is throw back my head and enjoy the ride.

When his giant hand leaves my thigh and wraps around my leaking cock, I know this is almost over. With the feeling in my ass mixed with the tight grip Miller has on my dick, my body explodes as cum shoots all over Miller's chest.

I ride out the pleasure and glance down at the beautiful sight just in time to see the last drops of cum fall onto his smooth skin.

I breathe heavy while Miller continues to move inside me until the friction in my ass almost becomes too much. I'm close to needing to ask to stop when he says, "I'm so close. So … fucking … clo—"

Miller grunts and releases inside me, and I suddenly wish there was no condom separating us.

I collapse on top of Miller, and he holds me close. We're covered in sweat, my cum is cooling on our skin, his cock is softening in my ass, and I know we need to move. But I don't wanna.

All I want is to recover and then do it again. And again.

Words like *forever* float around my brain, and I've never had that before.

"Shane?"

"Yeah," Miller croaks.

"You're so worth the risk. You're worth *everything*."

CHAPTER TWENTY-FOUR

MILLER

It doesn't take long for me to realize Talon's using positive reinforcement as a training method and even less time for him to realize I've figured it out.

We stay wrapped in our little bubble of training and fucking—and the occasional visit to my family—until my leg is better, and I begin to find hope again.

Reconditioning to get back to NFL level is harder than I thought it would be, and there are some setbacks, which have me wanting to tear my hair out and give up, but Talon's there to remind me of why we do this.

Football is in our blood. It's our lives.

Waking up on a Sunday morning in mid-spring, I reach for my phone, which is buzzing. It's the one morning a week Talon lets me sleep in, and some asshole is calling me at the ungodly hour of ...

Oh. It's eight fifteen. And it's also not my phone that's buzzing.

With a nudge of my hip, I try to rouse Talon. "Your phone won't shut up."

"Wha?" Talon reaches blindly for his phone, hits a button, and puts it to his ear. "Yeah. Speak."

A deep, rumbly laugh that doesn't belong to Talon or me fills the room. "It's a video call, dumbass. Nice ear."

Talon lifts his phone and squints at it. "Trey? What the fuck? What time is it?"

"Geez, you football players are so lazy. Only work for half the year and sleep in the rest of it."

Talon almost drops the phone as he yawns. "What's up?"

"Is that ... Is that Shane Miller?" Trey asks.

Fuck. I try to slip out of bed, but Talon pulls me back.

"Okay, wow, so you weren't lying when you said it turned out to be more, huh?" Trey doesn't sound weirded out, only surprised.

"What do you want?" Talon asks his brother.

"Was calling to check on you. Mom and Dad are being a pain in my ass, and that can only mean you've been avoiding them. They tend to pay me more attention when the number one son is busy."

"Fuck off. They love you for not leaving them. I'm only the favorite son because my success is measurable."

Trey eyes Talon warily through the screen. "Why do I feel like there's an insult in there somewhere?"

"If that was all you had to say, I'm gonna go back to sleep now. My boyfriend kept me up allll night doing gay things to me."

My heart stutters, but not at him telling his brother about last night. I trip on the boyfriend label, which I guess is what we are—we've been with only each other for months. But still, first time he's actually said it. But did he only say it to freak out Trey, or did he actually mean it?

Trey sighs. "If you're trying to freak me out by speaking fluent homo, you have to know I don't give a shit. I work with guys a hell of a lot gayer than you. I don't think you could shock me at this point."

"Let me sleeeep," Talon complains.

"Fine. But call Mom and Dad today. Please. For my own sanity."

"Will do." Talon yawns again. "Oh, and don't tell them about Miller, because I'm not gonna."

"Why not?"

"We're ..." Talon looks at me, and I try to keep my face passive. "We're still figuring this out."

Boyfriend label not serious then. And figuring it out? I thought we were past that.

"Fair enough, but when you do figure it out, maybe you should think about telling the press before they catch you."

"Why do you say that?" Talon asks.

"So you get to narrate your own story. Last thing you need is someone else doing it for you and getting it wrong. Like your teammate's story."

Talon purses his lips. "We should be fine. We're being careful."

Probably too careful.

"Talk soon, little brother."

They end the call, and I try to stay silent, but with one phone call, the bubble we've created on Staten Island just became a tad bit unstable. I expect it to pop any minute.

"Boyfriend?" I have to go for the easy target—taunting and preparing to laugh it off.

Talon puts his phone on the bedside table and rolls over to face me. His leg goes over my hip as he snuggles in closer. "It's what we are, aren't we?"

"I ... I guess? I mean, we're not seeing anyone else, and I've spent more nights at your place than I have my own ... so, uh, yeah, I guess so."

"He guesses," Talon says dryly. "You're totally in love with me. I can tell already."

I freeze, and with Talon wrapped around me, he notices instantly.

He shoves me. "I'm just playing."

"I know."

He's unconvinced, but it's hard to wrap my head around.

We've been finding our groove as a couple and still as teammates, but we don't talk about what will happen come training camp. In fact, we haven't talked about anything that doesn't reside on Staten Island.

When Talon said I was worth the risk, I think he meant I'm worth hiding for. There's no risk when there's no chance of anyone ever seeing us together.

Jackson had invited us to Noah's fundraising charity a few weeks back, which we fully intended to go to, but at the last minute, Talon distracted me with sex, and we didn't get out of bed for it. Maddox invited us to more bar nights, but I feigned exhaustion from training, because I knew Talon would make an excuse not to go.

We haven't left Staten Island since ... since he told me I was worth everything.

We live and breathe for training and each other, and if it were a possibility for our world to last this way, I'd jump at the chance to make it a permanent arrangement.

I know who I am with Talon. I know where I fit. I'm just not sure how the rest of the world fits in with us.

And sooner or later, real life is going to catch up to us.

"So, uh, what do you think about what your brother said?" I ask.

"About calling my parents? I'll do it later."

Not what I meant, and I wonder if he answered that way on purpose.

"Were you going to at least tell them? My mom knows."

"Your mom's not likely to blab about it to all of her friends. My mom's the worst secret keeper. I'd like to think she'd be good with something as big as this, but I could see her being all proud and telling her friends without thinking they'll tell someone else and then someone else, and then—"

"Right. Fair enough. And the media thing?" I don't know why I'm pushing, and with the way Talon's eyeing me, I don't think he does either.

"I thought we agreed that wasn't going to happen?"

"Yeah, but then we stopped going out in public at all. Don't get me wrong. I know we need to keep this quiet, but it's like this apartment is our entire freaking world right now, and while you might not mean it to, it's starting to feel like we're each other's dirty little secret."

"You want to go out?"

"I want to get off this stinking island. Leave our bubble."

Talon grinds his hard cock against me. "I happen to love our bubble."

God, I should not be this easily distracted. My hand runs down Talon's back and grips his ass, pulling him closer.

When I realize he's using sex to get out of this again, I shake off my lust and scramble out of bed. "Why don't you want to go out anywhere? I'm not asking you to hold my hand in Times Square. I just ... we need some vitamin D."

Talon, of course, grabs his cock. "I have your vitamin D right here."

I don't want to laugh, but he's so lame I have to. It stops again fast when I see Talon's worried face. "It seems like you decided we're going to be together for real, and then we don't see the real world for God knows how long. I've got cabin fever."

"You feeling a little like a princess in a tower?" Talon mocks, but it's forced. I hate that us going from friends to more has all these extra elements we have to think about, but if we don't address them, they're going to blow up in our faces, and we could lose everything.

Nothing is worth losing Talon over.

"It's like I'm only worth the risk when you take away the risk completely."

Talon slowly climbs out of bed, giving me a mouthwatering view of his naked form. His cock is hard, seemingly unfazed by our argument, unlike mine. Though it definitely becomes interested as Talon approaches.

"You want to know why I'm scared to go out in public with you?" he whispers. His body presses against mine, and his hands run up my sides, burning my skin.

Yep, my cock is definitely interested.

"Why?" I manage to get out, but it comes out gruff as Talon leans in and kisses me just under my ear.

"Because being in the gym without being able to touch you is hard enough." Talon's breath is warm on my neck, and it sends a shiver right through me. "And that's when I can take you upstairs and get you naked in minutes. In public? I might die."

"Die?"

"We may never be able to leave until I can squash the urge to touch you."

That's a good answer.

"How will we manage to do that?" I ask.

Talon sinks to his knees, and his tongue darts out to lick the length of my shaft.

"Holy fuck." I breathe heavy. "That's one way."

His hand grips my cock and gives a hard pump as he stares up at me. "I tell you what ..."

"Less telling, more blowjob."

Talon stares up at me. "We can go out tonight."

"That easy?"

"Not so easy." He leans forward and licks the drop of precum off the tip of my cock, and I moan. "You have to wear me the fuck out today first. And we're skipping the gym."

I tap into my inner Talon as I say something that would normally fall from his mouth. "Challenge accepted."

We decide our first excursions outside of the bubble should be small. Jackson and Noah are on vacation, so I message Maddox and fish for an invite to his and Damon's place in Brooklyn.

Their place near Prospect Park is nothing to look at on the outside, but the location alone would make it cost a pretty penny.

Guess Damon's making a name for himself in the agenting world.

As soon as Damon lets us into the townhouse, he claps Talon on the shoulder. "Finally let Miller out of his cage?"

Talon practically trips over his feet.

Maybe he's right and we can't go out in public.

Damon doesn't seem to notice Talon's little freak-out. Or maybe Maddox told Damon after all, and Damon's really good at hiding it.

I hold out the bottle of wine I insisted we bring, because it's what you do when you go to someone's house.

"Uh, thanks," Damon says, seemingly surprised I have manners.

Then I realize it's a double date thing to do, and then even I become paranoid.

Talon's getting to me.

And after an entire day full of orgasms, I don't think my brain is working too well.

"You're looking good. All the hard work's paying off," Damon says. "How's the leg?"

"Yeah, only took like a million months, but I'm finally getting back in shape for when the season starts again." I'm not there yet, but the confidence I have that'll happen is getting stronger every day thanks to Talon.

Damon leads us into their dining room and places the bottle of wine on the table. "Babe, they're here."

"I'm trying not to burn shit. I'll be out in a second!"

Damon smiles. "Maddox is actually really good in the kitchen. He's just excited you guys are here."

"You mean Talon," I say.

"Well, yeah, but I wasn't going to be rude about it."

I laugh. "I'm used to it. Man, all through college, all I ever got asked about was about Talon. I used to tell people he had a small penis."

"Hey," Talon whines.

"Hey, yourself. Even with that lie, you still got laid more than the rest of the team. *Combined*."

"Damn straight," Talon says proudly.

Maddox appears as we're taking our seats and places a large bowl of pasta in the middle of the table. The white sauce smells deliciously garlicky, and Talon and I try to beat each other to the serving spoon. He wins and grins at me triumphantly.

"It's your last contracted year with the Warriors, right?" Damon asks and pours me a glass of wine.

I look at Talon, asking for permission to drink said wine, and he gives me a look—one that says "Drink that, and you'll be heading to the gym when we get home."

After the all-day sex marathon, there's no way I'll be going home to have sex again, so I think *fuck it*. I'll go for a run later.

I turn to Damon. "Yeah. It's why I have to get my leg back to one hundred percent. The chance of being ditched this year is higher."

"What's Hewitt and Locke doing to secure your position?"

The question is a valid one, but it only makes me realize they're doing nothing to help my situation.

"I haven't heard from them since the initial injury. I called when I had my second surgery and left a message, but they never called back. I got an email thanking me for the update, but that was it."

Damon frowns. "They haven't spoken about sponsorships or endorsement deals with you?"

"I'm not a big enough name for any huge endorsement deals."

"No, but companies still pay athletes to wear their gear, get papped wearing it, and have their product all over the tabloids."

I'd have to be in public for that to happen.

"Or with your injury, you could endorse rehab equipment or—"

I knew not hearing from my agent wasn't a good thing, but I haven't even thought about what they could've been doing in the meantime.

Talon speaks up. "Maybe you should look at how to get out of your contract with Hewitt and Locke."

That surprises me, because I assumed he'd tell me to be loyal. He's been with Touchstone Sports and the same agent since he was drafted, whereas I've had a couple now. Still with my same firm, but I get passed around, because I'm not one of the big guys. Offensive tackles are the second-highest-paid players in the league next to quarterbacks, but like quarterbacks, you have to be one of the greats to earn that type of money and respect, and I'm not there yet.

"You think so?" I ask Talon. I hadn't thought about leaving my agency, but we haven't discussed the future either. It's like they're avoiding me.

"It sounds like Damon could do a lot more for you."

Damon does make sense, and he does seem more competent than my current agent. We're just numbers on Hewitt and Locke's roster. They don't care like Damon seems to. But something about the way Talon says it, it makes me think—

"Wait. Are you saying this because you think I'm not going to be ready for the season?"

One look at Talon's guilt written across his face, and I realize that he does think I won't be ready.

"I'm not saying that, but it won't hurt to have a backup plan. That's all I'm saying."

He's being smart, I know that, but it stings a little.

I take a sip of wine. "I'll talk to my agent."

"Whoa there," Maddox says. "I remember telling you to go with Damon months ago. What makes you think he has room for you now you're still broken?"

Talon scowls, but Damon breaks into laughter.

I smile too. "This is one of those times I'm supposed to ignore Maddox, right?"

Damon nods. "Definitely. I'll be happy to sign you if you're on board. I don't want to be a downer, but by the sound of it, they might be looking to drop you if they don't care about your injury."

"How so?"

"It's what they do. I know from personal experience and from witnessing it at my own firm. Injuries are hard to sell to teams and are too much work for some people. I often wonder if I had a supportive agent if I might've tried to rehab my injury instead of giving up. I won't let you give up."

We talk about my future some more, and as easy as that, Talon and I walk away from dinner a couple of hours later, me with a possible new agent and Talon with the knowledge that he can go a few hours without touching me.

When we get into the car, Talon hesitates with the key in the ignition. "Are you mad at me?"

"No, why would I be mad?"

"Because I said you might not be ready for the season. It's not that I think you can't do it. I just—"

I reach for his arm. “I’m not completely naïve or in denial. There’s still a lot of work to go. I’ll never be mad at you for telling me the truth.”

“Damon really does seem like a great fit for you. Actually, he seems like a one-of-kind-type agent. He’s gonna do some great things for queer athletes.”

“He already has.”

“Okay. Now home to hit the treadmill for an hour.”

I groan even though I knew it was coming.

CHAPTER TWENTY-FIVE

TALON

I have this thing. While watching movies, during an action sequence or something exciting, I don't watch the screen. I watch the face of whoever I'm watching it with.

Normally, that's more entertaining, but not tonight. Miller keeps staring at his phone as if he can will it to start ringing.

He's been trying to get a hold of his agent to no avail, and it's driving him crazy.

Right then.

I reach over and confiscate it.

Miller's quick to try to get it back, but I stretch out and lift it above my head.

He pins me to the couch and tries to climb me, but I press my forearm across his chest.

"Don't," I warn.

He reaches for it again.

"It's going off for the rest of the night."

"But—"

"Your agent hasn't called you back for days. They're not

going to do it at"—I hold the phone up and press the button for the home screen to pop up—"six forty-nine at night."

I feel the fight in him leave as his weight leans heavier on top of me.

"I'm sorry, baby."

Miller lowers himself onto me fully and buries his head in my neck.

My hand trails down his back. "Even if they're trying to drop you, Damon's expressed interest. You'll get another agent."

"Yeah, yeah. New agent, fixed leg ... it'll all happen."

And his words are so believable too. You know, if he wasn't so sullen as they come out.

I wish there was something I could do for him to make him believe everything will work out, but he knows, and I know, that's not how the industry works. Just wanting it isn't enough.

Miller's finally pushing himself again, and I don't want this crap with his agent to set him back.

If he can't believe it, I can at least make him forget about it for a while.

I push him off me and stand. "I'm gonna go run you a bath. It'll be good for your leg after training today."

"It's cute you think I could fit in that bucket you call a tub."

"It's a regular-sized tub, you big giant," I mumble.

Miller laughs.

"I'm running it for you anyway." I need him busy while I set up more distraction for him, seeing as movies aren't working.

While the bath fills, I get my phone out and put in an order on the same app where I get the groceries delivered from and check the box for the extra fee to get it within a forty-five-minute window.

I call Miller in when the bath is ready, and those warm dark eyes still hold skepticism as he undresses and eases himself into the tub that, okay, is a little small for him.

"I'll leave you to it," I say even though there's something oddly comforting and sexy about Miller having a bubble bath. I totally added the bubbles to mock him, but it's backfiring because it's filling some sort of soapy fantasy I didn't realize I had.

I force myself to leave the room, and despite Miller's complaints about not fitting in the tub, he's still not out of it by the time my supplies arrive.

"Just taking the trash out," I yell and greet the delivery guy at the door so I can take the stuff right up to the rooftop.

The delivery guy helps for an extra big tip, and when he says something about the girl I'm trying to impress, I grunt a non-answer.

I rush through setting everything up, but even so, Miller's waiting for me when the delivery guy leaves and I get back to the apartment. I'm flushed from rushing around and breathing hard. Miller's already dressed and cocks one dark eyebrow at me.

"What's up?" My voice goes high-pitched while I still try to catch my breath.

"Trash? Really? What are you up to?"

"Why's it so unbelievable that I took the trash out?"

Miller's arms cross his impressive chest while he eyes the pile of trash on the kitchen counter.

"Okay, fine. I lied. Let's go." I take his hand and take the stairs to the rooftop. It's only one floor, so he doesn't have time to question it.

"What are we—" He stops short at the sight of the picnic rug, pillows, and candles.

It's the best I could do on short notice. The area is barren apart from some old pieces of junk piled on the southern side of the concrete roofing.

I close the door behind us and block it off with a rusty old chair so no one can interrupt us.

The spring breeze still has a chilly bite, but the view of New York Harbor and the twinkling lights of Manhattan is amazing. I wonder if Miller takes the view for granted having grown up here.

"What did you do?" Miller asks.

"I know we can't, like, go on a real date or anything, but this is the closest thing I could think of. I'm trying to get us out of our bubble and you out of your head."

Miller turns to me with a wide smile. "Who knew you were a lame-ass romantic."

"Ha-ha." I shove him, but he's quick and takes hold of my wrist, bringing me against him.

"I love it." He holds me tight, our breaths mixing as he inches closer.

Before he can close the distance and kiss me, which would effectively throw us off course, I smile and grip his hips, spinning him in the direction of the picnic.

"That's not all." My arms wrap around him from behind, and we waddle our way over to where a basket sits next to the blanket.

"Ten bucks says you're about to pull out kale chips and tell me they're a treat."

My head drops onto his shoulder as I let out a little laugh. "You act as if I'm poisoning you."

"It tastes like you are."

I pull away from him. "All right. Sit down. You're in for a real treat."

"Is it your cock? Because I've already had that treat today."

"Shane ... I'm trying here."

He tilts his head and kinda looks like a bull mastiff pup when it's confused. "Trying what?"

"To make up for not being able to do this in public? I want you to relax and forget about *us*, about football, and your agent. Let's let tonight be you and me. Miller and Talon—best friends hanging out and drowning out all the bullshit."

"Best friends but with orgasms?"

"If you're lucky." That's not my intention with this, but hey, I'm not gonna say no.

Miller's brown eyes fill with something that looks part lust and part gratitude, but as he looks out at the harbor, his lips curve upward. "You know, best friend Talon is the guy who used to sneak me two footlong subs with extra cheese whenever Coach told us to diet."

I grin and reach for the picnic basket. "Well, looky here." Reaching in blindly, I pull out the exact sub he's talking about. He takes it and immediately holds his hand out for a second one. After I give it to him, I reach in again and pull out a container of wings.

His eyes widen. "Are you magic, or is that like a freak Mary Poppins bag? Best friend Talon would also pack beer."

"I know my man." I pull out a six pack of his favorite beer.

Miller reaches for the wings too but pauses just before he

can take them out of my grasp. "How much time in the gym am I going to have to do to make up for this?"

"None," I say.

"None?"

"I'm giving you a cheat day."

This time, when he leans in to kiss me, I don't stop him. I do stop myself from taking it too far. He's been complaining about being in our bubble, but when he kisses me like that, I never want to leave it.

"Come on. Eat up before trainer Talon turns up and changes my mind."

Miller wastes no time taking a seat on the rug and scarfing down his food. The moans he makes while eating the saturated-fat-loaded food should be illegal. The way he licks his fingers after the wings? Kill me now. It'd be less torturous.

After we eat unhealthy food, drink calorie-filled beer, and then stuff our faces with pie for dessert, we lie on our backs looking up at the city-polluted night sky.

Miller relaxes for the first time since I got here—maybe even since the start of last season when I turned up in Chicago. It's not sex relaxed, but *relaxed, relaxed*. He seems his normal, sarcastic but lovable self, and all his worries appear to be faded into the distance. At least for now. I'd do anything to make him hold onto this feeling going forward.

"Oh my God, I ate too much," he complains, but the smile on his face gives away the truth about how much he cares about that: not at all.

"I told you to go easy on the dessert."

"You also bought said dessert. Should never waste food, Marc. There are starving kids all over the world."

"And here you are, eating their desserts. You're a monster."

"Your sex monster," Miller retorts.

"That sounds highly unsexy."

"I'd show you how you're wrong, but I think if we even tried to have sex right now I'd throw up all over you. My stomach doesn't feel too good."

I roll onto my side and stare down at him while my fingers trace over Miller's food baby. "Poor Miller."

"So worth it."

"Which is better? Food or sex."

"Food," he says immediately without thought.

My mouth drops open, and I reach for the cushion behind me to hit him with. He blocks it but can't stop laughing as I try to hit him again and again.

"Okay, okay, I change my answer. Sex with you is at the top. Then food. Then sex with everyone else."

"Well, you can't possibly know that for sure unless you've had sex with everyone else."

"I had a busy senior year after you left me."

I hit him with the cushion again.

"I'm kidding! Even when I was with other guys, none of them compared to the way you made me feel back then. Or the way you make me feel now."

"And how's that?"

Miller cups my cheek, his thumb tracing my unshaved jaw. "Happy."

I relax and lean into his touch. Miller deserves pure happiness, and I want to be the guy to give it to him.

The call comes a few days later, and it turns out Damon was

right. Miller's agent was looking to drop him. It gets to Miller, and I can tell he's trying to put on a confident front. Having Damon ready to sign him helps, but I notice the shift in training, and it's obvious the reason he's still a tiny bit slower than he should be, not lifting as heavy as he was before his injury, and his all-round sluggishness isn't because he physically can't do it, but because his head's still not on right. It's all mind over matter at this point, and he isn't fully recovered from the hit his fighting instinct took when he tore his hamstring.

So, I push him harder every day, and he pushes me even harder at night. We venture out of our bubble occasionally to hang out with Damon and Maddox, but mostly, we train, fuck, and hang out.

It's almost exactly like it was in college except for one glaringly obvious detail. We don't need anyone between us now, because we know each other is enough. More than enough. The thought of sharing someone with him again actually makes my gut burn with possessiveness I never knew I had.

"Holy shit!" Miller says from my living room.

I'm fresh out of the shower with nothing but a towel around my waist. "What?" I call out.

"Talon, get in here."

"What is it?" I scrounge for some clothes in my drawers.

"Just ..."

"Just what?" Now I'm getting annoyed. How hard is it to tell me what he wants?

"Get your ass out here now, Marcus."

Marcus. Not Talon, not Marc. *Marcus*. Well, shit. I abandon my plan to get dressed and join Miller on the couch.

And there's a sight I never thought I'd see anytime soon.

Caleb Sorenson and Ollie Strömberg, two gay hockey players, coming out on national TV. Together.

"Whoa" is all I can say.

"Isn't Ollie one of Damon's clients?" Miller asks and takes out his phone.

I don't answer him, not only because I don't know the answer, but because I can't take my eyes off the press conference.

A million things run through my head at once. My initial thought is the world is finally changing and people aren't going to care about closeted athletes coming out, but if the NHL is anything like the NFL, this could be a one-off thing. These two guys might come out, and then nothing else happens. Everything will stay the same, and we'll still have to watch our every move.

I hate my brain goes there, because this should be an encouraging moment.

Miller's phone beeps. "Okay, so the deal is they aren't *together* together according to Maddox. They're just coming out together."

As Miller says that, Ollie admits on camera he didn't even know Caleb until tonight. He's coming out because of Caleb—because he doesn't want him to have to do it alone.

Have we been going about this the wrong way? Should we come out in support of Jackson instead of thinking we're protecting him?

Miller's hand lands on my knee. "What are you thinking about?"

"I'm thinking when does Jackson get back from Fiji?"

"He got back a few days ago."

"We need to talk to him."

A few days later, we arrange a meeting at Damon's offices with Miller, Jackson, and me.

Jackson enters the reception area with a confusion line across his forehead, which soars into his hair when he sees Miller and me.

"Is this an intervention?" Jackson jokes. "Or are we meeting about Talon's ego being nowhere near big enough. I agree, we should come up with ways on how we could stroke it more."

"Who invited him?" I grumble. Oh wait, I did.

"What's this really about?" Jackson asks.

Miller and I glance at each other.

"Ah. You two finally pull your heads out of your asses?"

"You said to tell you when I'm ready to talk about it," I say.

"I did. I'm wondering why my agent needs to be involved …" Jackson trails off as the reason becomes clear. "Y'all comin' out publicly?"

Miller looks around the empty reception area. "Wanna keep your voice down a bit?" The only person here is a girl behind the desk, but she's on the phone and doesn't pay attention.

"We're here to talk to you about that," I say.

"What have I got to do with it?" Jackson asks.

Before we can answer, Damon appears. "You boys ready?" He tips his head in the direction of the hallway for us to follow him.

When the door's shut, Damon takes a seat in his big boss chair. Jackson and I sit opposite him, but Miller wanders around the room, staring at Damon's sports memorabilia on his shelves.

"So, why are we here, how dead is dead, and where do we need to hide the body?" Damon asks.

"One day that joke's gonna backfire on you," Jackson says. "Your client may actually reply 'In the alley, super dead, and New Jersey. Because that's the only appropriate place to dispose of bodies.'"

Damon huffs. "Jersey's not that bad! Your and Maddox's aversion to it, I swear to God."

I take a deep breath, because the longer we sit here, the more antsy I'm getting, like that night at the bar with Maddox. "Miller and I are fucking," I blurt.

Miller laughs. "And you make fun of the way I told my mom."

I sigh. "Well, I don't see you speaking up."

Miller sits in the chair next to me, reaches over, and takes hold of my hand. "Talon and I are in a committed and serious relationship, but we have no idea how to come out or how it impacts Jackson's career."

Jackson leans forward to stare at me. "*That's* why I'm here? Think about your own careers. I've already been through so much that I can handle anything."

"No, they're doing the right thing," Damon says. "This will have repercussions on you and the Warriors."

I don't want to bring this up, because I didn't want Jackson knowing about it, but it's something we're all gonna have to face. "Henderson warned me during the season that my bromance with Miller makes us look like the fag team and that I need to be careful of hanging out with Jackson too much."

Jackson scowls. "You didn't say anything. Who else on the team has been saying shit behind my back? I thought ..." Hurt clouds his eyes. "I thought we were past all that—that we'd gotten past it during training camp. We won the fucking Super Bowl, and that's still not good enough for these assholes?"

"To be fair, this was before the Super Bowl, but yeah ... they've been good at hiding their disapproval. They caught on quick about keeping it from me too after I told a few of them to shut the fuck up. But this ..." I squeeze Miller's hand. "This could cause problems."

"Henderson's not the only one who's going to say it either," Damon says. "But I don't see it as a reason to live in the closet. We just need to devise a coming-out strategy."

"I don't recommend getting photographed blowing each other." Jackson winks. "Just sayin'."

Damon agrees. "Let's knock that one off the list."

"What we talking here?" Miller asks. "Press conferences, TV interviews, what?"

Damon leans back in his chair. "Actually, I think a softer approach with you two would be better."

I shift in my seat. "Softer how?"

"We wait until training camp and come out to the team and management first. If there are problems, one of them might leak it, but we can deal with that as it happens. There have been gay men in sports for years, where teams have known and the rumor mill has worked overtime, but it's never been exposed. Build a team of people you trust who know so you have support when it comes out. If it leaks, it leaks, and we can control what is said or be ready to defend if it's something we don't like. I also think a print interview would be better than an on-air press conference like Soren and Strömberg." Damon smiles. "And I know just the guy to do it."

"Who?" I ask.

"Strömberg's boyfriend is a journalist. Come to the Stanley Cup final in Jersey with us, and we'll introduce you."

I look over at Miller who seems a little stunned. I nudge him. "You okay?"

He nods but doesn't appear any calmer. He was fine a minute ago, wasn't he? Now he looks like he'd rather be anywhere but here. Before he can respond, Damon cuts in.

"We'll take this at your pace, guys. Talon, I'm gonna need to have access to your agent so we can work out something together. Until then, keep doing what you're doing. Train and focus on the upcoming season. I promise we'll make it work."

"I don't understand hockey," I say. "Skating is hard enough. Who decided to add sticks and a disc and call it a sport?"

Miller leans in and speaks quietly. "Shh. There's nothing scarier than hockey fans, and I'm too pretty to get beaten up."

"Pffft. You could kick all their asses."

He slinks down in his seat. "You're horrible, and I'm embarrassed to be seen with you."

"Aww. If there wasn't so many people around, I'd kiss you, you big sweet giant, you."

We're here at the arena early, and we're the first of Damon's posse to arrive. The stands fill with buzzing energy and a need to be victorious. The anticipation and the atmosphere is slightly different than the football crowd, but it still fills me with the adrenaline high of chasing a win.

"We're going for New Jersey, right? Because of that Soren guy?" I ask.

"Yeah, but if you ask me, Vegas has it in the bag."

I gasp. “You follow hockey? Do I know you at all?”

Miller shrugs. “I was reading up on Soren and kinda fell into a hockey hole.”

“Hockey hole ... I swear I saw a porno titled that once.”

Miller snorts.

Jackson and Noah are the first to arrive, and they sit next to us.

“You ready for what’s coming?” Noah asks, and we both give Jackson an inquisitive look. Did he out us to his husband?

“Six weeks until we report for training camp,” Jackson says and then mouths “Assholes” at our insinuation.

Oops.

“I think we’re ready,” I say.

“Sure,” Miller says, but I don’t even think he believes it himself. Training is still going relatively slow, and there’s no way we can definitively say one way or the other Miller’s ready to go back to work.

The other guys begin to arrive, and the last is Ollie Strömberg with his boyfriend, Lennon—the dude who’ll write our coming out article when we’re ready for it. He just doesn’t know it yet. Lennon’s adorably nerdy with his neat blond hair and glasses. Doesn’t help he’s next to his boyfriend who’s almost the size of Miller and covered in tattoos.

Damon said we should hang out with them, get to know Lennon, and if we’re not comfortable, we can use someone else, but as Lennon tells us he’s got a freelance gig writing editorial pieces about gay men in sports for *Sports Illustrated,* and Soren, Strömberg, and Jackson have all signed on, I already feel confident in his ability to write our story too.

Watching Damon and his friends is a weird experience. One I hope to be a bigger part of soon. Once the seed was planted, all I've thought about is being out with Miller and letting the rest of the world know how in love with him I am.

Should probably tell Miller first.

Oh, right. That. I'm waiting for the perfect moment. I dunno when that'll be, but I'm pretty sure while he's balls deep inside me isn't the right time. Or when I'm inside him.

These guys are so free with each other. The little touches, the obvious glances ...

Having sex with Miller earlier today didn't do the trick this time. I want to touch him.

Being put in a box and told to stay in there has never sat well with me, so I know, on some level, we won't be able to keep it a secret for long.

I thought it was the right thing to do, but it's become clear that this comradery between this group is what we need in our lives. This type of support. And we should give it to Jackson as well as ourselves. But we need to do it right.

Doesn't stop me from paying more attention to them than the game.

I find it almost ironic that any relationships I've had in the past have been exploited publicly. Not that any of them have been serious. Hell, I've never even said "I love you" to anyone. The one time I want to be in public with someone, and I have to pretend we're not together.

The group is planning to head to a gay bar afterward, but I don't know if I'll be able to handle that. Miller and I have been outside our bubble too long already. But as the game winds down, and the arena empties, Miller tells the others we'll meet them at the club.

"We're really gonna go to that?" I ask on the way to the car.

"You don't want to?"

"No, I want to. Probably too much."

Miller smiles. "Need a little road head on the way to tide you over until we get home?"

In the parking garage for the hockey arena, I glance around to make sure no one's within hearing distance. There's a crowd of people making their own way to their cars, and none of them are paying us attention, but I still can't do what I want to, which is take Miller's hand.

Miller knows me too well. He grabs my forearm. "You okay?"

"I'm just realizing shit."

"Man, you should write a philosophical self-help book and call it *Realizing Shit*."

When we stop by my rental, I resist the urge to pull him into me for a hug. Instead, I force myself to click the unlock button on my key fob and climb in the car.

As soon as Miller's in the passenger seat, he reaches over and rubs his hand over my cock. "Totally wasn't kidding, by the way." He leans in as if going to lower his head, but I stop him. He sits up straight again and frowns at me. "Okay, what's wrong?"

"This is going to sound weird."

"Oh, honey, everything out of your mouth is weird."

The term of endearment shouldn't make me all warm and fuzzy, damn it.

"I don't want sex," I blurt.

"Holy shit. That is weird."

"All I want is to hold your hand, kiss you, and claim you as mine."

"Aww, Marc. I am yours. Wholly and completely yours. Have been for years."

We lean over the center console, and our lips come together in a kiss unlike we've shared so far. It feels like permanence and a promise to each other.

Miller's tongue lazily strokes mine in an act of comfort and support. It's not urgent and needy, and I'm thankful for the tinted windows.

"Fuck," Miller whispers. "You might not want sex, but I do."

I chuckle. "Later. You told the guys we'll meet them."

"We can blow it off and blow each other instead."

"As fun as that sounds, we probably should make an appearance. That Lennon guy is there, and we have to make sure we want him to do our interview."

Something like hesitance crosses Miller's face. "Right. The interview."

"Having doubts?"

He forces a smile, and he must forget I know him well enough to know when he's about to bullshit me.

"Not about us," he says.

That doesn't really answer my question.

"Let's just go talk to this Lennon dude and see if we even gel with him."

"And if we get photographed going into a gay bar?"

"We follow what Damon says. We don't admit anything but don't deny it either. If there are unconfirmed rumors circulating, it'll make the fallout more cushion-y."

Miller shakes his head. "I still can't believe this is a conversation, you know?"

I shrug. "I went through something similar with Moxie, but that was more scheduling outings so we were intentionally photographed to make the world know our relationship was still going strong, even when it wasn't. It was kinda exhausting."

"It'll probably be the same for us once it's all out. You ready for that?"

Part of me thinks he's hoping I say no. I squeeze Miller's hand. "I'm more than ready, because it's different with you. With her, it felt like an obligation. With you, it's a necessary evil I'll gladly do because it means I get to be with you."

CHAPTER TWENTY-SIX

MILLER

Talon and I converge on poor Lennon while the others hit the dance floor. That Soren guy is sitting at our high-top table, but his gaze is firmly planted on Ollie who's dancing with Jackson's little brother. The tabloids are pushing for Soren and Ollie to get together, but from what I've seen tonight, Ollie and Lennon seem solid. Public I-love-yous give that impression.

While I know Talon and I can't have that relationship yet, we are taking steps to get there. I keep flip-flopping between wanting to do it and running the other way. We went from knowing this can't happen to organizing coming-out interviews in what feels like the blink of an eye.

And I don't know if I'm ready.

But we're here now, there was no paparazzi outside the bar, and this Lennon guy is right in front of us.

"Hey." I push a drink in front of him. "For you."

His eyes widen behind thick-rimmed glasses. "Thank you."

"So, the *Sports Illustrated* thing," Talon says. "That's cool."

Lennon's face lights up. "It's been my dream to write these kinds of articles ever since becoming a reporter, and it's awesome they're letting me do these editorial pieces. It's a brand-new avenue for the magazine. They're going to be more personal and call out industry problems when it comes to LGBTQ players, so it's an honor to be involved."

Score one for Lennon.

Talon and I share a glance.

I nod. "It's important, that's for sure."

Lennon's eyes get a sad shine to them. "Matt said what's been going on with the team behind his back. It's annoying it's still an issue."

"Yup." My throat goes dry, because it's one of those things, isn't it? It's something we're supposed to accept, but it's a hard pill to swallow. To be with the person I love, I have to take measures to make sure I don't lose my job over it.

And until the meeting we had with Damon, I hadn't thought of everything else to consider either—like the Warriors' ticket sales. They were steady this past year after Jackson came out, but we had a really good season. What will happen when the news gets out that we not only play for the same team, but we ... *play for the same team,* so to speak?

Lennon stares at me as if he said something, but I'd tuned out.

"Sorry, what?"

"How's your recovery going?"

I go to answer when I think better of it. "Off the record?"

"That bad? I promise it's off the record. I technically don't have a job right now. Well, I do, but it's for Ollie's team doing press releases. The *Sports Illustrated* gig is freelance, and it's restricted to queer men in sports, so you're safe." He winks.

"I, uh, well, yeah …"

He must confuse my stammering for a recovery issue. Not the second thing. "I'm sorry. It must suck not playing. Do you think you'll be ready for the season?"

If I'm honest with myself, no. I'm not where I should be, and I'm nowhere near where I was this time last year leading into training camp, but like I've been doing with Talon, I keep face. "I'll make sure I'm ready."

Because what else can I say? What else can I think? I can rehab for another year and hope to be picked up next season as a free agent when my contract runs out, or I can beg and plead with the Warriors' management team to sign me again, but I need to show them I'll be physically capable of doing the job.

"I'm depressing you," Lennon says. "Sorry."

"All good." I glance over at Talon again, and he nods toward Lennon with a smile. Guess he approves then.

Something doesn't feel right. I don't know what, but I wake with a knot in my stomach and the dreaded feeling that what we're doing today is too soon. Or wrong. Or we haven't thought it through properly.

I tell myself it's nerves. Coming out to the world is a big deal, and we didn't think it was going to happen this soon. Or at all. I mean, it's not like we're actually coming out today—we're just doing an interview that Lennon is supposed to sit on until we're okay with releasing it. But Talon went from talking about doing it in years to doing it soon, and now it feels like it's right this second. I've been hesitant but on board, but I'm wondering if that's only because it's been an idea, not an actual plan. Maybe I've been thinking it wasn't going to happen at all. Because faced with the reality of it, it's becoming too much.

Too much pressure. Too much of a risk. Just ... too much too soon.

Damon and Talon's agent, Alan, have organized for our interview to happen in a hotel suite in Manhattan, and it's all been very hush-hush. I don't think Lennon even knows why he's coming today.

"Are you sure you want to do this?" Talon's agent asks him. I want to answer *No, I'm not!* But he's not talking to me. They're huddled in the corner of the high-end hotel room whispering to each other as if I can't hear them. Newsflash: I can. And their conversation makes the knot in my stomach tighten. "This is risky."

Talon turns to glare at him, and Alan throws up his hands.

"Okay, fine, but don't say I didn't warn you. This doesn't affect Miller as much as it does you. You have further to fall. You've already pissed off some major endorsements with your 'scheduling conflict.' Meanwhile, you've been sitting on your ass training a lost cause."

Now I can taste bile. Nice. Talon blew off endorsement deals for me? I suspected as much, because huge stars like Talon generally have a busier schedule off season than when we play. Hearing it for a fact makes it worse—like it's the actual truth instead of an insecurity I can try to rationalize and dismiss.

"Last I checked, I pay you to support my decisions," Talon says through gritted teeth.

"You pay me to do what's best for you."

"For my career, you mean. Having Miller on the field with me is what's best for my career. You need to remember that."

There's a knock at the door, and Damon lets Lennon in.

"Thanks for coming."

Lennon smiles at him. "No problem. What's with all the secre—"

He stops short when he sees Talon approach me and land his ass on the ornate love seat next to me. I was reluctant to sit on it at first in fear of breaking it. It doesn't look like it can hold me, let alone Talon as well. Its flimsy legs still unnerve me.

Lennon's blue eyes shine bright behind his thick-framed glasses.

"This is all top secret for now, but I know I can trust you," Damon says.

"Of course." Lennon's glance flits between Talon and me. "But can someone tell me straight up what's going on? Because I think I'm jumping to all the wrong conclusions here, seeing as I've just been hired to write about LGBTQ players, and now I'm about to sit down with the biggest quarterback in the league and his college roommate. I'm trying not to salivate over here."

Damon claps his back. "You're not far off the mark."

Talon reaches for my hand. "Miller and I ... we're ... well ... our story is kinda complicated."

"Not that complicated," I say. "I've wanted him since we were teenagers, and I thought I'd never get him."

Lennon's hand goes to his heart. "Aww. This is so awesome."

"Rules," Damon interjects. "They can refuse to answer any question you ask, and Alan and I can object as well. This article is not to hit the stands until we give you approval, but it might have to be released at short notice if this gets out before we planned it. That's the only reason you're getting advance warning about this, and you're the only interview we've approved."

"Done, done, and easy. I won't tell *Sports Illustrated* about it until you're ready. They'll want an official photoshoot, but that can be done short notice if needed. After my last pushy editor, I'm not going to risk the story being released before any of you are ready."

Damon smiles. "I knew you were the right guy for the job."

"You mean apart from him being your client's boyfriend?" Talon quips.

"I trusted Lennon before he even knew Ollie," Damon says. "We ready to do this?"

"Yep. Let's do it," Talon says. His confidence hasn't wavered, but the ill feeling in my stomach won't go away.

Something isn't sitting right with this, and I don't know if it's because I can practically feel Talon's agent glaring daggers at me or if it's still the off feeling from this morning.

This is what I've wanted nearly my entire adult life—Talon and me together.

It's just nerves.

Alan stands over the other side of the room, his arms folded and a harsh scowl on his face. That makes it worse. I'm worried Alan brings up good points. He's right when he says I don't have much to lose. My career is rocky as it is. This will either make or break me. This might boost my career or kill it, but it will definitely give my profile a bump up in the celebrity world. I'll go from being in the background of paparazzi shots to being the one they want a photo of. Talon's already at that level, and his career has nowhere to go but down.

I don't want to be responsible for that.

Now the seed's been planted, it's only downhill from here.

We shouldn't be doing this.

Fuck, why did I think we were ready for this? We both went from knowing we had to stay quiet to suddenly sitting for articles that will paint us as a committed couple. Like the most committed couple to ever couple, and here I sit wondering if Talon is one hundred percent sure.

I should trust him. He's been nothing but open since this whole thing started, but it's fast. It's superfast.

You've been in love with him since college. That's not fast.

It's superfast for Talon. He only realized he wasn't straight a few months ago, and his agent certainly isn't confident in our relationship.

The rational voice in my head tells me that nothing's changed, but we've taken such small steps I haven't noticed how far we've come, and now we're here doing a coming out interview about our relationship, when we haven't even said *I love you* to each other.

Talon's putting a major risk on his career for a small chance this might actually work between us.

Everything flashes through my mind. I've spent years worrying about ex-lovers coming forward and outing me, and there's nothing to stop them doing that if I'm outing myself to the world. All those women we've shared, every single detail of our private lives is going to be splashed all over the news.

I knew this coming in, but now it's actually happening, I can't think properly. My heart pounds and sweat drops off my brow. I think I'm having a panic attack.

I force myself to take deep breaths but that makes it worse.

"Shane," Talon says, getting my attention.

“Sorry, what?” I glance around the room at the four pairs of eyes scrutinizing me.

“You okay?” Talon asks.

I stand. “Can we … have a minute?”

Lennon waves me off. “I need some time to get some questions together, so take however long you need.”

Alan looks hopeful that I’m about to pull the plug on this, but Damon doesn’t look happy. I take Talon’s hand and lead him to the bedroom of the suite, closing the double doors behind me.

“What’s wrong?” Talon asks.

“Nothing.” I run my hand through my hair. “Everything? Fuck, I don’t know. Alan has a point.”

“What point?”

“Don’t play dumb. I could hear you talking. He doesn’t want you to do this. I’m fucking everything up for you.”

“He doesn’t get a say.”

“Talon … I …” I close my eyes, because I can’t look at him as I say this. “Maybe this is too much.”

Talon realizes what I’m saying. “You don’t want to do this.”

“I can’t let us do this if we’re not one hundred percent sure.”

Maybe I’m lying to myself or maybe my words are the truth. Maybe I just need reassurance. I don’t know. All I know is I’m freaking out.

“You’re not sure? About us, about me … about what?” Talon frowns, and I want to do everything I can to make that go away, but I don’t know if I can do what he’s asking of me. Not yet.

“I don’t know. What if we’re going about it all wrong?”

“Wrong how?”

How can I expect Talon to understand when I don't myself?

"We've been doing this for how many months, but we haven't actually spoken about a future together. We're willing to risk everything, and for what? Tell me what a future with us would look like. You say I'm worth the risk, but what happens when this all falls apart? We might not have football or each other."

"We don't know what kind of fallout this is going to have. On you, on me, or on the NFL. It's impossible to know. But one thing I'm certain of is of you and me together. That will never be in jeopardy."

"What about when we're bombarded by paparazzi every day relentlessly with no break?"

"Won't be much different to my life right now, but there are ways around that. No one's bothered us while we've been training."

"Because they didn't know where we were. I need something more than a hope we'll stay together when our careers die and our teammates turn on us. I think being in our bubble has warped our vision. My family's supportive. Damon, Jackson, and that whole group of great guys are everything we need this world to be, but that's just it. The rest of the world isn't like them, and until Alan started saying shit about why this is a bad idea, I guess I didn't think about what reality would look like. Alan's just the beginning. The world is full of Alans and Hendersons."

"Alan will be fired if he doesn't get on board."

"As easy as that? You'll walk away from the guy who got you millions of dollars over the last however many years, because you didn't get your way?"

"Yep. Because this is more important to me."

"You're only saying that because you're impulsive and *always* get what you want. Maybe this is one time you need to step back and look at the facts. This isn't going to be easy, Marc."

I'm torn in two. The college guy in love with his best friend wants to do this—throw caution to the wind and do what I've wanted to do for years, which is tell people how I feel about Talon. The smarter or perhaps dumber part—haven't figured out which it is yet—wants to take more time.

If I can't even handle Talon's agent's negativity, how am I going to handle everyone else? The team, reporters, social media. It's going to be a bloodbath.

Does that mean I'm using him as an excuse? My head's all fuzzy right now, and I can't make sense of anything.

"I'm doing this," Talon says, "whether you're in or not. If you choose to walk out right now, the article will only be about me, but I'm still doing it."

I grunt. "Why the fuck are you so stubborn?"

"Why the fuck didn't you bring all this up before now?"

"Because I didn't realize this was an issue until today. You know how you sense shit on the field? It's like that. I can't explain it, but my gut is telling me we're not ready. Or … I'm not ready. Then your agent stood there and reminded me that you have everything to lose—more so than me—but I'm beginning to think that's not true. This could be the final nail in the coffin when it comes to my career. You're big enough to bounce back. I'm not. I've been fighting for the last few months trying to keep my career. Doing this could end it the second it gets out."

Talon hold ups his hands in a *just wait* gesture. "You're

ping-ponging all over the place. Is this about my career or yours? Is it about us now or what we'll become?" He steps closer and reaches for my arms, rubbing them soothingly from shoulder to elbow and back again. "What are you really scared of?"

I pull away and slink down on the bed. "I think I need time. I like where we're at. We're good. Why mess with it? Don't fix what ain't broke, right?"

"But don't you see it? The world is broken, which means we're broken. Having to hide this shouldn't be a necessity or a choice. It shouldn't be anything. It shouldn't even be a factor in anyone's lives but our own."

"And that's my point! It is a factor, and maybe I'm not ready to face that yet."

Talon's hand lands on my shoulder. "If this is a simple matter of you not being ready, then take all the time you need. I'm not going to force you to do anything here today, and if you want me to wait for you, I will. But can you sit there and tell me that's all there is to it?"

My heart rate calms down a little, but it does nothing to put out the raging inferno in my gut that just won't die down.

"I don't know," I whisper. "It's everything."

CHAPTER TWENTY-SEVEN

TALON

"I need some air." Miller's last words before he walks out of the hotel room don't exactly fill me with confidence.

I don't know what's going on with him—I don't think he knows himself—so I can't fix it. I'm a fixer. It's what I do. I want something, I go for it. Something stands in my way, I handle it.

I'm not used to this feeling of helplessness.

What am I supposed to do? Lie to him and say everything will be fine? That his worries don't hold merit? Because they do. They really fucking do. It's not going to reassure him any when he knows I'm lying. I can promise to do everything in my power to make this work, but what if that's not enough?

I'm used to getting my way, but a solid future in football and with each other might be one thing that's out of my reach.

So, I watch him leave, knowing there isn't anything I can do to stop it.

He needs time. Miller's a thinker, and he's analytical, and that's why we work well together. I'm impulsive, but he's smart about things.

He'll come back. He'll realize this is the right thing.

That's the lie I'll tell myself, because even though I have my shit together always, this is the first time in my life when I can feel everything slipping away.

What if it's not just cold feet and he's rethinking everything? What if he comes to the conclusion it'll be easier to walk away forever?

The living room of the suite is minus one agent when I gather the courage to go back out there.

Lennon and Damon stand together, both looking worried.

"Miller just needs to cool off," I say. "This is big, and he's been fighting for his career for months—pushing himself to get ready for the season. This has the ability to make all that work pointless."

I hope that's what his true issue is. Because that's fixable. We fight more, push harder ...

"I just wish I could reassure him about how this is gonna go over."

Damon nods. "It's better for him to have that freak-out now instead of when it's too late to take back."

"I don't know what to do. Where's Alan?"

Damon purses his lips. "You've got a lawyer on hand, right?"

My stomach sinks to my balls. "I can get one. Why?"

"Umm ... so, those doors aren't exactly thick, and you and Miller were loud. He was on the phone to Touchstone Sports basically the minute you threatened to fire him."

"Trying to find a way out of the contract?" I light up at the possibility. I need a supportive team around me, not someone who wants to drive a wedge between me and Miller.

Miller was completely fine until Alan opened his mouth.

Damon grimaces. "Trying to keep you locked to it more like it. You're their firm's biggest client. I totally understand why he'd be reluctant to let you come out, but the industry needs more guys like you to step forward. Matt, Soren, and Ollie are a great start, but in all truth, they've barely dented the surface."

"I want to do the article, but it feels wrong doing it without Miller."

"If you're worried about this affecting him, we could always redact Miller's name and replace it with someone else's to protect his identity, or we could not talk about him at all," Lennon says.

"I kinda have to talk about him. He's the entire reason I even discovered this side of me."

"Ooh, that's good. We can use that." Lennon walks over to his computer. "If you still want to do this, we won't publish it until I get the okay from you and your agent."

With Alan leaving half-cocked and Miller "getting air," I know it's not the time to do this. I want to tell the world my experience, because if someone had told me a year ago that I would be head over heels in love with a man right now, I never would've believed it.

Miller's blindsided me in more ways than one, and I can't imagine being with anyone else. Ever.

Just as my phone vibrates in my pocket, Damon says, "I'm gonna go check on Miller."

Miller: *I'm gonna catch a cab to the ferry and go back to Mom's. I'm sorry. I just can't.*

"No point. He's gone." I hold up my phone. "Who wants a drink?"

I head for the minibar.

Damon and Lennon don't say anything.

Drink in hand, I throw myself on the stupid love seat and hate that it's the most uncomfortable piece of furniture ever made.

Lennon closes his laptop. "For what it's worth, Ollie and I went through something similar. Had it not been for Soren, we still might be hiding in a closet."

I can't help thinking at least they would still be together. After Miller's freak-out, I don't know where we stand.

The emails from Touchstone Sports and Alan start coming in before I've even finished the mini bottle of scotch in the hotel room. Lennon, Damon, and I shoot the shit and laugh instead of doing the interview, and old stories of Miller and me pour from my mouth—mainly of what we did in college. You know, minus the three-ways.

"You're in love with him," Lennon says.

"I fell in love with him before I knew I was attracted to him. Does that even make sense?"

Damon smiles. "Makes total sense."

My phone buzzes with another notification, and when I look, it's my agent's firm again.

"What now?" Damon asks while I scroll through the email.

"Alan's been busy. This one's a copy of my contract from the Touchstone legal department with a whole bunch of ugly yellow highlighter everywhere. Either they dropped the whole contract in a vat of highlighter ink or they're telling me all the trouble I'll get myself into if I threaten to fire Alan again."

Damon huffs. "I hate agents like yours. I understand he

wants to get paid, but ultimately, our job is to do what's best for you, not your bank account."

Lennon nods. "That's exactly why you're going to be one of the biggest agents in the industry."

"I've been super lucky in scoring the big names I have," Damon says, "but my bosses keep telling me I need to grow my client list. I'm worried the more clients I have, the more neglectful I'll become, like them. I don't know where the perfect balance is."

"Well, if I'm getting out of this iron-clad contract, I'll be coming your way, but I don't like my chances."

"Can I look?" Damon asks. "I went to law school so I could understand the contracts I get all my clients to sign. If I find any loopholes you can use, I'll let you know."

"Thanks. What do you suggest I do until then?"

"There's not much you can do. You could always go above his head to his superiors."

"He's a partner in the firm."

"I'd go there in person if that's the case. Talk to his other partners. If you can't get out of the firm's contract, you might be able to get a different agent who's better at handling the big issues."

Damon's right. I need someone who'll spin my sexuality in a positive light, which means I need to come out to the partners too.

"Their offices are in L.A," I say.

I still remember the day Alan came to scout me at USC. I thought I was hot shit. Okay, who am I kidding—I still think that—but it's different now, because football isn't my only goal anymore.

Damon shrugs. "Up to you if you want to go all that way,

but it'll get done faster if you're there in person breathing down their necks. Ten bucks says they'll give you the email runaround if you're not there face-to-face. You might want to sort it before the season starts too, so you can focus on the more important things like football. That's what I'd do, personally, but you also need to talk to Miller about where you're going from here."

Damon's right. Touchstone will make an appointment for me if I push, but they're likely to ignore emails. Even if I am their biggest client. "Looks like I'm going to L.A."

First, I need to stop by a little house on Staten Island.

CHAPTER TWENTY-EIGHT

MILLER

"How'd it go?" Mom asks as soon as I walk in the door. She looks behind me, expecting to see Talon. "Where's—"

Her words stop short when she takes in my expression.

"What happened?"

I shake my head, because I still don't know myself. "I freaked out."

"*Why*?"

"I have no idea."

Mom gives me that look—the one that tells me to stop bullshitting her. I saw that same expression countless times when I was a teenager and I'd done the wrong thing.

"I think it was just too much. What happens when it doesn't work out?"

"When ..."

It takes a second to realize what I'd said. "*If*. Whatever."

"No, no. Your slip says a lot."

Shit, maybe it does.

I'm too wiped to get into this with her. "I'm gonna go lie down."

I'm thankful Mom doesn't follow me. I collapse on my bed face-first and bury my head in the pillow. If I could stay here for the rest of my life, that'd be sweet. Thanks, universe.

Continuing to hide from the world won't fix anything.

Ugh. Shut up, guilty conscience.

Walking away from the article felt freeing for about half an hour. Somewhere in the middle of New York Harbor, as I passed the Statue of Liberty, guilt took over the fear.

I didn't handle the hotel situation well at all. Maybe I should've said something sooner, or maybe I should've just swallowed it all down and did the interview. We had the option to pull it before publication if we weren't ready.

About one hour and countless thoughts of "What the fuck am I doing?" later, there's a knock on the front door, and Talon's voice drifts down the hall as Mom lets him into the house.

He appears in my bedroom doorway looking sheepishly hot.

Can't he look devastatingly exhausted just once in his life?

Double ugh.

"Hey," I say sleepily even though I didn't sleep. I couldn't with everything running through my head.

"Hey." His tone and demeanor make my blood turn cold.

"What's wrong?"

"So, uh, after I threatened to fire Alan louder than I intended to, he's already been onto his legal department and is trying to keep me locked to his firm."

I sit up. "Instead of talking to you about it, he got lawyers involved?"

"Yup."

"What an asshole."

"I think he's trying to scare me into stepping back, which is pretty stupid considering I'm doing that anyway because of you."

"Because of me?"

Talon glances away. "I was wrong earlier. When I said I was going to do it with or without you. It's both of us or nothing."

My lips form a thin line, because I don't know what to say to that.

"I don't mean that in terms of *us*. Just ... yeah ... maybe we do need more time before taking the next step, and we should do it together. We should both be ready. We're good, right? You and me?"

I know Talon's waiting for me to respond, but I've got nothing. We are good. Everything up until this morning is what I've wanted with him for *years*. Then why does it feel like the beginning of the end? I'm scared to take the next step because it's going to make us face obstacles we might not be able to survive.

I force myself to nod, but it doesn't appease him. If anything, his concern line across his forehead deepens.

"I'm gonna get the next flight to L.A. tonight and set up meetings for tomorrow to sort this shit."

"L.A.?"

"I'm going above Alan's pay grade for this one. He's creating more drama than what he's worth."

Impulsive as always. "Talon ... You owe your career to that man."

"I owe my career to years of training and hard work. All he did was paperwork."

I sigh. "I understand you're mad, but maybe you should think about this. Creating a rift between you and your agent isn't the best way to spin positive press when we'll have so much negative coming our way."

"I'm not the one who has to think anything through. I know what I want. While I'm sorting this agent crap, you should take the time to work out what you want. Because up until a few hours ago, I thought we were on the same page."

"We are," I argue. "I just want you without having to defend to the outside world why you're everything to me. I don't think that's too much to ask."

Except we both know that it is.

Talon approaches and kisses my forehead. "I already had to decide if what we have is worth facing that. Now it's your turn. I'll text you when I land."

Waking up without Talon next to me is already weird and unnatural.

My body is in training mode, telling me to get up and go for a run even without Talon being on my ass about pushing harder.

Days of running does little to clear my head, but my leg feels good, and even though it has taken an obscene amount of time, I'm finally getting back to my old self—the one who knew he had to train to stay on top of his game.

Talon and I text back and forth, but it's mainly agent related. He doesn't push me to make a decision, and I don't tell him my fears are still the same.

He's getting the runaround and is about to lose his shit. He refuses to tell me what they're saying in those meetings though, and if I had to guess, I assume they're telling him that I'm right. He shouldn't come out. Only their reason would be pure greed over Talon's lost endorsements. Because Talon has to know that this will lose him some campaigns. It'll probably gain him some too, but I can see some of them walking. They'll use terminology like "negative publicity" to describe it instead of "we're homophobic assholes," but it won't change the outcome.

College Miller wants to slap current me upside the head and tell me to chase after him and be there for him through all of this, but I don't listen to that voice, and I can't even say why.

When I'm with Talon, it's not only that everything is right, it's like everything else I've ever done without him was wrong.

But I'm scared being put under a microscope will be too much, and then I'll be left with nothing and the entire world wanting to know every sordid detail of my and Talon's sex lives. Not to mention all the shit that will follow.

Women from our past will come out of the woodwork telling their story, and there's nothing we can do to refute those claims, but telling the media it was all harmless fun and shouldn't have an impact is being naïve. Being on the queer spectrum will bring all the sexual deviant slander out, and add in threesomes and orgies? It'll perpetuate a stereotype that doesn't even fit who we are as a couple.

As friends, we were fine with sharing and having fun, but what we have together is so much more.

There's no way to positively spin that, and we're going to be a PR nightmare. I like my life being private. I've loved being the one in the background of paparazzi shots. I don't want my mom, sister, or niece to be dragged into this.

How do I get over that fear?

How do I tell myself to jump all in and have that blinding faith Talon has and I've always been envious of?

It takes a knock on my door for me to gain some real perspective.

When Lennon and Noah stand on the front porch of my mother's house, Lennon with a tentative stare and Noah with a somber expression, I seem to lose all my proper manners Mom ingrained in me from birth.

"Who is it?" Mom calls out.

"Some friends."

"Can we come in?" Lennon asks, still hesitant.

"Sorry. Of course." I step aside and lead them into the kitchen and dining area.

"You're probably wondering why we're here."

"Little bit. Are you going to try to get me to talk publicly?"

Lennon shakes his head. "No, I won't pressure anyone to do that before they're ready. I ... I actually wanted to share with you what I wrote about Talon."

My eyes widen. "I thought he didn't do the interview?"

"He didn't. Not a proper one. He sat there and talked about you the whole time. I won't publish this unless both you and Talon sign off on it, but I wanted you to read the words he said about you."

Lennon reaches into his laptop bag and slides papers over to me.

Mom comes into the room to introduce herself, but I'm too busy staring and focusing on the article in front of me:

Blindsided.

A one-twenty-yard patch of turf is the last place Marcus Talon thought he'd find love. He reserved all his affection on the field for the game, the glory, and his love of football.

That all changed this past season when he signed with the Warriors.

Shane Miller's job is to protect Marcus Talon's blind side, but it's their friendship off the field where they started seeing each other as more than teammates.

"Miller and I clicked the second we met," the three-time Super Bowl winner says of his college roommate. "It took me six years of missing him to realize I loved him—even back then."

Marcus Talon didn't understand his urge to follow Shane Miller and sign with the Warriors last season. He describes it as a gut feeling—the same instinct he has as one of the most successful quarterbacks in the league right now.

The move to Chicago led him to question a lot about himself and his life.

"Miller's been super patient with me while I've figured it all out."

Talon and Miller are teammates with Matt Jackson—the first out player to win a Super Bowl. When asked about Matt Jackson's influence over his relationship with Miller, Talon has only one thing to say.

"All Jackson has done has paved the way for others to explore what was already there. My feelings for Shane have been there for years. Jackson having the courage to be one of the first ones in this industry to speak out only gave me the motivation to go for something I've always wanted but never knew it."

Statistics show similar situations in other industries

throughout the world. In supportive and accepting environments, it's more likely people will be open with their sexualities. It's why we see families with many LGBTQ members and schools with clusters of queer students coming out at similar times. Just one person with the courage to come out can cause a domino effect, similar to what we have seen in the NHL in recent months with the simultaneous outings of Caleb Sorensen and Ollie Strömberg.

"Miller and I became friends over a shared dream. We always planned on winning the Super Bowl together, and that's still the goal."

The Warriors won this year's Super Bowl, but with Shane Miller out for the season due to a hamstring injury and missing twenty games, that's not good enough for the couple.

"A win where we're both on the field or it doesn't count," Talon says, his eyes shimmering with determination.

It's the kind of drive only a winner possesses, and with three Super Bowl wins in six years, this quarterback has the talent to pull off another trophy alongside his boyfriend.

In the past year, the NFL has seen its first out player since Michael Sam in 2014, and now it's facing the new dynamic of welcoming teammates in a relationship.

"I never saw this coming, but there's no doubt in my mind that Miller and I were meant to be. We were made for each other."

The article goes on and mentions our stats and the highlights from our careers, and the entire article reaffirms everything I've already known but has been drowned out by doubts and other people's negativity, but it's the last paragraph that kicks me in the ass and in the gut.

> *"It's not easy—loving someone you know other people will have opinions about. It's not easy being anything society doesn't expect you to be. But when you're with the person who was literally created with the sole purpose of being your other half, there's no way to fight it. There's only the choice to hide it or face it together, and I want to fight every battle and overcome every obstacle with Miller. I want us to help pave the way for others to be who they want to be and love who they want to love."*

Talon's words are everything I've wanted to hear for so long, but my cautious side hasn't allowed me to believe it. Waiting for him to freak out, to change his mind, to tell me we don't belong together after all ... I've been held back by my own disbelief.

But there it is in black and white. The thing I needed but hadn't realized.

Talon loves me.

Is that a fix to the problem? No. Are we still going to have to face everything I'm freaking out about? Yes.

Only, facing it doesn't seem as daunting now.

One L-word shouldn't change anything, but in my head, it changes *everything.*

Noah clears his throat, bringing me out of my revelation. "Matt's not handling this well."

My stomach sinks. "The Henderson stuff?"

"He thought he was making a difference and that there were no problems with the team. He had buried his issues with Carter and thought everything was fine. Now Henderson is making him question everyone. I don't want to put pressure on you to come out—that's not what this is about—but on the off chance you guys are still worried for his sake, I want you to know it might actually be good for him."

It doesn't have anything to do with Jackson, and I can't help feeling guilty and selfish over that. He needs our support.

"Is he okay?" I ask.

A coy smile crosses Noah's face. "I'm there to comfort him. Constantly."

"It's true. I live directly below their bedroom." Lennon turns to Noah. "Why do you think I'm spending most nights at Ollie's?"

"Like you're not doing the same thing over there," Noah says.

"True, but he doesn't have any roommates."

The pang of jealousy that hits me at them casually talking about their relationships makes me realize I'm a fucking coward. But being closeted isn't the coward part. I'm running away from what-ifs, and that's no way to live.

CHAPTER TWENTY-NINE

TALON

The idea of coming to L.A. to sort this shit between my agent and me is proving to be useless. I've probably spent more time on the phone with them than sitting in their offices, and every time I've spoken to one of Alan's partners about the situation, they've expressed their concerns about me coming out. One even called a publicist and put them on speaker phone so I could hear their thoughts on a hypothetical NFL superstar coming out.

They said after Jackson another coming out might be pushing our luck. One is something that can be handled, but two could cause boycotts.

Whoever says the world is different now is full of shit.

One of the agents decide to lecture me for an hour on sports not being the only fucked-up industry. Musicians, actors, and the whole entertainment industry is still full of closeted stars.

Anyone in the public eye is open to scrutiny, which is why coming out is still a big deal when it shouldn't be.

The one young partner who isn't over the age of fifty sees where I'm coming from and sympathizes, but even he expressed concerns.

I've been in contact with Damon, and he hasn't been able to find any escape clause in the contract, but he suggested I get a contract lawyer out here to go over it too.

It seems the fight's already begun, and I haven't even officially come out yet.

And this is exactly what Miller is worried about. I understand it, I do, and being out here on my own has kind of driven his point home.

So even though I miss Miller like crazy, my slightly crushed ego is preventing me from calling him and telling him he was right. I don't want to call him until I have a solution.

"How much can I pay them to go away?" I ask my newly appointed lawyer.

He sits behind his big desk in his fancy law firm and purses his lips. He looks as frustrated as I am. Then again, he's about to make a lot of money off me, so maybe he's happy they're fighting this and feigning sympathy.

Miller's voice echoes in my head: *Everything comes easy to you, and you've never had to fight for anything.*

Now, here I am, trying to pay off my problems, and I want to take it back immediately. If Miller's going to have faith in us, then he needs to know I'm not going to do the easy fix.

"There's nothing in your contract saying you can't get outside representation, but any jobs your second agent gets you, you're obligated to pay ten percent to Alan's firm until your contract with the Warriors is up."

My five-year contract that still has four years on it. That's millions of dollars to the assholes who are trying to get me to stay quiet about me and Miller.

A true agent who had my best interests at heart would've stayed and talked to me that day instead of bolting and lawyering up over the contract. That only made me want to get out of it more.

I have to report for training camp soon, and Miller and I haven't even sorted our shit out yet either.

For the first time in my life, I'm not in control, and I have no idea how to handle that.

Leaving the meeting dejected, I begin to think Miller's right. Maybe this is too much. It's not like he's here telling me to fight this. He's probably happy they're trying to put a stop to me coming out.

And maybe that's what I have to do? Just ... keep it to myself. Even if I've never felt this way about another person in my whole life and I want nothing more than to celebrate that.

It's not lost on me that this is the type of shit the entire LGBTQ community has gone through for *decades*. I've only had a taste of it, and I've never experienced anything more difficult. No one should have to defend who they want to be with. Ever. They shouldn't be worried about image, their career, or what anyone else might think or say.

I thought being a celebrity was invasive enough—I could handle that—but this ... the only way I see Miller and I surviving this is if we're in it together.

I'm distracted by my thoughts as I enter the hotel room, and I don't notice it right away. My shoes and socks come off, and I dump my phone and wallet on the table in the entryway before freezing at the sound of someone in my bedroom.

Why the fuck is there someone in my room?

I should totally run away, right?

"Hello?"

Shit, I totally just became the stupid chick in a horror film.

It's probably housekeeping or something, but now, all I can think of is some masked serial killer is going to kill me.

Because I'm completely rational when I'm confused. Clearly.

It's not a maid in a hotel uniform or a serial killer who steps out of the bedroom door.

No, all six-foot-five and wide-as-fuck Shane Miller stands there, his impressive arms folded as he leans against the doorjamb.

"How did you … where were … and … you're here?"

He grins. "You're not the only one who can flirt their way into somewhere."

I itch to go to him. I've never missed someone so fucking much in my life. We may have spent most of this year apart, but being stuck here has been the hardest. Before, it didn't really matter where we stood with each other. But now … now, everything is different because the man standing before me is my world. He's all that matters.

Miller takes tentative steps toward me. "I came to tell you—"

"Don't," I say and rush him. Within a second, my mouth's on his, and my tongue pushes past his lips.

Miller lets me have what I want for about three seconds before he's pulling away way too soon.

"No, no, no," I murmur. "No talking."

He pulls back even more. "We have to."

Damn, that can't be good.

Miller wouldn't fly across the country to break up with me, right? If he wanted to do it in person, he'd wait for me to ... Shit, it's not like he's gonna do it at training camp. Or over the phone or text.

The look on Miller's face almost has me dropping to my knees and begging him not to do this.

Instead, I blurt, "You were right." At the same time, he says the exact same thing.

"What?" I ask.

"Have you ever wanted something so fucking much that when you get it you're scared it's not really happening, or you're worried you'll mess it all up, or you can't actually believe you have it?"

"Umm ... no."

"You've never thought to yourself that instead of having constant dread hang over your head that it'd be better to give up completely because at least then you'd have an answer?"

"Still no."

Miller huffs a laugh. "Bottom line is, I want to be with you. I don't want to live without you. I'm not even sure I'd know how to anymore."

Exhaustion weighs down my words. "I want the same thing, but it doesn't have to be publicly. After all this contract drama, I can more than see your point."

"Going that well, is it?"

"We're not even out yet, and I'm already dealing with the blowout from it. And you were totally right in saying I have no idea what it'd be like, because the mere fact I have to fight a team of people who are supposed to be on my side means this is just the beginning. It's only going to get worse. Turns out I have no idea what to do when I don't have control of a situation."

Miller's eyes are sympathetic. "Those who shout what year we're in and say it's easy to just come out have no idea. This industry wants to chew us up and spit us out."

"Spitting is never good etiquette."

He levels me with his *shut up* look. "I'm trying to have a moment here."

"Sorry. Continue."

Miller covers my mouth with his hand so I don't interrupt again. "There are a million reasons not to do this. There are a few good reasons to go for it. But there's only one reason why I'm here. It's you, Marc. Always you."

I'm not even sure when he removes his hand from my mouth or who moves first, but next thing I know, I'm kissing him again.

Fierce and claiming.

Heat travels over my skin when Miller lifts the hem of my shirt and his fingers skim down my stomach. I'll never tire of his touch, his mouth, his body against mine. It's where I've always belonged, but I was too busy looking at everything and everyone else to notice.

Miller grounds me, makes me less impulsive, and settles the ever-buzzing energy I usually have.

He makes me more human, and I love him for it. Not just the love I've always had for him, but the type I never knew existed.

"I love you," I blurt.

Miller pulls back and smiles. "'Bout fucking time you caught up."

I try to shove him, but he holds me firm.

"We should do the Lennon article. Actually ... I'll rephrase. We've done the Lennon article. We should tell him to print it."

"What?"

"Lennon wrote an article on what you guys talked about that day we were supposed to sit down with him, and I had him rework it so it involves both of us and the truth about coming out in this industry. Why it's still hard. Why, even though there's been an athlete in nearly every sport come out, they're still lonely fish in a big pond. Statistically, there has to be more."

"But what about—"

"The fallout is gonna suck, but we have a great supporting network around us even if your management team isn't involved in that. We can get through it if we promise we'll get through it together. That we're in this together. Just us ..."

He hasn't brought up the threesome thing since the day with his PT, and while I can't be sure he's hinting at that or is going for a us versus the world thing, either way, my answer is the same.

"Only us," I say.

He's all I need, and if Miller had to step back to become more confident in what we have, then I can't complain about his freak-out. I think deep down I knew he'd come around after he had a chance to think it through, but that one little voice in my head telling me he could walk away damn near broke me.

"I have something to show you." Miller disappears into the bedroom, and I follow him. He pulls out some stapled papers from his bag, flips to the last page, and hands it over to me. "I want to give you everything you want."

At the bottom of the page, the last line of the interview reads:

When asked how he feels about Marcus Talon, Shane Miller smiles. "I've been in love with Marc since before I knew the possibility of having him was a reality."

"I thought everything we did in college was just about sex. That it was a kink I had to want to share women with you, but it wasn't. I was falling for you way back then."

"About ... uh, that. I have a surprise for you." Miller glances toward the bathroom. "It's kinda a compromise on the three-way thing."

I follow his gaze and narrow my eyes. "Is there a hooker in the shower? Because I feel like this is a test ... in which case, my answer is no. I don't want the super-hot, super boobish hooker in the bathroom, thank you very much."

Miller laughs. "No hooker. Although, I'm sure if I'd asked, I could've gotten the desk clerk up here. She's a USC alum, and she'd heard stories about us."

"Our reputation precedes itself."

"Dunno if that's something we should be proud of."

"Is that slut shaming I hear again?"

Miller grins, and I'm thrown back to that morning in my bathroom after we took home those girls ... wow, a year ago already.

"What?" Miller asks.

"What, what?"

"You look weird."

"Thanks."

Miller huffs. "You look like you're concentrating. It's alarming."

"Ha-ha. I'm having one of those 'How did we get here?'

moments. It's kinda surreal to think of where we were a year ago."

"Probably not as surreal as this." Miller takes my hand in his and leads me to the bathroom, and as soon as I see his compromise in the shower, I have to laugh.

"Only your true love brings sex toys as compromises."

"It was super fun bringing that through security at the airport."

I laugh, but Miller wraps his arm around me from behind and leans in to kiss the side of my neck, and I no longer find it funny. I tilt my head backward, giving him more access.

"I was thinking about that threesome scene we love. You know, where there was a guy in the middle ..."

"You want me to fuck a Fleshlight while you fuck me?" My cock leaks at the thought.

"I may not want to share you with real people, but I don't see you falling for an inanimate object anytime soon."

"I dunno, inanimate objects don't talk back."

"You know what else doesn't talk back?" Miller asks.

I wait for him to continue.

"Guys who have their mouth full of cock."

I laugh. "You better get to work then."

Miller tilts his head. "Hell no. I meant you."

"You want my ass, you have to suck my dick."

"They should make that into a bumper sticker." Despite Miller's protest, he sinks to his knees.

He makes quick work of my pants while I shuck my shirt off and throw it somewhere.

"I'm gonna prep you while I'm down here, so spread your legs a little more."

I do as he says, and he reaches for the lube on the bathroom counter.

When slick fingers grip my balls, I can't contain a loud moan. He's barely even touched me, and I'm ready to explode in his face.

God, now I'm thinking about cum dripping off his cheeks, his chin, his upper lip, and I have to quickly grip my dick to keep it under control.

"Someone a little too excited?" Miller mocks. "Need to come first, or can you hold out?"

"Hold out," I rasp, and it sounds like a lie.

Miller chuckles. "We'll see about that."

The challenge in his voice makes me nervous, but as soon as his fingers make their way between my ass cheeks and press against my hole teasingly, I'm brought back from the edge by one finger slipping inside.

It's still awkward, that first touch, and I have to remind myself of how good it'll get once I loosen up. It's a hell of a lot easier to remember that when Miller takes my cock in his mouth, and it's so warm and wet I barely register when the finger pushes in farther. I have a stubbly mouth on my cock and fingers in my ass, and although the sensations are still new and a little uncomfortable, I can't get enough, because no sex has ever been as good as when Miller's inside me. Owning me.

Miller adds a finger and works me open until I'm panting and dangerously approaching the edge once again. He must sense it, because he stops.

His fingers slip from my ass, and my hole pulses, trying to bring the full sensation back.

Standing, still fully clothed, Miller reaches for the lube

and passes it to me. "Get your cock lubed-up and ready to go. I want to watch you use the toy for a bit first." Miller slowly undresses while I stroke my cock, watching him. Shirtless now, but still with pants on, he swats at me. "Get in the shower already."

Under the spray, I run my hands over my hair and enjoy the heat beating down on my body.

"Talon," Miller barks.

My eyes fly open, and I love how he becomes impatient. When I line my cock up with the Fleshlight suctioned to the tile wall, I make sure to keep my eyes on Miller. That is, until they roll back into my head. Damn, who knew these things felt so good?

My hands fly to the wall, trying to grip onto something but fail. I still and take a few breaths, and when I finally find my composure, I test out a few small thrusts because I don't know how sturdy they make these toys, but I quickly have no control over what my hips do anymore.

A groan comes from behind me somewhere. "So fucking sexy."

And then Miller's hands are on me, slowly moving down my back and gripping my hips. His hard, latex-covered cock rests against my ass cheek, and I find myself sticking my ass out as I continue to move in and out of the toy.

"Do we need the condom?" My voice comes out as a breath.

"Want to go bareback? Are we okay to do that?"

"I am. Haven't been with anyone but you since the last team health check."

"Same. Guess we don't need this then." He pulls the condom off and drops it to the tiled floor.

Then his fingers are back, sliding straight into my ready hole.

"Need your dick." I don't have to tell him twice.

Miller applies more lube, and with one swift move, he thrusts inside me, all ten million inches of his huge-ass motherfucking cock, and I feel like I'm being torn in two.

I love it. My ass pulses around him.

"Feel any different?" Miller's voice rumbles in my ear.

"So good. So fucking good." Not as good being filled with his cum will be.

"You gonna take all of me?"

I nod.

"Can't hear you."

"Yes," I hiss. "All of you."

"Might wanna brace yourself."

Miller moves slowly at first. A roll of his hips, a tiny thrust. Every move he makes, I do the same to the toy, and I swear I'm two seconds away from passing out. Pleasure rolls through me, from my head to my toes and then back again.

I never want it to end, but I fear it may kill me if it doesn't.

When he goes harder, my hand slips, and I almost headbutt the wall. I have to rest my forearm against the tile instead.

Miller pounds my ass until my vision blurs and the water runs cold, but the heat between us is enough to keep me warm.

The magnificent drag of Miller's cock over my prostate over and over again has my orgasm hitting out of nowhere. My whole body trembles, and my moans vibrate off the walls, but Miller continues his punishing pace.

While I spill into the Fleshlight, every time Miller moves

inside me, it drags out my orgasm. My legs go so weak the only thing holding me up right now is Miller.

"Tell me you're mine," Miller grunts.

I turn my head to look at him. "Yours."

Miller's arms wrap around me as if holding on for dear life as he comes. My cock becomes oversensitive, and I have to pull out while Miller slows and catches his breath. "Always?"

"Forever."

CHAPTER THIRTY

MILLER

Damon's plan works to a tee although the timeline is moved up. Team management is informed, but the public article goes to print before we get a chance to tell our teammates. It starts with rumors and is confirmed by Lennon's article. And that's how our lives have imploded.

Everything we feared would happen has.

We're photographed constantly.

We can't step outside our houses or go anywhere without someone following.

The articles spreading hate about gay being contagious and pulling Jackson into it are fewer than expected, but they're a lot harsher than anticipated. The fearmongering is out of control.

Worse yet is all those people we were scared about coming forward have—guys I hooked up with in college and girls Talon and I shared. Although it's interesting to hear we were hooking up with each other even back then. It was news to us, but apparently, these women remember it differently.

We know to let it go, but it's hard when there are lies out there mixed with the positive things about us. And there is positivity among the negative, which we're both thankful for.

But social media is the evilest thing to ever evil. The positive sometimes outweighs the rest but not always. Yet, I can't seem to stop checking it. Masochism is a shitty trait to possess.

Football is a man's sport #nohomo

If Marcus Talon and Shane Miller get married, their celeb name would be Sharcus.

Who cares who bones who? #loveislove #teamSharcus

#ConGAYgious. First Matt Jackson. Now two more. Soon the whole NFL will be gay.

I thought San Francisco was the gay city #herecomesChicago

The reason football players wear helmets is to stop them from kissing.

TALON AND MILLER ARE SO FREAKING CUTE! #teamSharcus

I wonder who plays wide receiver in the bedroom.

Ugh. Ugh. Ugh.

"You on Twitter again? I told you to stay away from that bullshit," Talon calls out from his kitchen. I must be making my grumbly noises aloud.

"Would you believe me if I lied and said I wasn't?"

"Well, no, because you just told me you're lying."

"Oh. Right." I stare at my phone again.

Talon appears and throws himself down on the couch next to me. "Anything new?"

"Same old, same old. Although, Henderson is getting more passive-aggressive every day." I show him Henderson's latest tweet that's a picture of guys in military getup.

These are real men.

Talon points to the photo. "Bet you that one on the end is a total bottom."

I snort.

The hashtag #teamSharcus trends for a week after we come out. Worst 'shipped name ever, but we'll take it. We'll accept any of the positivity that has the power to drown out the negative noise.

"You ready to head out?" Talon asks, and if I'm honest, the answer is no.

Facing our team for the first time? Excuse me for not jumping for joy at being reunited with the guys who gave Jackson hell when he first joined the Warriors.

As if sensing my dread, Talon reaches for me. "It'll be fine."

I scoff. "Uh-huh, sure."

The drive to Jackson and Noah's place is silent because we're both mentally psyching ourselves up to do this.

A year ago, we were on Jackson's doorstep in Chicago trying to convince him to come out with us to meet the rest of the team. This time, we're here for a different reason, but the same queasy, *maybe we shouldn't be doing this* feeling is there. Last year was for him. Now, it's for us.

After I knock, Noah answers the door.

"He's not coming with you guys," he says quietly. "He doesn't want to make it worse for you, and he definitely doesn't want to have to justify all of you being on the team and all that other bullshit."

"We get it," I say. "But thought we'd try anyway."

From what little Noah's told us about how Jackson's doing, we know he's still hurt, and we can understand it. He thought he was making progress. He played his heart out last season, and the team has a championship ring to show for it. But now it's like he's back at square one and last season didn't matter.

Noah looks over his shoulder and then back at us. "It's not that he doesn't support you two—"

"We know," Talon says.

We'd prefer showing a united front on this, but we completely understand if he can't face the team yet. We figured it'd be easier doing this in a casual environment than when we have to report for training camp.

Noah sighs. "I'll talk to him again. I think it'll be good for him to see the team is still the same team he was on last year, minus the few closed-minded assholes."

"Thanks," I say, but when the door closes, we don't bother waiting around.

We both know he's not coming with us, and who could blame him?

The stalkery paparazzi are waiting for us outside the bar as expected. There's no real secret way to invite fifty-odd people somewhere without word spreading. Especially when we don't know how many of those fifty people are on our side.

We hold hands and wade through the crowd, because we can do that now—hold hands in public. And while it's ruined by camera flashes blinding us and people yelling inappropriate questions at us, we're facing it together like we promised.

It's not easy—not by a fucking long shot—but it's out there now, and we just have to deal with it.

Talon and I wake up next to each other knowing whatever comes we're ready for it. When either of us worry it's getting too much, the other is there to block tabloid sites and hit us over the head to snap out of it.

Which I might need right now as we step into the safety of the bar and away from the cameras, because I'm freaking out again.

Talon squeezes my hand. "You still with me?"

I nod, unable to form words, which he picks up on and immediately knows I'm lying. Of course.

He pulls me close to him. "What do you need from me? To give you an out, tell you to snap out of it, or hold your hand tighter?"

Talon couldn't be more perfect. His willingness to give me what I need without hesitation still amazes me, even though it shouldn't. Talon's always been like that even when we were just friends. I lean in and kiss his cheek. "Just don't leave my side."

"Done. Let's get this over with."

As much as I'd like to keep holding his hand, I know it's not smart. We should ease the guys into this and not throw it in their face.

Approaching the tables with a lump in my throat, I'm thankful Jackson didn't end up coming with us, because when we're spotted, the whole group goes silent, and as if sensing the tension in the air, the entire bar seems to quiet down too.

I quickly do a head count, and of the main guys from the team, only about half are here. Fifty-fifty isn't bad, but it's not really what I was hoping for. I've been hoping one thing we expected would surprise us by being the opposite or not as bad as we'd thought, but nope. Hasn't happened yet.

"There's one way to make an entrance," Talon says and forces a laugh. "We're gonna go get drinks."

Talon pulls me by my shirt sleeve toward the bar.

"Chicken out?" I ask.

"Yup. You? You didn't say anything."

"Yep."

"Why didn't Jackson want to come when we're having so much fun already?"

I snort.

"Okay, I got an idea." Talon gets the bartender's attention and orders a shot for everyone back at the group of tables they've taken up.

"We're gonna get them drunk?" I ask. "Because giving angry, testosterone-filled guys liquor might not be the best idea to get them on our side."

"The way I figure it, they made the effort to come here, so they're willing to hear us out, at least. We'll give them a peace offering and tell them we're still the same guys we were last season."

It's a solid plan, but when does my man ever stick to those?

We place the trays of shots down on the tables, and the guys are more welcoming this time, so the first part of the plan works.

But as they go to reach for the drinks, Talon says loudly

"Go ahead. Unless you're scared being attracted to guys is in the alcohol and you might catch it."

I try not to laugh, and I have to cover my mouth.

A few of the guys pause, and I'm two seconds away from thinking calling them out on their shit is gonna backfire. I give a hopeful glance toward the married guys on the team, but surprising me, DeShawn Jenkins is the first to take a shot.

"Give me as many of these as you want," he says. "No amount of alcohol will make any of you uglies hot."

It's the perfect icebreaker. If anyone doesn't take a drink, they're admitting that, with enough alcohol, they could be tempted. I think Talon and I let out simultaneous relieved breaths when the others hold up their drinks before knocking them back.

Talon smiles and crosses his arms. "Good. Is this sorted or do we need to stand here and tell you our whole story?"

"We've read the articles and seen the tabloids," Bell says. "You both like guys and girls but love each other." He shrugs. "Whatever, man, don't really care. All I care about is kicking ass on the field again this year."

There're shouts of agreements all round.

"Good, because if anyone doesn't like it, you can all go bitch and moan quietly—or not so quietly—with Henderson and Carter."

"Hey, what did I do?" a voice yells from somewhere.

We turn and see Carter at the end of one of the tables.

"Sorry. Didn't realize you were here. We just figured—"

"I already told Jackson I was sorry for the way I acted last season, and I meant it. We're all here for football, and I can admit when I'm wrong. I was wrong to think Jackson was using his sexuality as a gimmick, and I sure as fuck know you two aren't with how much heat you've brought on yourselves and the rest of the team. No one willingly does that."

"Heat?" I ask. The team's been getting heat from it? I know we've been hit pretty hard on Twitter, but I've spoken to Damon a few times, and he hasn't said anything about Warriors' management worrying too much past ticket sales.

A few heads cock toward us in confusion.

"You don't know, do you?" Bell asks.

Talon frowns. "Know what?"

"Henderson didn't re-sign," Bell says. "He'd been demanding more money than he was worth and was still negotiating his new contract. When your news came out ..."

"He walked." I shake my head. Unbelievable. "Who'd he sign with?"

"No one. He's a free agent. And I doubt anyone will be interested when they see all the hate he's been spewing on social media."

I scoff. "He threw away his career because he'd rather give up football than play on a team with us?"

"Someone's protesting a little too hard there," Talon says. "Can anyone say overcompensating for something?"

A few of the guys chuckle nervously, but I shake my head again, because I still can't believe hate can be that powerful. Then again, I see it all the time in the news. Hate is the number one reason for all the bad shit going on in the world. "If he's that upset over this, then I actually feel sorry for him."

"Don't." Jackson appears at my side and reaches for one of the remaining few shots on the table. "He's not worth it. And neither is anyone else who can't see you two were made for each other." He downs the shot and turns to Talon and me.

"Sorry I'm late. I had to get over myself and realize not everything is about me."

"Says the guy who just signed a twenty-five million-dollar, three-year deal," Jenkins calls out.

Jackson's one of the highest paid tight ends in the league now, which is better than his last contract. I'm guessing management felt the need to make it up to him.

Jackson smiles. "Guess next round's on me?"

And *finally*. For the first time, something does go better than I expect, and it's a weight off my shoulders knowing at least half the team has our backs.

Training camp is as grueling as ever, but the team is strong off the Super Bowl win. If anyone who didn't come to drinks that night has a problem with Talon and me, they keep their mouths shut.

Talon's lawyers have eventually managed to get him released from his contract, but Talon had to pay a ton of money to do it. It's not ideal, but Talon lost all faith in them when they gave him the runaround and tried convincing him to stay in the closet.

So now we share the same agent, the same team, and, soon, the same house. We just have to get through to the end of today.

Training camp hasn't been going well for me, and it's the last cut day. I'm guaranteed my salary because of a stipulation in my contract, but that doesn't mean they won't cut me.

As much as we love our coaches, it's on days like this one you don't want them to approach you in the weight room.

“Miller,” Coach Caldwell says.

The air in the room stifles everyone, not just me. Rookies look at me in horror, as if they can’t comprehend me getting cut over them, and the veterans stare at me in sympathy.

My heart pounds wildly as I make my feet move, and it feels like I’m walking my very own death march.

Melodramatic maybe, but this is my life on the line. Maybe not my physical life but the one I’ve lived for since I was twelve years old and put on my first set of football pads.

I can’t bring myself to look at Talon, who’s slowing the treadmill as fast as he can to come over to me, but out of the corner of my eye, I see Jackson stop him, and I’ve never been more thankful.

I hold my head high as I walk through the halls of the university where training camp is held and into the offices the coaches have commandeered while here.

Coach Caldwell takes the seat behind the small desk, and I sit in front of it.

“I’m done?” I ask. I need him to jump to the end, because I can’t handle the explanation first.

“You’re slower than your usual self.”

“I’ve had two leg surgeries in the last ten months, so …” *Fucking duh* is so not the appropriate thing to say so I bite my tongue.

“We know. And we’re not cutting you.”

I should feel relief, but there’s a reason he called me in here, and it can’t be just to have a chat.

“But we’ve got powerful rookies this year.” He’s talking about the guy who stepped into my spot last season when I was injured, and I’ve noticed a new kid who was just drafted. “They’re going to take starting positions.”

"I'm being demoted to backup." Meaning, this is most likely going to be my last year in the NFL. My contract is up, and no one's going to recruit me after sitting on my ass for a year.

"We'll see how the season goes and get you in with the team trainer to keep rehabbing that leg of yours to get you back to where you were. You're talented, and we don't want to let that go to waste. You'll probably still play some games."

I try to hold in my scoff, because chances are small. I'm not as versatile as the others. I can step in for right tackle if needed, but I'm better on the left—it's where my skill lies.

I'm fucked.

"You're not cut," Coach says again. "I wanted to let you know so you're not taken off guard when the rosters come out."

Yay for small mercies. "Can I go now?"

I don't want to throw a hissy fit, but this is what I've feared more than anything else I almost ran away from.

All the work Talon and I did over the break, all that psychological bullshit and positive reinforcement ... I actually believed we'd done enough, which makes this crushing disappointment so much worse.

My career has an expiration date, and I have no idea what to be when I grow up. Add this to all the public bullshit, and I'm so ready to give up. Just throw in the towel and say fuck it.

Then I remember Talon. Our dream.

We're not even going to get that before I'm forced into retirement.

I've still got this season. I've still got this season. Nope. No matter how many times I say it, the dreaded feeling of the end won't go away.

I leave in a daze and wander around aimlessly before directing my feet toward the team's hotel.

Meanwhile, I keep chanting in my head, *It's not over, it's not over, it's not over.*

Only, it is. I won't even be dressing for games. I'm benched. Indefinitely. Unless some miracle occurs. Perhaps I can hope for an injury of another player, but after what I've just been through this past year? Not only is it vindictive but karma would kick my ass so hard.

It doesn't occur to me that it's the first time in weeks that I haven't been followed, but as soon as I arrive at the hotel, I realize why I've been left alone. Talon must've come straight here when I got called into Caldwell's office thinking this would be my first stop afterward.

I wade my way through the photographers and ignore their stupid questions—one asks if I've been cut from the team.

My footsteps are heavy, and when I step through Talon's and my hotel room, I find my boyfriend, my partner, the love of my life, pacing the small space for me.

He stops wearing tracks into the carpet when he hears me come in. "Are you leaving me?"

"What?"

"Well, if you're cut, you're going to try for another team, right? Which means you could be across the country, and I know it's only for half the year, and then we'll be together, but I don't want you to leave. We've done this whole thing practically long-distance, and I've only had a short time of having you in person, and I don't want to do that again."

I let him ramble, because he's on a roll.

"I'll do it if we have to because I would never hold you back from your dream of playing in the NFL—I'm not that much of an asshole—but damn it, I'm super selfish and don't want you to leave me."

"You done?" I ask, a smile finding my face. Weirdly, Talon freaking out about this makes me calmer, because he's right. This could be so much worse than it is. I could've been cut. They could've thrown me out on my ass. But I'm here. I get to stay with the team and be in Chicago—even if I don't get to play too many games. If any.

"What? What did they say?"

"I'm benched because McLaren and the new kid are faster than me right now."

The fight leaves Talon in a visible whoosh as he relaxes. "You're staying?"

"For this year at least." Next year, probably not, but I don't say that. We'll face that when we need to. I have an entire season to figure out my future.

Talon begins pacing again. "No. You'll be here next year too. We'll make sure of it. More training, more PT, more—"

"We'll figure it out."

"Together. We'll figure it out together ... right?"

I nod. "I'm not going to run again. I know what I want."

Talon being here, supporting me, planning our future together is all I want.

"Whatever I do, whether this is my last season or my leg gets better, it won't matter. So long as I'm with you, I'll be happy."

Talon's expression softens, and he approaches to wrap his arms around me. His head fits just below mine, and his shampoo smells like the crappy hotel stuff. "We can still do this. I'm sure of it. Do you remember that night a billion years ago where I promised it was gonna be you and me winning a Super Bowl together one day?"

"Yeah," I mumble into his hair. "I thought you were full of shit."

Talon laughs. "I think even back then the dream was about us together. Not the championship. I fell in love with you without even knowing that was possible."

My chest warms and fills with happiness. "So maybe we should make a new dream. Anything else that involves you and me."

He playfully slaps the back of my head. "That'll be Plan B. We can still do Plan A. It might just take some time."

"Lucky I'm willing to keep your ass forever."

Talon pulls back and cocks his head. "Just my ass?"

I shrug. "I guess I'll take the rest of you too."

With a wry smile, he leans in and softly kisses me. "You're so good to me."

"Sarcasm. It's how I love."

"Holy shit, you must love me a fuck ton."

It's my turn to kiss him. "More than a fuck ton."

"I love you too, Shane."

CHAPTER THIRTY-ONE

TALON

THREE YEARS LATER

Okay, so dreams take fucking longer than planned in real life, but the important part is we're here. Whether it was fate, the universe, or pure will, Miller being demoted only lasted half a season before he was called up because the rookie choked when it counted. Miller worked his ass off, and we fought as a team, but we'd had too many losses in the first eight games to come back. We missed out on even the playoffs that year, which crushed our egos considering we were the defending champs.

Last year, we at least made it close to the end but were knocked out one game from the Super Bowl.

We're a strong team, and we've proved that, but it was still never enough for me.

Now, as we're about to be presented with the Vince Lombardi Trophy—something I've won four times now—nothing, and I mean nothing, has been a bigger win for me.

Because this night has been over a decade in the making, ever since the night Shane Miller walked into my life.

It's also the night I never thought would come—the night I ask someone to be my forever person on paper and not just in our hearts. When I told my family my plan, my mom said I was romantic, Dad said I had balls of steel, and my brother said it was douchey.

Thanks, Trey.

When the announcer is done talking to the coach and GM and he calls me up to give an MVP speech, I've never been closer to shitting myself on national TV.

In the three years since coming out, two more players have followed suit. One from Baltimore who's near retirement and a kid named Whitman who came out not long before he was drafted to San Francisco. Is the industry more accepting? Not quite, but it's getting better.

My hand shakes as the trophy is handed to me and my GM gives me a hug.

I've thought about taking this step with Miller for three years now—ever since we chose each other above all else—but maybe doing it in front of a hundred million people or so is too impulsive. It's me, so it wouldn't be a Talon thing to do without a little flair, but I'm thinking this could be too much.

Look at me, being mature. Go me.

I talk with the announcer, but I have no clue what words come out. When he's about to move on, reflexes take over, and I pull the microphone back to my mouth.

"There is one thing I wanna do before we wrap this up." I turn and glance behind me at the crowd of teammates at the bottom of the steps to the podium. "Shane. Where are you?" I wave him up.

People say you shouldn't propose unless you know the answer will definitely be yes, and while Miller has said we're in this forever, we've never actually spoken about marriage.

In the four years since I turned up in Chicago, marriage hasn't been mentioned once. If he wanted it, surely, he would've said something by now ... maybe. Come to think of it, I haven't mentioned it either, but here I am. God, what if it's something he doesn't want? Valid question this day and age.

Fuuuck.

Maybe I should just give him a hug.

When he makes it to the stage, his eyes are slightly widened, but he's got a smile on his face—a winning smile, because we fucking did it.

My doubt and worry melt away, because even if he doesn't want to get married, I want him to know that it's me and him forever. Whether we take this step or not, it doesn't matter to me, because I'll still have him.

I go to hand over the trophy to him but pull him into a hug at the same time, squishing it between us. God, he smells incredible. Like Miller mixed with football. We're still in our heavy pads and sweaty and dirt-soaked uniforms, but this moment couldn't smell any sweeter.

The crowd seems to get louder, but it's all drowned out by my heartbeat in my ears.

Most people propose with a ring. I'm doing it with the Vince Lombardi Trophy. But hey, at least he can never complain about me half-assing it.

My brain and body seem to be on the same wavelength for once, and instead of doing the big, public, over-the-top marriage proposal I'd been thinking about, all I do is turn my head and whisper in Miller's ear.

"Marry me, Shane."

He pulls back abruptly and lets go of the trophy, which slips out of my hands at the same time. Considering neither of us are receivers on the field, I'm impressed when we both catch it again.

We laugh, but it fades when our eyes meet.

"Say it again," Miller says. "So I'm sure it actually happened."

"Marry me. Be my husband. My best friend. My life partner. My everything."

It's only now I realize the announcer has shoved the microphone in our faces again, and the entire eighty-thousand seat stadium heard. Everyone gets to their feet.

Oh fuck ...

Public proposal it is after all.

Miller just smiles and leans in to the microphone.

With a simple word, my whole life becomes complete. "Yes."

THANK YOU!

Thank you for reading Blindsided. Talon and Miller were one of those couples who just would not shut up and needed their own story.

Another pair who are dying to get a book is young Jet with hockey hunk Soren. They're up next in the Fake Boyfriend universe, but like Talon and Miller, they will most-likely not contain a fake boyfriend trope.

Jet was supposed to run off and live his music dream in a music world. Turns out, he might not want to leave big brother's world behind. Release date TBA.

To keep up with Eden Finley news, the best place to do it is in my reader group on Facebook. https://www.facebook.com/groups/1901150070202571

Alternatively, you can join my mailing list:
http://eepurl.com/bS1OFH

ALSO BY EDEN FINLEY

FAMOUS SERIES

Pop Star

Spotlight

Fandom

Encore

Novellas:

Rockstar Hearts

FAKE BOYFRIEND SERIES

Fake Out

Trick Play

Deke

Blindsided

Hat Trick

Novellas:

Fake Boyfriend Breakaways: A short story collection

Final Play

STEELE BROTHERS

Unwritten Law

Unspoken Vow

ROYAL OBLIGATION

Unprincely (M/M/F)

BOOKS COWRITTEN WITH SAXON JAMES

Power Plays & Straight A's

Face Offs & Cheap Shots

Goal Lines & First Times

Line Mates & Study Dates

Puck Drills & Quick Thrills

ACKNOWLEDGMENTS

I want to thank my betas: Leslie Copeland and Jill Wexler.

A special mention to my other early readers: Crystal Lacy, May Archer, Anita Maxwell, Jenn Taylor, Sam Desity, Aimie Jennison, and Kimberly Readnour.

Deb Nemeth for the wonderful editing.

Thanks to Kelly from Xterraweb copy-editing/proofing.

And to Lori Parks for the last read through.

Kellie Dennis from Book Cover by Design, you are always a rockstar.

Lastly, a big thanks to Linda from Foreword PR & Marketing for helping get this book out.

www.ingramcontent.com/pod-product-compliance
Lightning Source LLC
Chambersburg PA
CBHW020942310726
48980CB00001B/20

* 9 7 8 0 6 4 5 1 4 6 6 6 0 *